MW00488541

YEARS
SIMON &
SCHUSTER

THE
SLEEPWALKERS

SCARLETT THOMAS

Simon & Schuster

NEW YORK   LONDON   TORONTO
SYDNEY   NEW DELHI

1230 Avenue of the Americas
New York, NY 10020

First Simon & Schuster hardcover edition April 2024

SIMON & SCHUSTER and colophon are registered trademarks
of Simon & Schuster, LLC

Simon & Schuster: Celebrating 100 Years of Publishing in 2024

For information about special discounts for bulk purchases,
please contact Simon & Schuster Special Sales at 1-866-506-1949
or business@simonandschuster.com.

The Simon & Schuster Speakers Bureau can bring authors to
your live event. For more information or to book an event,
contact the Simon & Schuster Speakers Bureau at 1-866-248-3049
or visit our website at www.simonspeakers.com.

Manufactured in the United States of America

1   3   5   7   9   10   8   6   4   2

Library of Congress Cataloging-in-Publication Data has been applied for.

ISBN 978-1-6680-3298-5
ISBN 978-1-6680-3300-5 (ebook)

For Mum and
for Gordian

Contents

a) Letter 1, torn, partial, burn marks, blue ink on hotel notepaper

b) Letter 2, rain damage, black biro on paper (I)

c) Moleskine notebook pages, lilac ink on cream paper, burn marks

d) Note 1, intact, blue ink on shop receipt

e) Note 2, slight bloodstaining, turquoise ink on paper doily

f) ~~Set of black-and-white photographs, some marbling on edges~~ (removed)

g) Sketches, charcoal on paper

h) Audio transcript 1/1, original file (uncorrected)

i) Letter 2 (continued), scuff marks, rain damage, black biro on paper (II)

j) Hotel guest book pages, four in total. Very damaged.

k) Smythson spiral-bound notebook pages, ten in total, some water damage

l) Letter 3, black ink on hotel notepaper

m) Letter 4, turquoise ink on hotel notepaper

n) List of images

September 23rd, 2022

Dear Richard,

You'll no doubt think I owe you some sort of explanation for what I've done, so here it is.

Of course, I don't know where to begin. Just before our first proper date, when your mother told me the color black washed me out and that I should borrow her white silk blouse instead? Or that moment at our wedding when we both knew—but never actually said—that our love was forever cursed? Maybe I'll start in a more dignified way with the small plane we took to get here almost two weeks ago, all the tiny islands like a map beneath us, the plane's slender propellers naked and somehow savage, cutting through the air like white machetes.

Or perhaps I should skip to the moment when we turned up at the Villa Rosa and first met Isabella. *Isabella*. I find it so hard to write her name. But you have to face the things you fear, so here it is again: *Isabella*. *Isabella*. *Isabella*. But of course if I start with her, it's already over, and the dogs have won, and we are now just piles of bones.

So maybe I'll simply start with the night before we checked into the Villa Rosa. The beachfront taverna, moonlit and warm; only us, our friends and the beautiful people left on the island by then, or so it seemed.

The beautiful people? Well, I don't think you listened to anything I ever said about them, although perhaps you know who they are now. When I go over it all in my mind I can still see her so clearly, the prettier girl, the dark-haired one, a sleek heron in a black bikini and a thin orange sarong. She was walking down the road in the sun carrying a bag that said *Istanbul is Contemporary*.

She really was the most beautiful person I'd ever seen.

Amidst all the usual traffic on that narrow beach road—rusty utes carrying mineral water and bottled Coke, or Greek men on mopeds with their "amusing" cargos that Paul loved to point out: a large side-saddle wife, a massive watermelon, a white poodle—there she was. She was alone and free and, well, sometimes I look at young women and remember what it was like to be them, but I don't remember ever being her, with those sharp, wingish bones and her extraordinary long calves.

I imagine you reading this letter too fast in the hot and windy dark, or maybe in the calm of tomorrow morning, skimming to get to the headline, the facts, having decided that this lead-in is irrelevant. You are probably wondering where I am. Because I am going to go when I finish this. It's time, don't you think?

I see you holding this letter, having found it on the pillow where I plan to leave it later. You probably have that look you get whenever I try to explain something, and I start at the very beginning—or at least what the beginning was for me—and you act like you are struggling through bracken and maquis and dense thicket until I mention something you recognize as part of your story and only then do you stand still for a second and listen. But neither of us really wants to go back to the start, do we?

So feel free to skip ahead if you like. That's the beauty of a letter, after all: it's not a forest, not a complicated under-growth, not a loud argument. Take your machete and fuck all of this. Take your soft-mouthed dogs and beat out the birds and sight them and shoot them down and then you'll know.

That was the only time I saw her on her own, the beautiful girl. Most of the time she had her shorter, blonder friend with her, and the two boys trailing after them. Those beautiful boys. When they weren't trailing after the girls they were flittering down the street with their shirts off, carrying bottles of local beer, which they actually took care to put in the recy-cling bin once they were empty. Or they were strutting with their rooster chests high and proud, eating fruit or throwing a ball. One of the boys was skinnier than the other, with long bony fingers that fluttered through the air like the legs of a tiny creature that did not want to be picked up.

I kept wondering where these kids had come from. They looked rich to me, or, at least, expensive. I pointed them out one night over dinner in George's Taverna, but you weren't interested. You just thought they were normal young people, nothing unusual about them. You assumed they were from a British private school like the one you and Paul had both gone to, and didn't think it was at all interesting when they started speaking in a language none of us knew. I decided it was Turkish. You could see Turkey from the beach. And, well, *Istanbul is Contemporary.*

It gave me something to talk about with Beth at least. We had nothing in common otherwise. Since I'm an actor and she's a makeup artist, we should have had a riot. But I'm mainly in sweaty plays and she "does" politicians for the BBC News, so when I tried to ask her what she thought the best mascara on the market currently was, she just looked at me blankly while I burbled on about Chanel, and how hard I found it to tell the difference between the waterproof mascara I wear in sad times, and the normal one I prefer because it is more black, like the very bitterest depths of the night. Like now.

Paul seemed to have chosen Beth the way he picked all his girlfriends. She was to be adored yet hated; violated but also revered. She had that rubbery sex-doll look of all his women, but there was something human and raw about her too. Something in her slightly pimply skin and visible contact lenses; and the way she would let her DD boobs flop around in her strappy lemon sun dress without even a bikini under-neath. I once suggested to you that Paul had made her wear the dresses that way and you said you didn't know what I meant. Instead, you wondered about the etymology of the word seersucker, and why you'd never heard of it. You have always seemed so innocent, and mostly I've loved that.

Or, I did love it, once.

During those last, hot days, while you and Paul swam out as far as you could, beyond the buoys and the yachts, racing each other in that subtle way you do, Beth and I wondered whether the beautiful people had come from one of the boats. One day we saw four figures on the deck of the largest yacht, and we said that was it, that was them. But it wasn't them. Even from that distance you could see the small, puffy rolls of fat on the women. There was no fat on those girls. Not on the boys either.

Then one day we saw their shoes. Four pairs of dirty espadrilles, all with holes and signs of over-pronation. What is it about poverty and pronation? The beautiful people were out of place in a way we couldn't figure. Beth and I brainstormed what beautiful boys like that would become when they grew up, but we found it hard to imagine them as parents, or at a dinner party. What on earth would they talk about? What shoes would they find to wear?

While you were swimming, we speculated about what it would be like to sleep with boys like that. Our friendship had warmed up at last. What would it be like to be touched by a boy whose limbs were not made from money, but crafted from something different, like hope, or hard work? I recollect a photo on your mother's dresser of you in a short-sleeved linen shirt somewhere tropical, and even then you had a flush in your skin that those boys didn't have. A ripeness. Like a polished apple.

During those last days I became quite obsessed with the thin dark girl, and her friend. I suppose I wanted to sink into other lives that were not my own. I could see their rivalry, something you'd tell me I was imagining, probably, but the girl from Istanbul, the one you showed me photographs of later, was flirting with both the boys: the blond one in his faded pink shorts, the dark skinny one in faded lime green. Touching their tanned, slim arms—all muscle, of course, but not the sort you can get in a gym. The other girl noticed, but she never touched their long, lean lines herself. She frowned and, just once, looked tearful.

Perhaps the boys' muscles were from tying knots? We thought maybe they were staying on the white catamaran, Beth and I. It was a large, impressive vessel from which speed boats shot every night like sharp pellets, perhaps taking the beautiful people to hot, glamorous parties in the hills: you couldn't really tell in the dark. But then the catamaran went and the beautiful people were still here, on the island.

The summer itself was slowly creeping away. All the other yachts left. The swallows flitted across the water for the last few times and then they all flew off together, heading for Africa.

The other tourists were long gone.

The motorcycle man closed his shop and no longer asked me if I wanted to rent a scooter every time I went past him. The strange wreath in front of his shop remained, though, commemorating the υπνοβάτες, or *ypnováres*: the "sleepwalkers," a married couple who'd drowned in that part of the sea the year before.

George's Taverna stopped serving fresh fish, because the fisherman had taken his wife to Athens. Those last days of

Greek salads with old dry feta and toasted bread, because by then even the bakery had closed. Those last days. Our last days together. I will always treasure them, even though they were so very tainted.

The fat, slow hornets; they were still there. And the beautiful people. And us.

That last night before Beth and Paul went too, and left us alone for the final part of our honeymoon, we agreed that the island was the most incredible place we'd ever been. What was it? The zealous bougainvilleas, perhaps, or the rest of the greenery, so much more lush than on other Greek islands we'd been to before? There were eucalyptus trees and fig trees and pomegranates. Little whitewashed houses that seemed stuffed with peace. That soft heat in which everything slowed and made life back home seem almost insignificant. The kind of heat in which secrets melt, like beef tallow.

We made plans to return, earlier in the season next time; maybe even get an apartment for me to write in, if I carried on writing, of course. The only shadow over everything was that my second one-woman play hadn't been picked up for TV in the end, and my finances were a bit grim. I couldn't sponge off you, even now we were married, so I was probably going to have to apply for a permanent teaching job when we got home. I'd remortgaged the small house I owned via some complicated arrangement only you and your mother understood. Before the summer was out I was supposed to have written something new, something to finally bring back the success I'd grown so fond of, and to make me feel like myself again.

But when was I supposed to finish writing another play? Certainly not before we came on our honeymoon. The gift had been well meant, you insisted. A week at the exclusive Villa Rosa, recently reviewed in both *Vogue* and the *Daily Telegraph*. But the only way we could honor your mother's wedding gift and fit it into our lives was by changing the date of the actual wedding and then coming to the island a week before the suite was available. A slightly shit honeymoon while we waited for the perfect one to be ready. The kind of logic you'd grown up on.

The first week was so cheap we paid for Paul and Beth too. Our hotel rooms cost forty-five euros per night and had whitewashed balconies looking out to sea, with wire clothes-drying racks, orange pegs with rusty hinges, and handheld showers. When I first saw the showers I wanted to cry. But I got used to them in the same way I'd got used to your mother hijacking our engagement with her gift of a honeymoon in the first place.

"A little treat," Annabelle had said to me, handing over the envelope just after our engagement lunch, her voice booming oddly like a master of hounds in the tiled entrance hall of your childhood home. "Somewhere to write, perhaps?"

I'm still not sure why she felt the need to do it. You must have hundreds of thousands in your various funds and ISAs. You're not poor. I am not without good taste. Did she think you were ten years old again and had to have your holiday chosen by Mummy? And who actually works on their honeymoon? The whole thing was just terribly inconvenient, but you forbade me from ever mentioning that.

I ended up enjoying the handheld shower, anyway. I felt rustic and ordinary again, briefly, and my skin glowed with a new kind of exfoliation that made it seem as though I sparkled, and was clean, at least on the outside. There was no shortage of hot water in the cheap hotel, and I needed an awful lot of hot water after our wedding.

Maybe you felt the same after Luciana, with her dark peach dress and long shining hair, spoke the words that ruined us? But I guess we'll come back to that, because I'm not sure you know exactly what happened, even now. I'm not completely sure I do. And yes, this is me saying it, the thing we silently decided not to acknowledge. Or at least, I'm building up to it. I mean, did you even hear? But you must have done.

You can't have known all along, surely? The thought makes my flesh creep.

We left for our honeymoon right after the wedding reception, with Paul and Beth due to follow two days later, when she could get off work. We had a sweaty silent layover in Athens before catching the propellor plane first thing the next morning. In Athens we were so wrecked we didn't even leave the airport hotel. None of the windows opened, and the air-con drifted around like a lost phantom—but you'd been pleased you'd got some extra air miles from booking it. You ended up drinking Scotch with some golfers from Finland while I sat on my own and drank an entire bottle of sweet rosé that tasted like rancid petals.

You said later that I'd been determined not to like the Villa Rosa right from the start. You implied it was because it was your mother's gift, but I'd always got on surprisingly well with Annabelle, and the Villa Rosa was objectively a good choice. The antique wooden floors, the tulip paintings, the white muslin curtains that waltzed sleepily in the breeze. Everything was so timeless and relaxing. I'd recently realized that my style, the authentic one I'd been able to discover only after making a significant amount of money, was quite similar to your mother's. Antiques, old mirrors with wooden frames, high ceilings, slightly stained maps, old-looking documents and letters tied with string.

And so I should have loved the Villa Rosa, because it was exactly that, but in a hot place—and I like hot places, I really do. The candle lamps, the lazy white ceiling fans and mosquito nets. But I felt out of place here from the very beginning. Maybe because at heart I am still the kind of girl—woman—girl—who wants to get married in a field. Maybe I am just that. The field was my choice; the Villa Rosa was the corrective.

But I'm getting ahead of myself. There we were on our last night with Paul and Beth, in George's Taverna at the beach: them due to go home the next day, us due to move from the cheap hotel to the Villa Rosa. We sat at our usual table under the palm trees with the sea lapping gently by our feet and George talking again about the fabled storm that we didn't really believe in.

"It will come," he said, putting down a basket of slightly stale bread. "End of September, it always comes and takes away the beach. The water will rise up, high, high, over the stones, and the road. My chairs and tables here—all gone.

Until April. Then another storm will come and bring the beach back and the summer will begin again."

George looked ready for the end of the season. His eyes were tired and his clothes and footwear had become more ragged even in the eight days we'd already been there. It seemed he spent the entire season running back and forth from the water's edge—where the tourists ate—across the road and into his taverna where groups of elderly Greek men sat in the darkness under a ceiling fan laughing or shouting things at him. The motorcycle man was George's brother or cousin, and he sat there every night as well, looking sadly into the bottom of his glass of *tsikoudia*, a Cretan spirit I also rather liked.

"How could a storm 'take away the beach'?" you said when George ran off in his shredded trainers to get our second carafe of white wine. "That's just ridiculous."

"I think they make it all up," Beth said. "Stories for the tourists."

I caught Paul's eye and I could tell he liked the violent romance of it as much as I did. He tossed a stale bread roll into the water and we both watched as the fish came to eat it like a milk pot gathering itself to the boil, a strange little volcano under the water's surface. Paul glanced at me again and his look lingered for a few seconds longer than it should have. But I broke the connection first, I promise.

That night the beautiful people were sitting with some elegant older men; they were perched on the very edges of their chairs, all angles and pointy elbows like pallid birds in a modernist painting. They were the only people in the restaurant with bare feet. I sat with my back to them so that I didn't just stare. It probably didn't help, all my staring, although I can't say you ever noticed. I couldn't work out whether I was more fascinated by the thin dark-haired girl who walked with such an air, or with the boy with the long fingers, who I'd seen one day with a streak of gold glitter on his face.

I joined in as we shared stories of our school days. I'd gone to the worst comprehensive in my area, where the other girls carried knives and MDMA, and I'd hidden from them by going to drama club, where everyone was very deep and sensitive and into Chekhov and Stanislavski. You and Paul had gone to the most expensive school in the same small city where I'd gone to university. You were always so awkward talking about your youth, but Paul was hilarious, with endless stories of the disgusting habits of private schoolboys. Is it strange to have a friend come on your honeymoon? I never thought so. Your mother found it a bit odd, though, which was another reason for her gift. "So you can have some time alone together without Paul for a change." Yep. That went well.

Anyway, that night we started talking again about another of our favorite topics: what we'd do if we lived here all year round. Like if we got a villa and just moved here, to the island.

"I'd be a day trader," said Paul. "Laptop and deck shoes. Who needs more than that?"

"Deck shoes?" said Beth. "Please no."

"Paul's deck shoes are probably Gucci," I said.

Did Paul do something to Beth under the table then? She

sort of winced, just for a second, then covered it. He never liked being teased by his girlfriends. Only I could ever get away with that. I sometimes thought I was the only woman he actually respected.

"Dior," he said to me, with a half-hidden smile.

"It would get boring," you said, not noticing. "There's nothing to actually do except lie in the sun."

"You could chuck out your vitamin D tablets," said Paul.

"You could do an honest job in the day," I said, "and read or party at night. It would be like being retired, but young. Best of both worlds."

"You just used the word party as a verb," Paul said. "Why is that exciting?"

"Because it means to have sex," Beth said. "You know, like in tabloids? When the celebrities or whoever 'partied' all night?"

"Like Christos," Paul said.

"Christos doesn't party all night," I said. "He works all night."

Christos was American and—don't quote me on this—possibly related to George in some way. He'd come to Europe on a year-abroad program and never returned. On the night when you and Paul climbed up to the ruined castle and left Beth and me to have pre-dinner drinks alone in the harbor, we talked to him. He told us all about his favorite authors and how he spent every night reading until three a.m. before getting up at nine a.m. to open the taverna. He worked at the taverna until three p.m., and then read for an hour before crossing the island to work his evening shifts in the expensive fish restaurant in the harbor. I'd suggested he go home and do his master's in American literature but he said he was happy here, being a waiter. He was living his dream, he said. He'd found his treasure already.

There'd been an awkward moment after that when Christos had frowned as if he were not that happy; as if the dream had gone sour. He'd looked as if he was about to say something important, then didn't.

"You should come and see my books," he'd said. "I have a whole library up in my apartment. And the view is to die for."

He'd pointed out across the harbor to a ramshackle group of old villas and tavernas with several floors.

Now you snorted. Does that sound wrong? Maybe just "laughed" is better. But it wasn't immediately clear what was funny.

"Christos is wasting his life here," you said.

"Is he?" said Beth. "Or is he actually living the simple life we all dream of?"

"You can't live that life when you're young," said Paul. "It's cheating."

"He'll have ten kids by the time he's forty," you said. "And an enormous gut."

"A hernia and a porn addiction," added Paul.

"Why is he called 'Christos', anyway?" said Beth. "He's American, right?"

"He's gone native," said Paul. "Which would be another danger."

"I think he's got a massive secret," I blurted out, before I'd really thought about it. It was one of those moments when you don't realize you believe something until you actually say it.

"You think everyone has a massive secret," you said. I suppose you meant it to sound fond, but it actually sounded like you already thought I was crazy.

"Maybe everyone does," said Paul lightly.

Then there was a strange moment when you sighed, shook your head and glowered at him, and he picked up a small packet of sugar and crushed it in his fist while pretending not to notice. Then we talked about other things while George ran back and forth with more carafes of wine and small bowls of Greek yogurt and preserved lemon.

But perhaps there was a slightly strained atmosphere between you and Paul for the rest of the evening? Things hadn't quite been the same between you after the row you'd had the day Paul and Beth had arrived on the island, a row I had not understood at all. It seemed to have been just another thing that had gushed out of the black cloud we'd both been under since the wedding. The row—or, I guess, fight—had started in the curio shop, and I wasn't at all sure what had triggered it. But I'm going off track again, and I know how much that annoys you.

We had sex on that last night in our cheap bed in our cheap beach hotel. The mattress was so thin I thought we might go through it, or bounce it off its plywood frame. While you pounded me I imagined I was a glamorous but sad nightclub dancer, and I'd picked you up that evening and didn't know your name. In that scenario, you looked a bit like Paul.

We'd left the balcony doors open and the curtains flickered

occasionally, although there wasn't much of a breeze. I don't think either of us noticed how humid it was becoming, how sultry, how close.

The Villa Rosa was so near that we didn't know how to get there. We couldn't call a cab to take us 400 yards around the corner. In the end we decided to walk there with our suitcases.

You insisted on dressing up, because we were now going to what you called a "proper hotel." You wore your white shirt and your navy chinos. I dressed as usual in my beach stuff. I was the one who read instructions and itineraries, so I knew we probably couldn't check in yet and would have to leave our bags. I was ready to walk back to the beach after that and just have a normal day. I didn't want anything to change. I wanted to lie on the same lounger on the same patch of beach and feel the sun knead the back of my thighs like hot dough while I tried to plot my new play.

"I wish we didn't have to go," I said to Marlena, the manager of the cheap beach hotel, as we checked out.

"You will be back," she said, smiling. "Next year."

"Next year," I agreed, and she squeezed my hand. "Have fun in Italy," I added.

She was leaving that day to visit her sister. She'd been telling us all about it. Her sister had been here helping with the refugees on the north of the island, but had got burned out and had to leave. The hotel was shuttered and locked up, except for our room. Paul and Beth had already taken the early boat. Marlena now gave us two pieces of homemade coconut cake wrapped in foil—the same sort she'd made for the refugees, she said—and made us promise to come back later and get our beach towels for the day as usual. The way it worked here was that the sun loungers half belonged to the hotel they were in front of, and half belonged to the public. To claim one, you had to put a towel on it. If you were staying in a hotel, they gave you the towel.

"I'll leave them with Raoul," she said. Raoul was the barman. Tomorrow he was departing for Athens too.

"I'm sure they'll have towels at the Villa Rosa," you said.

"But probably not until after we check in," I reminded him.

We couldn't officially check in until two o'clock, but we were going to try our luck now anyway. We'd promised Marlena that we'd check out early so she could get to the airport in good time. She was worried about the plane to Athens, especially in the wind that was due to pick up later that day. We didn't want her to have to hurry as well.

I'd forgotten how heavy my leather handbag was. It cut into my shoulder as I wheeled my two suitcases out of Marlena's hotel and down the tarmac road. We took the first turning on the right. It was a narrow back street, dusty and still, with overhanging trees and pale green cactuses with dying flowers. Our suitcase wheels kept getting stuck on hard seed pods, or churned up with small stones. I had to yank mine along and the movement was so awkward that at one point I ripped a fingernail.

It seemed to get hotter as we walked. The houses were not like the whitewashed squares along the seafront. Here were darker, grander villas, with tall gates and long fences. Dogs barked, and every gate had a sign saying *Beware of the Dog* in

Greek. Outside one of the bigger houses, a collarless, ragged-looking Alsatian ran hard along the fence as we passed, then growled at our backs as we walked on.

Eventually, our suitcase wheels red with crushed berries, we turned into the driveway of the Villa Rosa and walked past more tired-looking cactuses, exhausted lemon trees and big, sleepy hornets. A massive pomegranate tree slopped its bruised fruits onto the path. There were still dogs barking in the distance, always the sound of the dogs barking, but there were no dogs at the Villa Rosa.

There she was, in the shade of the stone veranda, in a prim white dress. Isabella. I can barely even write her name. From now on, everything I say I will imagine you disagreeing with, saying, "It wasn't like that" or "You're not being fair" and all I can do is bow my head slightly and say, "OK." And then just not react. Because I don't know what else to do. There's no point arguing anymore. And yes, perhaps it wasn't the way I say, and perhaps I'm not being fair, and perhaps leaving at the first sign of the storm easing, as I am about to do, to walk to the airport (a mere seven miles), to take the first plane out of here in secret, and to never see you again—perhaps that proves I am the one who is mad. But it no longer troubles me that you think that. I am at peace with what has happened, and the knowledge that this is goodbye. I hoped we could get past everything, but you've proven that this will always be impossible.

When we arrived, you in your travel outfit, and me in my bikini and flamingo-print silk playsuit, there they were: the beautiful people. They had been staying here in the expensive place approved of by your mother; of course they had. The roosters were not yachtsmen. The boys were kicking a tennis ball in the dust while a pair of cool, comfortable-looking men—the same ones as the previous night—sat at a table smoking and looking down at their tablets, both of which had covers the color of bluebottles. A couple of guitars were propped up near them. The prettier girl, the one I never was, lolled in a hammock with a notebook and pen. The other girl had a ping-pong bat and a ball which she was hitting up in the air, *tap, tap, tap*. They completely ignored us. Well, almost. The darker boy caught my eye and stared at me for a couple of seconds too long. I could see more glitter, this time around his cheekbones, as if it had not quite been scrubbed off.

Isabella came out from the shaded stone veranda, worry in her large eyes. We must have looked dusty and out of place. And who arrives on foot to a hotel like this? We should have got a taxi.

Behind her, the Villa Rosa loomed, grander than any other structure we'd seen on the island. The large veranda was flanked by a series of terracotta brick columns. Above the veranda was a balcony, with plants in terracotta pots. All the windows had aubergine wooden shutters, and the main house was built from large pale bricks. It was grand, but also somehow rustic. Its effect was to make one feel small, but also overcomplex, too attached to the modern world and its kerfuffle. It was the sort of place you'd hand over your mobile phone and go around in a dressing gown all day.

Except this was no spa. I'd looked it up online and been baffled about why it cost so much and was always fully booked. There was no swimming pool, no sauna or hot tub. Our room didn't even have a balcony or a sea view. Of course, none of the rooms had a sea view, because the hotel was not by the sea.

"*Kalimera*," I said, sing-songing the word for "good morning" the way the maids did in Marlena's hotel. Marlena always seemed to like it when I tried to speak Greek.

"Yes?" Isabella said in lightly accented English. "Can I help you?"

I gave her my name but she still looked worried. She had the air of a serious child who has been left in charge while her neglectful parents nip out to the pub or go on holiday somewhere, but she must have been my age or a bit older.

She stood there like a picture from a children's book, hands behind her back.

"The other guests," she said, frowning, "they have not left. They are still here."

"I know," I said. "I can see. But can we leave our luggage?"

"Well, yes," she said uncertainly. "I suppose."

"The big bags can go on the veranda," you said. "I'm sure it won't rain."

She beamed at you. "Yes," she said. "Good." The smile had disappeared by the time she turned back to me. "You can check in at two o'clock," she said. Isabella then turned to go into the villa, so we followed her.

"And my handbag?" I said. "Can I . . . ?"

The lobby was all cool tiles and wood and smelled of polish and fine incense, like the stately homes and medieval churches my mother used to like to visit. The interior was dark and impressive, with high ceilings and stained-glass window panels. There was an antique chiffonier with a thick guest book. Beside it, a bundle of old-looking documents tied with string.

To my right was an impressive pair of wooden double doors with shining brass hinges. They were closed. Ahead of me was another wooden door, which was open. Isabella glided across the tiled floor and closed it.

"Anywhere you like," Isabella said, gesturing at a chair upholstered in salmon velvet.

"It's got my passport in it," I said. "And all my money."

"You would like me to put it in the cupboard? Or under my desk?"

She gestured toward the door she'd just closed.

"Oh yes. Thank you." I smiled.

"But why?" she said, not smiling back. "Everything is safe here. The whole house is completely open. Nothing is locked. We have no reason to worry here."

"OK then," I said. "Fine. I'll leave it on the chair."

"If you really want I can find somewhere else."

"It's fine. Really. The chair is great."

You gave me a look, then, that I didn't understand. I was being perfectly polite.

We walked back through the dust and the bleeding berries and the dead fruit smell while the dogs barked and snarled at us, and I was sure I could still hear the *tap, tap, tap* of the girl with the bat and ball. A man had watched us leave: a gardener, holding a sharp-looking machete. His eyes had followed us past the cactuses and the lemon trees as if he were a guard.

"She seemed nice," you said. We didn't yet know Isabella's name.

As I write your dialogue here, I realize I want it to be more nuanced, but it wasn't. It was as if some spell had taken hold of you the very moment you saw her. Maybe it was our wedding curse. I want to write instead that, at that point, so early in the whole thing, you took my hand and asked if I was all right. But you didn't. You completely ignored the fact that I'd just been instructed to leave my valuables in a shared hallway. You must know that I'm not exactly a locked-room person myself. You made me feel like I was an uptight, weak little victim; but of course you can't possibly have done that with only one sentence. So perhaps it was just me.

I glared at you and didn't reply, and then the silence closed over us like a scab.

The day was getting hotter and stiller, and by the time we got back to the beach I almost felt as if I were breathing underwater. We were the only tourists left. We sat on our usual sunbeds as the tepid wind began to swirl around us and choppy waves appeared on the surface of the water. You read a novel as if everything was normal, and I brooded and waited for you to go first. You did not.

I walked to the edge of the water but your eyes did not follow me. When I swam, the fish underneath me seemed to move more urgently, shivering back and forth as though preparing for something. Then it began to drizzle. The rain was warmer than I expected it would be.

Two taxis passed us as we walked back in the rain. Through the window I could see sharp shoulder blades, shiny dark hair, bluebottle tablet covers and lean, tanned arms. So that was it. The beautiful people were gone too. On the afternoon boat I guess, because the plane had gone at eleven. I'd heard it take off, the sound of its engines snarling through the air like an angered beast.

When we went to collect our room key, Isabella looked distracted, and almost—this will sound odd—frightened. A man was leaving the house—I realize as I write this that it was the dapper little man from the curio shop, but I don't think either of us noticed or cared about that at the time. We just wanted to check in.

Isabella was holding a basket of bruised red fruits that looked like pomegranates, which she put on the chiffonier before showing us to our room. To get there, we had to go outside again and up the staircase behind the veranda to the patio above. The stone tiles gleamed with the recent rain, and the flowers in the terracotta pots appeared to tremble. It had stopped raining, but the wind still flapped around like an invisible lost bird, fluffing things up, fluttering.

At the end of the patio was a large window which was slightly open, with a thin white curtain drawn across it. The curtain jerked in the breeze like a pinned butterfly. The aubergine shutter that went with the window was weather-stained and looked as if it had been kept open for a long time. The brass hook holding it against the wall was green and tarnished. At a right angle to the window was a fire door that wasn't in keeping with the rest of the hotel. It seemed municipal somehow. It was propped open with a rock. We walked through it to a tiled corridor.

The corridor was dark and had the same woodsmoke and incense smell as the lobby downstairs. It had four doors leading off it, and a narrow, darkly carpeted staircase. Next to the staircase was an ancient sign that I could just about see had once said "Attic Suites 1 and 2" in a cursive script, but this had been struck out and it now said "Staff Only."

Three doors were wide open; each led to identical neat guest rooms with four-poster beds and freestanding white enamel baths. I've never understood that, by the way, when hotel rooms have baths in the main room, so you can't even bathe and prepare yourself for your lover in private.

Next to each of the four-poster beds was an antique transistor radio and a small stack of old hardback books. Each room had a dresser with a floral ceramic washbasin, and a little bundle of letters and documents tied with string, just like the one I'd seen downstairs on the chiffonier.

We reached the closed door at the end of the corridor and Isabella unlocked it.

"You have the best rooms," she said, sounding as if she'd rather have given them to someone else. Or perhaps I imagined that. How many ways there are to say a simple sentence, and how hard it is to agree on what the speaker really means.

She said "rooms" because our accommodation was actually a suite, made up of two bedrooms and one bathroom. Although there was much more space in our suite than in the other rooms, it was clearly less desirable than them. The beds didn't have headboards, let alone posts. There was no bath. As we walked around we realized that the bigger, lighter bedroom was the one with the large window overlooking the patio at the top of the stone staircase; thus the drawn white curtain. But the other bedroom was extremely dark and poky, so we wheeled our cases into the big one.

"Will we have to keep this curtain closed?" I said.

"This is up to you," said Isabella.

But clearly we wouldn't be able to open it. Even when it was closed, the curtain moved about in the breeze and anyone coming up the stone steps would be able to get glimpses of the bed, and whoever was in it.

"The other rooms," I began. You glared at me. I'd promised not to do this here. Of course, that was before we knew we were cursed, when promises still meant something.

"Yes?" said Isabella.

"Well, I just noticed that they seem a little more private, and—"

"You want more private?"

"It's fine," you said. "This is wonderful."

"Your mother choose this room," Isabella said to you, warmly. "She has good taste." She looked at me, and her tone became colder once again. "One of the new rooms was free three weeks ago, but your mother-in-law look at the website and see this room is better. It is the Honeymoon Suite."

I must have gone pale at that. So we could have had one of the nicer rooms at the time we actually wanted? But no one ever questioned Annabelle. I blinked back my pathetic tears, thinking again of how the gods seemed to want us undone, cursed as we were. There was nothing auspicious about our union; nothing.

But, of course, I was overreacting as usual.

Isabella explained how to operate the fans, and where the insect-killing plugs were kept. Her white dress was stiff as she walked. It really did look like a child's outfit, and she still had that faint air of abandonment about her. Her legs were slim, tanned and surprisingly muscular. Her sandals were the same whitewash color as so many things on the island: the buildings, walls, even the trunks of trees. She looked awkward and fragile despite her suntan and her muscles.

"Thank you," I made myself say. "*Efharisto*. It's all so lovely. Your house is beautiful."

The wind picked up outside. Something fell over with a clatter. The curtain fluttered, and its edge lifted like a buffeted wing until the entire patio was visible. Our bedroom was on display for anyone walking past.

"The storm is arriving," said Isabella, her mood seeming to darken, like the sky. "You are here at the wrong time."

Indeed. As she'd handed me the envelope, your mother had specifically told me that the Villa Rosa was fully booked for the rest of the summer. She'd talked about how long it had taken her to make all the arrangements, how well reviewed this place was, how gilded.

"Yes, well, I wanted to come earlier," I began to say.

"We don't mind a bit of weather," you said.

Isabella looked at you and giggled, as if you'd made a joke. Then her face fell once more. "Excuse me if I am emotional. I have just said goodbye to the most wonderful guests." Isabella closed her eyes for a moment. She breathed in slowly and then out again, making a sad little noise as she did so. "We have actually all just been crying," she said, forcing a brave half-smile. "Crying and playing the guitar and singing. These were such beautiful guests. I am so sorry to see them leave. We all cried," she said again, and closed her eyes.

When she left, you started to unpack. The suitcases were only slightly damp from being on the uncovered part of the veranda during the rain shower.

"Oh my God," I said, rolling my eyes.

"What?" you said, unfolding a pair of cream chinos and shaking them before putting them the way you like them on the hanger.

"Come on. Really?" I laughed. "'We all cried'? Nice way to greet your new guests. How are we going to live up to that?"

"It isn't a competition," you said. And you smiled, or half-smiled, to reassure me. Or maybe I just made that bit up and there was no smile. But smile or not, I never said it was a competition. I just thought, at first, that it was weird and funny, like the time the overweight motorcycle man broke into an earnest jog when he saw me running, and I caught George's eye and we both laughed. But from the day you and I got married, it's been harder for us to catch each other's eyes in that easy way and share a moment.

We had a restless first night at the Villa Rosa. We'd gone out for dinner as usual but the only place open on the beach had those caged birds I don't like. They are for sale every-where here: goldfinches locked up and singing for a mate, or for their freedom. The songs were loud and beautiful, but also unsettling. Our food had too much garlic, and the tzatziki was warm. When we got back to the Villa Rosa—the dogs all barking hungrily in the dark, me using my phone as a torch—the wind died and the stillness returned. It felt hotter than ever.

Even though the air was still, the curtain over the window separating us from the patio fluttered back and forth. But maybe I imagined that. I closed the window anyway. But of course that made the room even hotter.

"Is there no air-conditioning?" I said as we got ready for bed.

"The fans'll be OK," you said.

"Right," I said. "But they're noisy."

"Air-conditioning is noisy."

"OK."

"I think I prefer it without air-conditioning."

"Right."

"It's better for the environment."

You wanted to have sex and I didn't. I felt too hot and, even though I can't explain this, too unlike the beautiful people. I felt that my bones were hidden too deeply inside me. The patio light shone through the thin curtain and gave the room a pale, osseous color. Shadows of insects danced on the ceiling.

Before I put on my sleep mask I contemplated the tulip painting above the chest of drawers. The oil paint had been thickly layered, as if the artist fancied themselves as a Dutch master, and the red flowers looked like large wineglasses full of blood, or—and I have no idea why I thought this—stuffed with meat. When I eventually got to sleep I dreamed that the beautiful people were sleek gundogs running through a field a lot like the one we got married in, except full of badly painted tulips.

At some point toward dawn there was a strange banging, and the sound of a door slamming. And, in the distance, dogs barking and roosters crowing and a fluttering sound that was unfamiliar. The patio light had remained on.

The next morning, as I got dressed in my bikini and play-suit, something began to trouble me. I realized it was the mirror in the door of the antique wardrobe. It made me look absurdly short and fat. In the mirror at the beach hotel I'd seemed taller, leaner, younger than normal. The light from the sea picked up my tan and made me look healthy. Here I looked old, English, mangy. My eyes and skin looked dull and unhealthy. All skin and fat and no bone, like a pile of cheap supermarket poultry pieces.

When we left our suite the corridor was quiet. The doors to the other rooms remained open. As far as I knew, there were no other guests. The door to the patio was propped open with the rock again, and there was a note taped to it that I was sure hadn't been there yesterday. *PLEASE do not lock this door over-night, it is necessary to be open for ALL the guests. You need not worry about intruders as we have had no problems in last 20 years.*

"Odd," I said.

"It's good," you said. "Too many people are paranoid about locking doors."

"But you may as well lock doors," I said. "An unlocked door has no actual benefit to those inside."

You frowned, but didn't reply. It was the kind of thing you'd be more likely to say than me. Comments on efficiency and practicalities were your area, not mine.

We walked down the stone staircase and into the

courtyard. The garden was dry after the rain. It wasn't yet eight o'clock but it was already so hot.

"Where's breakfast?" you said.

"I think we sit at one of the tables in the garden and wait," I said.

"No," you said confidently. "It'll be through there." You pointed into the dark lobby with its pink velvet chairs and the pair of polished wooden doors. They were still closed.

I was pretty sure that those doors led to Isabella's part of the house, but I couldn't stop you as you blundered into her private space. She didn't seem to mind, though. I heard giggling and reassuring noises coming from within.

Once you'd been put right and we'd sat in the garden at a wrought-iron table, Isabella appeared. Her outfit today was more masculine. She wore navy jodhpurs and a crisp white shirt. How strange. You had been wearing almost the same thing the day before. Well, OK, you didn't wear jodhpurs, but something about her outfit was peculiar. She'd color-matched you exactly. But of course it can't have been deliberate. Her thick golden hair tumbled down her back like a waterfall and her shy brown eyes flicked this way and that before finally settling on yours.

"What would you like for breakfast?" she asked. "We have pastries, breads, jams, yogurt, eggs—whatever you want."

"Bacon and eggs?" you said cheerfully.

"Oh, I'm sorry," said Isabella. "We are a vegetarian hotel. Perhaps you did not know."

"You *did* know that," I hissed at you. "I'm so sorry," I said to Isabella. "We did know. We just forgot." What an incredible faux pas, I thought. But the two of you acted as if nothing had gone wrong. You ordered scrambled eggs on wholemeal toast, and she beamed at you.

"I'll just have fruit," I said when the shy eyes finally moved to mine.

"No bread?"

"No, thanks."

"Maybe gluten-free?"

"No. Just fruit. If that's OK. Thanks very much."

"OK." She raised an eyebrow. Caught your eye. Looked back at me. "Just fruit," she repeated, as if she were practicing a foreign phrase. She went to walk away, but then paused and turned back. "Any fruit in particular?"

"Just whatever you've got." I said. "Maybe some melon, if you have it."

"No, I'm sorry, we do not have melon," Isabella said.

"OK," I said. "Just whatever, then."

While we waited for breakfast you talked enthusiastically about the garden, about the house, about the run you were planning for later that day. I found myself wishing I were wearing white linen rather than thin safari-print silk, and that I had a bag that said *Istanbul is Contemporary*, and that I was younger and shinier and had brighter eyes.

When breakfast arrived, you were presented with a large plate of thick-cut wholemeal toast topped with a pile of yellow steaming eggs, all fluffy and beautiful. You were also given a bonus bowl of Greek yogurt with preserved lemon and pomegranate seeds, and a big pot of fresh coffee.

I was given a child-size bowl containing—and I promise you I counted—two strawberries chopped into quarters, three blueberries, one raspberry and one unripe apricot chopped into eighths. I'd asked for tea, which here, as so often in Europe, meant a pot of warm water and a teabag still in its paper wrapper.

"*Efharisto*," I said. "Thank you."

Isabella nodded, then smiled at you, did a strange action that was like a little curtsey, and left.

"Wow," I said, thinking the contrast pretty obvious.

"Great, isn't it?" you said.

"I, um, don't have much," I said.

"Well, you did only ask for fruit," you said.

"I know, but ..." I shrugged. "This ... And where are my pomegranate seeds?"

"What do you mean?"

"Well, you have pomegranate seeds and I don't," I said.

"Everything here's fresh and in season," you said. "Maybe they just don't have much fruit at the moment. Maybe there aren't many pomegranate seeds. It's not like at home where you can just go to the supermarket."

"I've been to the shop," I said. "There are different fruits in the shop. There are watermelons and cantaloupes and grapes, and there are actually pomegranates growing on trees right here and—"

"I'm sure she did her best," you said. "Do you want some of my eggs?"

"No, thanks," I said.

After a while, Isabella came back out to collect the plates.

I wonder how different everything might have been if you had answered her next question instead of me.

"Can I get you anything else?" she said.

"Oh, yes," I said, before I'd even thought how to phrase my request. "Er, beach towels. We need beach towels. How do we ...? I mean, do you give them out, or should we ...?"

"Towels?" said Isabella uncertainly, as if this was something she might have to ask her parents. "For the beach?"

"Yes," I said. "If that's OK."

"Well," she said. "I don't know. I could give you two of the white ones, I suppose."

"Great," I said.

A few minutes later she returned with two perfect fluffy white towels. They were folded into plump cubes. She held them out to me, but not quite all the way.

"I'm not sure these will be so good on the beach," she said. "It is very dirty."

It was true. The beach was mainly pebbles on top of a reddish sand that was slightly sticky and must have had clay in it. My beach strategy was to stay on a lounger in the sun as long as possible, but keep a patch of shade nearby for when it got too much. My shade sessions were on a towel on the pebbles. Marlena had never minded this.

"OK," I said, a little confused. "Well, we'd better not take them, then."

"Also, water is big problem here on the island and we try not to wash too many towels."

"Well in that case we definitely won't take them," I said.

But now she thrust the towels toward me. "Please," she said.

"No, thank you," I said. "Really. It's fine."

"Please," she held them out to me. "You can take them."

"No," I said. "We'll do without them. Thank you anyway."

"Please," she said again.

"I couldn't possibly," I said.

She looked as if she might cry.

When she went back inside with the towels I looked at you but you wouldn't catch my eye. I'd expected something. A raised eyebrow would have been fine. A mumbled "Well, that was weird" would have been perfect. I mean, that *was* weird. It actually was. Had the beautiful people had beach towels? I couldn't remember.

Back in the room, you were quiet. I returned to contemplating myself in the mirror. I just looked so wrong here. And my skin! It looked like old wolfskin, blistered and cracked like a leathery hunter's bottle. But to be truthful it was just the speckling on the antique mirror. I've always found that strange, by the way, when the surface of a mirror degrades: it's like reality itself bubbling and bursting. Which always makes me wonder.

"Please tell me I don't really look like this," I said.

It's a thing I used to do with my mum. If ever we were both in a lift or a changing room with a strange mirror I'd look at her reflection, her striking face not yet so puffed up, and say, "You don't look like that in reality, you know," and she'd be relieved and say the same about me and then we'd make faces in the bad mirror and it would be one of the few bonding experiences I ever remember having with her, especially in those hard teenage years when everything

I did was wrong and I got caught shoplifting and smoking and having sex with the wrong boys and everyone was so happy when I finally got a place at university and left with my bags full of outlandish outfits and makeup I'd never paid for.

"What?" you said, without looking at me. "Sorry?"

"Do I actually look like this? Please tell me I don't."

"Like what?"

"Like in this mirror. It's extremely unflattering."

"Don't you have more important things to think about than that?"

"Sorry?"

"Aren't you supposed to be writing?"

"It's 8:30 in the morning. I don't understand why you—"

"I don't understand why it always has to be about appearance with you anyway."

"What? What the hell does that mean? You didn't seem to mind when I was on a diet to look good for your fucking family wedding photos."

You sighed then, and it was a long, drawn-out, pre-argument sigh.

"What's the matter?" I asked, although really it should have been the other way around. I was the one who'd had a horrible breakfast, and the upsetting conversation about the towels. On the wall behind you there was a lonely and strange picture of a mauve tulip. It looked as if it had been done in such a hurry that the background had been forgotten. It hung in the white space like a sagging balloon, its stem a thin green string. The scene seemed to freeze for a second, and it was just me and you and the single tulip in the entire universe, and nothing had a background anymore.

"Why can't you be nicer to Isabella?" you said.

It was the first time I'd heard her name. You must have learned it when I was otherwise engaged.

I blinked. "Excuse me?"

"You were downright rude before. It was embarrassing."

"Seriously?" I said. "You really think that was me being rude? What's wrong with you?"

"Don't start on me now," you said, emphasizing the *me*, as if I was a ragged Alsatian about to attack anyone I could get my teeth into; as if I was dangerous, rabid.

I shook my head, confused. "So you *don't* think that was the most passive-aggressive thing you've ever seen?"

"What?"

"The business with the towels."

"She was just trying to save water. I don't know why we have to have new towels every day anyway. It's not good for the environment."

"So you don't think it was weird that she offered us those towels but basically said we shouldn't take them?"

"They're probably the only ones she has."

"She runs a hotel near a beach! Surely she has beach towels."

"Yes, well, not everyone wants to lie on a beach all day." You didn't catch my eye then. You breathed in, a bit haughtily, I thought; as if just by breathing you could rise above me, a mighty zeppelin floating high above a flightless dog gnashing its teeth and pawing the ground.

"What is that supposed to mean?" I said.

"There is more to life than spending every day lying on a beach and looking at yourself in the mirror."

"Oh really? Thanks, Oprah. I never would have known what life was actually about if you hadn't enlightened me. What the fuck? Why are you doing this?"

"And we're not in America. Why do you have to talk like that? Why is everything sarcastic all the time? And 'weird'? And don't say 'What the fuck?' like that to me. You know I hate it. And I don't know who Oprah is."

"Yes, you do."

"No, I don't."

"Your fucking school even protected you from Oprah?" I said. "Good job."

Paul had recently told a "funny" story over dinner about the headmaster at St. Mark's giving a talk every year on why it was important to avoid the girls from the nearby grammar school. The headmaster apparently never mentioned the comprehensives and certainly never thought to warn you off the girls who ended up at the local university, the bad one that only asked for a couple of grade Cs to do theatre studies.

St. Mark's did such a good job of hiding knowledge of girls that perhaps it was inevitable that so many of its alumni would end up with ones like me who don't know how to use cutlery properly and deep down think all beds need a valance.

Now, of course, we are, or were, married, until death or— just as bad—divorce did us part. I could feel tears coming.

"All I wanted was for you to support me. To agree with me."

"You just want me to be your yes-man? A sycophant? Is that what you're saying?"

"No. Come on, please. Why are you doing this?"

"I'm not doing anything," you said. "I am simply trying to have a nice time in this beautiful place that you have decided to hate, presumably because you are jealous of Isabella."

"Oh, fuck you," I said, and went into the bathroom and locked the door.

When I came out, you'd gone. For a run, according to the neutral note you left.

I spent the morning trying to write. But I kept replaying our argument, or scripting the next one. Of course, neither of us was addressing the moment at the wedding when Luciana cursed us forever. Had you heard? Perhaps not.

What was I going to say when you got back? The sensible thing would be to drop it, of course; I knew that. And you often would come back after an argument and act like it hadn't happened, which you thought to be measured and mature, but I sometimes felt was just repression and acting like your father. Go for a run and wait for the hysterical woman to pipe down. Wait for the growling dog to go back in its kennel. Take a tablet, get a rabies shot. Close your eyes and ears. Go to bed.

I typed the beginning of a bad scene on my laptop until my torn fingernail annoyed me so much that I ripped at it and then it started to bleed on the keyboard. I was determined not to give in and go to the beach. Not until I'd written something good.

I tried putting something a bit like our argument into

the new play, which was about a dinner party that leads to the tragic downfall of a young woman who says the wrong thing. As you know, I'd had my last grant application rejected because my work was too unbelievable and "gruesome." But a commercial director was interested in me and my "voice," and we'd had a meeting booked for, well, tomorrow actually, which naturally I'd had to cancel because we are, or were, still on our honeymoon.

What your mother had really done was screw up my one chance of resurrecting my ailing career. I'd asked her if we could change the dates, but she'd said the booking was non-refundable. Of course it was.

You know, I still can't believe how quickly I fell. I'm not sure we ever really discussed what happened with my career, and I'm not sure if it made things easier between us, or harder. I went from housekeeper with an MA in Theatre Studies and a script for a one-woman show to fringe-sensation with my own TV series to washed-up failure in a period of just over six years. I have a magnificent wardrobe and a lot of gold and diamond jewelry and not much else. Oh, and a husband.

What did you make of those years? You never exactly said. You found my show exciting, but also distasteful, I think, more so once it was honed for TV. Not that you ever quite admitted it as we sat in the Groucho with you looking worried and out of place while I drank Skinny Bitches (you called these "tequila, lime and sodas") and did lines of coke in the loos. I suppose you must have known about my brief issue with the various powders I needed to get through all the endless days of rehearsals and auditions and diets and table reads and shoots. It's all over now. The only powder I'm interested in now is the crushed black elderberry I take to ward off infections. And the Dior loose face powder that smells of roses, which Beth said she hadn't ever tried.

My show was about a girl who sleeps with her boss and believes she groomed him, not the other way around. It was fine until it was on TV, at which point people started to find fault with it, and an opinion piece in a national newspaper said it was basically an apologia for the patriarchy and should never have been created. This inspired others to attack the show for being unoriginal, plagiarized and even culturally appropriated.

I tried to respond with a small column for the newspaper but it was given an unfortunate click-bait headline which caused a small but significant Twitter pile-on. After that my remaining invitations and auditions dried up and I sat at home and cried while my career was extinguished like a campfire in a sudden downpour.

But perhaps I deserved it? No one ever spotted the real problem with the show, except perhaps your mother and father, but they never actually said anything. Like you, they love silence. When things get really tough? Zip it.

So I pulled myself together and wrote a new play, entirely different, about a heightened, Gothic safari where almost everyone ends up eaten, either by animals or other humans. It was supposed to be funny. A dark comedy about canni-balism. No one liked it, and I was left with a large tax bill and only a very slim hope for the future. Still, I will survive. I always have.

But it is hard, once you've been up in the air, to come back down again.

Do you remember the morning of our engagement party? Perhaps not. I'm not sure what you were doing before the lunch. It was at your parents' house near Canterbury, where I'd lived in as their housekeeper for four years when I was at university. Once we were engaged, everyone decided to forget I'd ever been a housekeeper at all, which was a relief in many ways.

That morning last spring I was in the dim, cool dining room searching for napkin rings. It was a bright day, and your mother had decided we should have the lunch outside. I was looking out of the French windows when I saw something sharp-beaked and magnificent. A sparrowhawk! Your mother's garden was always the most lush, most jungle-like in your street. And now it had its very own top predator.

Your father was a keen birdwatcher, and we had once spent a long country walk stalking a grey heron while you and your mother discussed what to do about your eccentric aunt Sylvia who was plowing rather too much of the family money into the publishing house she'd set up, seemingly to print the work of her friends and students. I know you remember that day, because you were troubled by the idea that anyone could have so much to say to your father. But we'd always been close, even before I really knew you. Your mother was frequently away for work, and when you were at Durham it was often just Peter and me in the house.

On our engagement-party morning, I'd just seen him approaching when I noticed the sparrowhawk, and so I'd called to him in that kind of low hiss reserved for those situations when you want to alert somebody to the fact that there is something interesting to see, without alerting the thing you want them to look at.

"Peter?" I breathed, the P of his name pushing out of my mouth like the puffed-up chest of the bird on the lawn. "Peter?"

The sparrowhawk, sharp-beaked and haughty, was in one of those dips in the lawn your mother was proud of for a reason that I can't remember. Its feathers flared on its legs. It was pecking away at something, quite violently. It seemed to have made quite a mess of the lawn. Was that black stuff earth? It seemed almost too dense and peaty. Was the sparrowhawk digging something up? As your father came to stand beside me, I realized that it was a blackbird. The sparrowhawk was killing a blackbird by sort of rubbing it into the lawn. It was burying its face in it.

"Everything all right, Evelyn?" said Peter, too loudly.

I put my finger to my lips, but it was too late. The sparrowhawk took off, the blackbird now skewered on its talons. It came down on the other side of the garden, near the stone birdbath with the ivy wound around its stem.

"Sparrowhawk," I whispered, pointing.

Peter saw it. "I'll get the binoculars," he said, touching my arm, just once.

Later, after lunch, when your mother had just opened the second bottle of champagne, we tried to describe what we'd seen.

Your father's eyes shone, not quite as gold as the hawk's had been, but with a similar intensity. I, too, felt different. Charged. Aloft with adrenaline and blood.

There had been something so disgusting, but also unexpectedly beautiful, about seeing one bird killing and then plucking another. Nature, red in tooth and claw—as Peter said several times—but also absurdly, slasher-film violent, almost sublimely so. The blackbird's head had flopped from side to side as the sparrowhawk tore out its feathers, trying to get at its flesh. I thought I'd seen the blackbird open its beak then, and the idea that it might still be alive had made me gag and run for the loo, but instead of throwing up as I'd thought I was going to, I found myself laughing uncontrollably. It's hard to explain now without sounding like I was unhinged then in the way I know you suspect I am now. But your father felt it too.

"When Evelyn got back, the sparrowhawk had just eaten the blackbird's eyeball," said Peter, after sipping his champagne. "Missed the best part. Looked as if it were rather chewy."

"Now I understand why you didn't eat your caviar," said Aunt Sylvia. She was right. That was exactly why I hadn't eaten my caviar. But I couldn't get my brain and the rest of my body to catch up with my queasy stomach.

My arms were still tingling with the viscerality of it all. All the tiny hairs on my body were charged with electricity, puffed up like a cat's tail. When I swallowed the chilled champagne, it was like hot blood in my throat, and I felt more alive than I ever had before.

When we made love that night, I pretended you were your father. A harmless and natural fantasy I'm sure most girls have. But perhaps you knew, or suspected? You'd been quiet earlier that evening as I'd tried to play the role of the enthusiastic new member of the family, even though this wasn't exactly what I was: laughing too hard at your father's jokes, and touching his arm every time he said something interesting. I'd met your father when I was at university, and then I'd become his—well, your family's—housekeeper. Now I was to be his daughter-in-law, and I was doing my best to get into the role. Now, if I act like that, you tell me to quieten down, but back then you were still shy.

Anyway, on our first morning at the Villa Rosa, you came back from your run all sweaty and hot just before lunchtime.

"It's true," you said excitedly.

"What is?"

"The beach," you said. "It's gone."

"What do you mean, 'gone'?"

"Well not exactly *all* gone. But the man in the motorcycle shop says it'll go completely when the big storm comes tonight or tomorrow."

"Right."

"Oh well, at least you'll be able to concentrate on your writing," you said, and gave me a damp kiss on the cheek. "I'm sorry about before, by the way. Can we just forget it?"

"Sure," I said. But of course, it was easy for you to forget because I hadn't said anything bad about you. But me? Too fat, too gauche, too American, too lazy, too narcissistic. But OK, for the sake of peace I decided to let it all go. Almost.

"She is a bit strange, though, don't you think?" I said.

"What, Isabella?"

"Yes."

You sighed then. "The towel thing was a bit odd, yes."

"Thank you." I kissed you on your sweaty lips.

"But I think she's nervous around us. We should try to be nice to her."

"OK."

"Can you do that?"

Why you have to push things the whole time, I don't know.

"Sure," I said. "Fine."

"You might ask her for a restaurant recommendation for tonight?" you said. "While I'm in the shower."

"I'm in the middle of a scene," I said. "We can do it later."

I went back to my laptop, and my finger bled some more, and it was the color of the awful tulips. I got into my scene but I knew it was bad. I was trying to write about the beautiful people. I don't know why I thought I could put them in a play about a dinner party. They kept turning into queer, undead, cannibalistic creatures. I couldn't stop them. I decided that in the story no one sees them until the sun has gone down. Had they roosted somewhere in the large Gothic house all day? Haha! They were not roosters, but roosters. Bats. Dark, with folded wings.

But describing people as vampires does not make a good scene, and, in any case, I was not supposed to be writing about vampires. How could I do a one-woman show about vampires anyway? And I was definitely supposed to be done with cannibals.

Nevertheless, telling myself I needed to loosen up, I started writing a scene that was very tasteless, just for the hell of it. You would have hated it. You liked writing to be clean, minimal, stylish. This was a kitschy, garish scene in which the vampires, dressed as hunters, lured two innocent couples to a candlelit picnic where the other guests were animals and taxidermists and crazed balloonists, and in the hot, waxy forest light they raped and murdered the couples and left them immortal, beautiful and perfect, their wounds healed with fresh green leaves.

They didn't eat them, I promise.

I wanted to find some way of showing the thick swirl of blood and ripping flesh and the hot excitement of the kill, but all I could think of were the tulip paintings. The one above my makeshift desk began to bother me. It was bad, of course; all the paintings were. Its petals were the color of meat, but dried and curled, like dead tongues. The dead tongues were wrapped smugly around their erect green stems.

You came out of the shower.

"How's your scene going?"

"Fine," I said, shutting the laptop. "I'm distracted by these terrible paintings."

"What terrible paintings?"

"All the tulips."

"Evie," you said, sighing.

"What?"

"Well you must know that she does them? I saw her easel set up downstairs."

"Oh," I said. "Well, that doesn't stop them being awful." I stretched and put my glasses away in their case. "It must be time for lunch soon?"

"Isabella's put some sandwiches out for us," you said.

"Oh. Right. But I thought we might go to the beach, or what's left of it."

"Nothing's open. George's Taverna's shut. Raoul's gone. The sun loungers aren't there anymore. It's all closed down."

"The shop must still be open, though? I thought we could get some bread and cheese and sit and look at the sea."

"Well, we can't just leave the sandwiches. She's gone to a lot of trouble."

It was then that I had the feeling I was never going to see the beach or the sea again.

The sandwiches were on bread I don't like (poppy seed), with smelly, bloating fillings I don't like (hummus and red pepper; egg and tomato), but I ate them anyway and did not complain. After lunch Isabella disappeared completely and there was no way of getting a cup of tea or coffee so we just drank water we'd bought from the shop the day before. Still, you'd managed to get a restaurant recommendation from Isabella: she'd even rung and booked for us. It was a place on the other side of the island. We'd need a cab to get there. She'd booked that too.

I spent the afternoon writing and deleting things while you read a thin novel your mother had recommended. You always read more than I did, even though I was supposed to be the artistic one. I read infrequently, partly because every book changed me, right down to the level of my DNA. I didn't want to be changed so often. But you were able to hoover up contemporary culture without so much as a little belch afterwards. You just carried on being you.

At six, I put on my black dress, the one I know you like. You wore your white linen shirt with your dark blue chinos and your Ralph Lauren boat shoes. I hadn't worn much makeup this whole holiday, but that night I did it all: foundation, which felt like thick butter on my face, full heavy eyes with mink eyelashes, and red lips.

I told myself I was doing it for you, but really I was doing it for the mirror. In any case, it didn't work and I still looked like a pile of guts and marrow but this time with red lipstick. You're not supposed to have heavy eyes and red lips together, by the way, because all the women's magazines say it's slut-tish, like offering yourself up as a piece of meat, a craven dog. But men don't know that, and you always liked me in a lot of makeup. You actually once described this look as "natural," but men don't know what is natural and what is fake most of the time.

"You look beautiful," you said.

Even though everything has gone so horribly wrong, I'll always remember that. Thank you.

While we waited for the cab, the gardener sat on a low wall with his machete next to him, smoking and watching us. Isabella was beyond him in the still sunlit garden, pick-ing pomegranates and putting them into a wicker basket. She must have picked a lot of pomegranates in her life, but she was picking these ones as if the process was new to her, yanking them off their branches with unnecessary violence. It wasn't efficient. Her basket was full of stalks and leaves. As she ripped the fruits off their stems, her small breasts bounced in her white shirt. She quite clearly was not wearing a bra.

"Oh," she said, turning and seeing us. "You are here."

"Just waiting for our cab," you said.

"This is Kostas," she said, indicating the gardener. "He helps me in the garden."

Which is exactly how your mother always described workers as well: "helpers."

I helped your mother quite a bit. And your father, too.

Kostas nodded at us. You walked over and shook him manfully by the hand. While he shook your hand, his eyes crept over my body. You didn't notice.

The cab driver was unfriendly and spoke no English, although he did at least respond to my *Kalispera* with a gruff mumble. His crackly car radio was playing Bob Dylan's "One More Cup of Coffee for the Road." It was oddly proleptic, hearing that song then, because in fact it's all I can hear in my head as I write this letter.

We sat together in the back of the cab and you held my hand. The driver didn't turn toward the beach but instead went up into the hills behind the Villa Rosa. The sun was going down and pink clouds were thickening overhead, like sauce that might easily curdle. After about fifteen minutes we reached a small bay with a wooden pier and some fishing boats. We hadn't been to that side of the island yet. In high season perhaps there were a lot of people there, but that night it was just us. The wind was too strong for us to sit outside by the water, so we went into the taverna. The television blared with a Greek game show.

"This is so authentic," you said.

"Right," I said. The tables were laminated with sticky

plastic. The chef was smoking. The waitress, who was also clearly his wife, had her left arm in a sling.

"It's great to be able to come somewhere real for once."

"What do you mean?" I said. "George's Taverna was real."

"It was for tourists," you said.

"OK," I said. "But we are tourists."

The waitress brought us the menus. I felt sorry for you then. It was the worst we'd seen on the island. All your least favorite things: deep-fried cheese balls; deep-fried halloumi; deep-fried baby shrimp. There were no salads. When you asked about fish of the day you were told that the fisherman had not been out today. In fact, the waitress said, there was no fish at all except for something that was supposed to be a bit like "cod-fish," which was prepared in a way similar to fish and chips. We both ordered that, and a carafe of white wine.

The waitress then brought us a bowl of taramasalata, and small white rolls that had obviously been defrosted and then heated in the microwave. An *amuse-bouche*.

"Mmm," you said. "Fresh bread."

I couldn't tell you it wasn't really fresh, just as I couldn't tell you that the taramasalata was mainly breadcrumbs and ketchup. You wanted to like everything so much, and I loved you for that. But you wanted to like this place more than usual.

"I bet you can't find this in the Lonely Planet," you said happily.

"No," I agreed.

Had you ever even read a Lonely Planet guide? I can't imagine you doing so, except maybe on your gap year. You traveled mostly for work, rather than pleasure, and the whole thing was always a complex game for you, an augmented reality of platinum cards and hotel memberships and collecting as many loyalty points as you could, for things you could afford to pay full price for anyway. Don't take this the wrong way, but you were never the world's most authentic, earthy traveler. But I never thought you wanted to be.

"We are close tomorrow," the waitress said. "Go to Athens before storm."

Just like everyone else.

"Why are they all so sure a storm is coming?" you asked in the cab home. We were drunk. We'd ordered three more carafes of wine to make up for the terrible food, which you kept saying was great, right until the very end when they brought an ice-cream sandwich of the sort my mother used to give my father and me for dessert—which, yes, we did used to call it. I don't think you'd ever seen one before, but even you couldn't pretend this was an authentic Greek experience. But you still didn't say anything: you just ate it and smiled. Your class is always so positive, don't you find? Doesn't it ever annoy you?

When we got back, Kostas was smoking at one of the breakfast tables. He didn't say anything to us. His smoke curled above his head in thick petals. The moon was high and full, with clouds rushing in front of it like dark chariots on their way to a big event.

There was a new mirror in our room. A full-length antique mirror on a stand. It was an oval shape, with brass hinges that looked like wings. Odd. But I didn't think about that then as you pulled me onto the bed.

"Shhh," I said. "Kostas is still out there."

Our window was open, even though I was sure I'd left it closed. The thin curtain lifted in the breeze.

"He can't hear anything."

Another thing about you: you have never believed anyone can hear anything through open windows. But as we made love I imagined Kostas listening. I thought about him appraising my body the way he had before. I imagined him coming up the stone steps and pausing there on the hard tiles, watching us through the window. I imagined him unzipping his work trousers.

When I orgasmed, you believed you'd done it.

Before I fell asleep I wondered where the mirror had come from.

The next morning, I had a hangover. We'd drunk more than I'd realized, and the wine must have been cheap and full of sulphites. I looked bad enough in the old mirrors, but in the new one I was jowly and pale, like a bleached-out St. Bernard that had drunk its little barrel of whisky a long time before, and whose only hope in life was to find another one.

"Where do you think this mirror came from?" I asked you, before we went down to breakfast.

"What mirror?"

"This one."

You peered at it, and then at yourself in it. I don't know what you saw.

You looked away, as if disgusted with yourself.

"You don't look like that, by the way," I said, before I'd even thought about it. But you didn't. And it made me feel better because I realized the mirror had distorted me too. In fact, as I looked at it properly I realized how horrible it was. The glass was cheap and smeared in places. The varnish on the wooden frame was thick and ugly.

You sighed. "Wasn't it here before?"

"No," I said. "Do you think ...?"

"What?"

"Isabella," I whispered. "Did she listen to us yesterday?"

"Don't be silly," you said, and kissed me on the top of my head. "Let's go and have breakfast."

As we left the room, Isabella was on the patio, sweeping up leaves and dead insects and presumably not listening to us. She was wearing army-green shorts and a white T-shirt. Again, with no bra. I could clearly see the bloom of her dark nipples through the thin cotton, and I was sure you could too.

"Please," she said. "You must leave this door unlocked overnight."

"We did," you said. "I'm sure we did."

Actually, I locked it when you weren't looking. Because, well, just because. We were drunk, and about to make love, and Kostas with his strange eyes was down below and ... I don't know. I'm provincial. Petit bourgeois. Uptight. Afraid. Like most women, I don't want my dark sexual fantasies to actually manifest in real life.

"Sorry," I said. "I'm just used to locking doors at home. I must have done it without thinking."

"It is safe here," Isabella said urgently, with that fear back in her eyes.

"OK," I said. "But we're the only guests. Does it matter?"

"We are safe here," she said again. "No need to lock."

We sat at the same table again for breakfast. The pomegranate trees looked dull in the odd morning light. It was
cloudy and the air was dense, even more so than yesterday.
The day had the feeling of a large balloon that was too heavy
to take off, because its skin was too thick and its basket too
full of people.

The dapper little man from the curio shop was there again,
in the tiled hallway, putting documents into a soft and battered brown leather briefcase.

Paul and I had begun calling him the "dapper little man"
after we'd first seen him in his curio shop. I'm not sure you'd
ever really noticed the dapper little man, but Paul and I had
developed all kinds of theories about him. There was something waxy and doll-like about his skin, and he was slight
and short. We imagined him dressed in all kinds of miniature
outfits, like an aged, Gothic Ken, or a decommissioned Action
Man. We'd invented racks of little felt paisley waistcoats and
bow ties, a moustache-grooming set and a cupboard full
of monocles.

Paul and I had so many little in-jokes and references, and
you shared none of them. Sometimes we could communicate
with only our eyes. A little flick here or there, or just a tiny
flash, and we always knew what we meant, what we were
finding ridiculous, or suspect. Why was it never like that
with me and you? The one time I tried to communicate with
you using only my eyes you asked if I might need to go to
the optician.

We'd discovered the curio shop the day Paul and Beth

had arrived on the island, two days after us. It had taken us only an afternoon to exhaust the main village by the harbor, and it seemed that the few tourist shops all sold the same things anyway: brightly painted ceramics, cheap jewelry, lavender sachets, lemon balm tea in decorative tins, and dried seahorses and starfish.

The curio shop was just beyond the village. It also had the seahorses and the starfish, but they were different, somehow. Maybe they just seemed fresher, and less dead? Almost every-thing in the curio shop had been part of a living creature once—antlers, leather packing cases, feather boas, riding crops—and I fancied I could sense a faint pulse in every one of the objects, as if the creatures were simply asleep, or under some kind of spell. Beth put her hand mindlessly into a drawer full of dried seahorses and sort of swirled them around, but I was too squeamish. I couldn't touch anything in case it woke up.

The dapper little man had been sitting on a high stool in a dark corner at the back of the shop, twisting a piece of wire with a pair of sharp-looking pliers. On the counter in front of him was a half-completed birdcage of the sort we'd seen in other shops and restaurants—the ones the goldfinches were kept in. Behind him were shelves holding bundles of documents tied with string, seeming to be little antique archives, or collections of old love letters—just like the ones Isabella had at the Villa Rosa, on the chiffonier and in the four-poster rooms.

Now, I noticed the dapper little man flinch only slightly as Isabella brushed past him, a bit closely, I thought. He snapped the bronze clasp on his antique briefcase and hurried away across the courtyard to his scooter. Isabella paused for a moment by the chiffonier, but I couldn't see what she was doing. The scooter sped away.

Isabella came out.

"Good morning," she said, with a smile directed at you. It was as if we hadn't just spoken to her upstairs, as if we hadn't yet seen her today.

"Morning," you said back.

"*Kalimera*," I said. But she ignored my attempt at Greek, just as she had the day before.

"So," she said, biting her lip. "You went to a different restaurant in the end. It was good?"

"What do you mean?" you said.

"The restaurant call and say you did not come."

A few beats then while we all realized what must have happened.

Then you laughed. "Oh dear. Did we go to the wrong one?"

"It seems so," said Isabella.

"We went to the one the cab driver took us to," I said. "He pointed at the door."

You and Isabella locked eyes and laughed, as if this were the funniest thing ever. So we'd eaten terrible frozen food for no reason? I did not find this funny. If only you'd been more honest about how bad it was we might have realized our mistake. Authentic, indeed. You laughed and laughed. In fact, Isabella laughed so much she had to grab your arm, perhaps to stop her from falling to the ground with the sheer hilarity of it all.

"I bring you eggs on toast again?" Isabella said to you once you'd both stopped laughing and she had finally let go of your arm.

"Thank you," you said back, touching her arm now. All this arm-touching all of a sudden, but I was not part of it, not at all.

"And 'just fruit,'" Isabella said to me, I thought a little mockingly.

"Thanks," I said.

Breakfast arrived. Yours was the same as yesterday. Mine was a bowl of melon. Just melon with—and I pointed this out to you, and you know it is true—one pomegranate seed on the top. One. I tasted a bit of the melon. It was hard and unripe.

"Wow," I said.

"What's wrong this time?" you said.

"It's a bowl of melon," I said. "Just melon. Loads and loads of melon."

"Well, you did ask for it."

"OK, but I usually eat all different fruits for breakfast. Why just melon? Don't you think it's weird?"

"You've got a pomegranate seed as well," you said, with a half-smile.

"You must agree that that's odd," I said. "Who puts one pomegranate seed on a bowl of melon?"

"It does look quite pretty," you said.

"It looks like a tit," I said. "A cubist tit."

"A cubist tit could still be pretty?" Your face was still flushed with the aftermath of all the laughter. You raised an eyebrow. You were being playful. Light.

"I'm not eating it," I said.

"Evelyn," you said, groaning. "Don't."

"If she wants a passive-aggressive war then she can have one," I said. "I lived with my mother for twenty years and yours for almost five. I can win against this pathetic attempt if I have to."

"Look, she made you a bowl of melon because you asked for it yesterday. Why don't you just eat it?"

"One pomegranate seed," I said, shaking my head. "Please." And then for a moment it did seem almost funny, and I smiled, and you smiled back, and I remembered you stroking my hair last night and telling me you loved me, and the storm didn't come, and the clouds moved away.

I popped the single pomegranate seed in my mouth.

After breakfast you got ready for a long run. Once you'd left, I found it hard to get into my writing. I tried to compose something about the wedding, but it was too hard, and then I started tinkering with the plans I'd already made for my new one-woman show about a girl who is raped in Freshers' Week at university. I tried different forms for this—even using an epistolary structure at one point. But nothing was working.

Instead, I tried to look up the beautiful people on Tripadvisor. Would one of them have left a review by now? I wanted to know if they were Turkish, how old they were, whether any of them had an Instagram. I couldn't imagine not being able to follow them digitally now that I couldn't follow them in real life.

I told myself that's all I was doing on Tripadvisor, but then I found myself reading all the reviews of the Villa Rosa. I know this is awful, but I wanted them to be bad. They weren't.

I wanted them to say how peculiar Isabella was, but they didn't. One said, *The charming owner is such a free spirit and so inspirational. In an area surrounded by high fences and guard dogs, she chooses to have an open house.* Another said, *The breakfast is magnificent. All that wonderful fresh fruit picked from Isabella's delightful garden.* Another said, *Isabella was so kind to us after the loss of our parents in such tragic circumstances. We arrived on the island in* ... The entry was long and I skipped over it. Unlike me, I know.

The beautiful people were not on there. But why would they be? They were not the kind of people who left reviews. They were, I thought then, more the kind of people who received reviews. Were they some sort of band? That would explain their beauty, the glitter and the presence of the older men, who could have been managers or agents. The guitars and the singing, too. I googled *Turkish band four members two boys two girls*, but before the results could come up the lights flickered and the Wi-Fi went off. The universe telling me to go back to my play, I thought. Not that the universe had given me any other indications that it wanted me to carry on writing, or performing. There was a low rumble of thunder outside, and I expected it to start raining, but it didn't.

I wanted to walk to the beach but in truth I was a bit afraid of the dogs, and I knew you'd be annoyed if you got back and found me gone. You'd made it clear, after all, that the days of lying on the beach were over. I was supposed to be writing. But I knew you wouldn't object to a wholesome walk, for inspiration, as long as it was not to the beach. I wrote you a note, and then started the long process of applying sun cream and insect repellent. I changed from my playsuit into my long khaki shorts and a white shirt. Then I closed the bedroom door, went down to the garden and started walking up the steep hill behind the Villa Rosa. I didn't lock the door, because, well, I'm such a free spirit. And you didn't have a key.

The air was hot and moist, and the hill was scrubby, with ancient-looking roots poking out of the earth, and bits of old birdcage strewn around. I knew it was a birdcage because the little yellow perch was still attached to a rusting piece of wire. It was the only colorful thing up here.

On and on I went, higher and higher, sweating. I realized I hadn't brought any water with me, and made myself slow down.

When I reached the top of the hill I sat and tried to think about my writing. I could see the coastline below me, and the next town just across the bay. Beyond that was the Turkish coast, with its rugged cliffs, and the wind farm that resembled a marching army of long-legged white birds. It looked as if it was nighttime there. Why was it so dark? Then there was a flash in the sky and I realized that there was a big storm going on. From up here it looked like war, or the end of the world. Every few moments the dark sky was illuminated yellow and white like the cracking of a giant bird's egg. One would expect a lot of noise with a spectacle like that, but in fact it was completely silent. Was this the storm that was due to come here? It was enormous.

My mouth was dry. I wondered if I could still speak, and so I said the word *parakalo* a few times, up there on the hill on my own. I'd become a little obsessed with the word. I loved hearing Greek people say it, and it always seemed like a sort of reward for trying to speak their language.

Efharisto was the most difficult basic foreign word I'd ever had to learn. All that effort just to say thank you. Four syllables, and all that rasping on that middle H, which completely broke the rhythm of the word. It was not at all onomatopoeic, unless the effort required to say the word did have some actual tangible meaning; like, I am making such an *effort* to thank you by spitting out this uncomfortable word.

If you did manage to say it, the other person would say back *parakalo*, and that word had such a contrasting fluency, and such a pretty, birdsong feel, even more so than the happy lilts of both *kalimera* and *kalispera*. *Parakalo* was another four-syllable word—they all seemed to be—but it was one that Greek speakers seemed to like to draw out. Pa-ra-ka-LO, they would often say, leaving the stress until the last syllable, just when you thought there might not be any stress at all. But the second syllable could be stressed too. It meant *you're welcome*, and also, *please*.

I realized then that I'd never said it out loud before. Why would a Greek person say thank you to me? I simply had no need of *you're welcome*. I wasn't sure if I'd ever said *please*, either. In English, *please* has an aggressive edge—"Would you bring me a bowl of melon, please?"—and we are far more likely to use *thank you* or *sorry* instead. "Sorry, would you mind bringing me a bowl of melon?" "Could I have a bowl of melon? Thank you." *Efharisto*. I realized I said thank you all the time here in place of sorry, too, which I did not know how to say in Greek. That was why I heard *parakalo* so much. It followed me around, trailing in the wake of my *efharisto*s.

I practiced saying *parakalo* again as I sat there watching the Turkish storm. I wanted to be able to say it to someone. *Parakalo*. My tongue felt massive in my mouth, and twisted, like one of the tulip stems. What on earth could I do to make Isabella or Kostas or a taxi driver or a waitress thank me, so I could chirp back *parakalo*? I was determined to find something. Now, every time the lightning flashed I replied. *Parakalo*, I said to the sky, and then the sea. *Parakalo*. You're welcome. Please. I imagined Kostas walking up the hill then, sweaty from gardening, and me drawing him closer as he touched my arm the way Isabella had touched yours. *Parakalo*. *Parakalo*. *Parakalo*.

Then I thought I heard a scuffling noise behind me, followed by a bang, and then another one. I stood up and looked around. Over the brow of the hill was an old shepherd's hut. The wooden door was banging in the wind, as though someone had just left without closing it properly. I used to feel afraid in situations like this, but lately I've noticed I simply feel numb instead, as if I'm encased in a skin that is not my own, and that can't be pierced or penetrated. But anyway, there was no need to feel any fear, because there was no one there, at least not anymore. Nevertheless, I set off back down the hill, perhaps a little quicker than I'd usually walk.

Just before I reached the place where the path split—left for the road; right for the Villa Rosa—I heard another noise; it was the *pat, pat, pat* of a runner. I thought at first it was you, but the steps were lighter than yours. I turned and saw it was the dark-haired boy, the one with the glitter, although there was no glitter on him now. He was wearing acid-wash skinny denim shorts and no vest. He looked so bony, like someone had already eaten all his flesh, as well as any garnish he may have had. He caught my eye, only for a second, and I thought I saw fear again, as well as a sort of uncanny desperation, as he ran past. He was holding something that I first thought was a dead white bird, or wool from a sheep, but was actually a plastic packet of paper doilies.

When I got back to our rooms you were in your running clothes, looking worried.

"Where were you?" you said.

"I went for a walk," I said back. "Are you OK?"

"A walk where? The beach?"

"No. Up the hill. I left you a note."

"A note?"

"It's there," I said, pointing at your bedside table. "On your glasses case."

I knew you'd put on your glasses when you got in. Your case was always a safe place to leave a note. You never noticed much about changes in your surroundings, so I had to be canny if I wanted to get your attention. And I knew how you hated it if I didn't leave you a note. You preferred these to be real notes rather than texts, for reasons I had never fathomed.

"There wasn't a note there," you said.

Typical. You'd opened your glasses case without even seeing it, and the note had fluttered like a broken little wing onto the floor or under the bed. I began searching, but there was no note.

"I wish you'd remember," you said.

"What?"

"I wish you'd just remember to leave me a note. You must have forgotten."

"I didn't forget," I said. But perhaps I had, because there was no note anywhere. I searched the whole room. While I was searching, I noticed that something else had changed. The light in the room was different, and it wasn't because of the clouds, or the pre-storm weather. What was it? What was it?

"The tulip paintings," I said, getting up from my knees. I'd been having one last glance under the bed. "Look. They've gone. Isabella's been in here and taken the paintings and taken your note too. I don't know why she'd do that. I—"

"Will you stop blaming Isabella for everything," you said. "It's becoming really tiring."

"Well, where are the tulip paintings, then?" I said.

There were light square patches on the walls where they'd been. These absences somehow looked even worse than the paintings had.

You sighed loudly. "Well, I don't know. Did you take them down?"

"Me?"

"Yes. You kept going on about how much you hated them."

"Right. I actually think I said one thing about them being awful paintings, which they are. I'm not going to take them off the walls, though. Are you insane?"

"No," you said. "I'm not insane."

Did you slightly stress the *I'm* in that sentence? So much

is in the delivery, after all. It's fascinating how different that sentence is if you stress the *not*, or the *insane*. One way makes me mad; one way makes you mad; one way makes neither of us mad. At this moment I honestly don't know which way it was. But I think you did stress the *I'm*, just a little: just enough.

"What the fuck is that supposed to mean?" I said.

"Nothing. I'm not insane."

"And you're saying I am?"

"How does me not being insane make you insane?"

I sighed. "This is ridiculous."

"I agree. So where are the paintings?"

"Maybe you should ask Isabella."

You shook your head then. "I'm going to have my shower," you said. "And maybe you can do something about your jealousy while I'm in there."

"I fail to see why I should be jealous of a glorified maid who can't even make an acceptable breakfast," I said.

You slammed the bathroom door.

"*Parakalo*," I said quietly. It didn't come out quite right, though.

The Wi-Fi still wasn't working. I went downstairs to see if I could find Isabella to ask her about it. I also thought I might inquire about where the paintings had gone, not because I cared, but so I could prove you wrong.

There was no sign of her, but someone had put up the trestle table where the sandwiches had been yesterday. Today there was a single block of feta cheese laid out with some sliced bread and more melon. The unripe melon must have been on special offer somewhere. Maybe it was a job lot.

Nothing was covered, and there were flies buzzing around. I didn't feel hungry. I wanted to phone someone, a friend.

Who were my friends? Did I even have any? The last few years had been like an intact birdcage. All my most important emails coming from producers and the media and a few fans. And you, me and Paul becoming so close that we didn't need anyone else. The comedy value of Paul's stream of ridiculous girlfriends was the only variety we seemed to require. But even if I did have someone to phone, there was no phone reception as well as no Wi-Fi.

I was going to take a piece of unripe melon but I suddenly had the feeling that it would contaminate me, that the sugars would swirl in my mouth and create bacteria and putrefy in my stomach. I imagined myself as an autopsy afterwards—after what, I don't know—and I didn't want there to be anything for them to find. I didn't want them to say, "Her last meal was . . ." I wanted them to be as baffled about my last meal as I was about the tulip paintings. I could see Kostas standing by a lemon tree with his machete and I also wanted to be pure when I spoke to him. I approached him slowly, as if he was a game bird and I was a gun dog with a soft mouth, always a soft mouth.

"*Kalimera*," I said when he noticed me.

"*Kalimera*," he said back, nodding.

"Isabella?" I said. "Where is she?"

"Where she is?"

I nodded.

He shrugged. "She paint." He mimed it and then smiled in an odd, cruel way.

"OK."

"Inside." He pointed.

"OK. Thanks. *Efharisto.*"

"*Parakalo.*"

He looked at my breasts again. I let him.

"The storm," he said. "It come today. Big rain. Stay in room."

"All right," I said. "OK." I said it in a light, girlish tone and then smiled.

"OK," he repeated, using a similar light, girlish tone. I didn't know if he was mimicking me to make me sound stupid or because he wanted to get the accent right, or for some other reason.

He picked up his machete then, quite suddenly, and pointed it at me. I could see the hazy sun reflect off the sharp tip. The machete moved toward me and the sunlight scattered all over the place like bits of bright shot.

"What are you . . . ?" I began, but before I knew what had happened he had used the machete to flick a hornet from my chest. It fell to the ground, swollen and fat, its back half bright as a bullet, drunk on the end of summer and the glut of fruit. After a couple of seconds it heaved itself up like an over-laden zeppelin and flew away toward the pomegranate trees.

When I got back to the room you were out of the shower. Your hair was still wet and you were rubbing it with one of the fluffy white towels.

"What were you talking to Kostas about?" you said. So you'd been watching from the window.

"The storm," I said. "It's coming today."

"I thought you didn't believe in the storm," you said.

"No, I know," I said. "But earlier I could see it over Turkey. It's huge."

You scowled. "You saw what over where?"

"The storm. It was really intense. I could see it over Turkey, from the top of the hill. Dark clouds with lightning going through them. Big flashes."

You didn't reply. Perhaps you didn't believe me.

"Kostas says we should stay in," I said. "For the rest of the day."

"What are we going to eat?" you said.

"There's lots of food downstairs," I said. "I'm going to get on with my writing."

"Right," you said. You wouldn't catch my eye.

"What's the matter?" I said.

You sighed. "Just ... Nothing. It doesn't matter."

"OK."

"Actually, though ... All right. It does matter."

"What?"

"What you said about Isabella before."

"What did I say about Isabella before?"

"About her being a glorified maid."

"She is a glorified maid. Why does that matter? Oh, wait. I see. You think my treatment of servants is vulgar because I say what you really think, what people like you and your mother really think."

"What's my mother got to do with this?"

"Good question."

"I really just meant that with your background ..."

"What?" I laughed then, even though it wasn't at all funny. "Oh, I see. You're saying *I'm* a glorified maid."

You looked at me the way Kostas had looked at the hornet as it wriggled on the ground trying to right itself.

"Are you OK?" you said, with a heavy sigh.

"What?"

"Are you feeling all right? Has the sun got to you or something?"

"Sorry?"

I could feel myself making a face then. Isn't it odd how during an argument people try to make themselves as ugly as possible? It's not even conscious. Well, not usually. But right then I could feel my face twisting and crumpling like a piece of burning silk.

"You don't seem quite yourself," you said.

My heart jolted. Was this your lead-in to talking about the wedding?

"I'm absolutely fine," I said.

"Well, can you please just try to be a bit nicer about Isabella? It's upsetting me."

"And it's not upsetting you that she isn't being very nice to me?"

You looked at me then with a horrible kind of pity, as if it were a shame that I was so mad I could not see the truth.

"She's being perfectly normal to you," you said.

"But I don't—"

"Evelyn," you interrupted. "You are seeing things that are not there."

"Don't," I said. "Don't do this. It's not fair. You know it's not—"

"You have become very paranoid," you said slowly.

I bit my lip. "That's what you really think?" I said. "Even after—"

"Sorry. I just think it's time for us to . . ."

Were you going to say something else then? Were you going to drift into the swirling waters of the unsayable? I didn't let you.

"Great," I said. "You think I'm mad. As well as . . ." But I couldn't say it either.

You wouldn't catch my eye. "You are working quite hard."

"Right." I sighed. I looked around at all the bright white spaces where the tulip paintings used to be. They blurred in my eyes.

"Evie?"

"What?"

"Come on. Don't cry."

"Why not? This is our honeymoon! And you've decided not to believe what I say. I'm your *wife*. And Isabella is a hotel owner whom we've known for all of two days. I just don't understand why you're taking her side."

"It's not about sides."

"It is! I mean, I wish it wasn't, but it is. You need to take my side."

"What if I think you're wrong?"

"This is our honeymoon," I said again. "For God's sake. Give me the benefit of the doubt."

"Quite a long honeymoon," you said quietly.

"What does that mean?"

"Well, it was bound to get strained at some point, don't you think?"

I sighed and closed my eyes. Why weren't we saying it?

"Especially once Paul had gone," you added pointedly.

"What's Paul got to do with anything?"

"I'm going to go and see about the Wi-Fi," you said. "And get some lunch."

While you were gone I tried to write, but my hands were shaking. It didn't help that I'd had no lunch, and I wasn't sure where we were going to get dinner. Isabella seemed always to disappear in the afternoons, and there was no way of calling a taxi or booking a restaurant without her.

I walked around the room with my phone trying to get mobile reception. There had always been 4G down at the beach. But I could hear rumbles of thunder coming from that direction. *Stay in room*, Kostas had said. I started trying to write about the storm—not the one in real life, but one I might put into a play—but it kept coming out wrong, like a distorted reflection in a mirror. It had jagged machete lightning and clouds the color of ashes.

When you came back you looked more relaxed, almost happy. You were holding something in your hands that looked like a deck of cards but a slightly different shape.

"Any sign of the Wi-Fi?" I said.

"Isabella's trying to fix it," you said. "She's getting Kostas to look at it. They say it's because of the storm coming."

You came over and kissed my head. "You OK?"

"Yep."

"You sure?"

"Yeah."

"Isabella gave me these to show you."

"What are they?" I said.

You passed me a stack of maybe fifteen black-and-white photographs. They were old-fashioned Polaroids with white edges and high-contrast tones. They were all of the girl. The one I wasn't. The one I'd first seen walking down the dusty street like a haughty heron. The most beautiful of the beautiful people. She was posing against a wall, her tiny shoulders thrown forward like a young bird about to fledge. Her teeth were dazzling. I realized I'd never seen her smile, but here she was, relaxed and charming and happy. The photographs were beautiful in every possible way. They were the most perfect pictures I'd ever seen. There was only one that was a little troubling. In it, the girl wasn't smiling. The thin strap of her top had fallen down over her bony shoulder and half her breast was revealed. No nipple, but the shot was still somehow wrong.

"Isabella thought you'd like them."

"Really? Why?"

"What do you mean?"

"Well for a start I don't even know who this girl is."

"Yes, you do. She's one of the people who were here before. Isabella took the pictures. She was showing them to me just now and I thought they were great. Then she said she wanted you to see them too."

"But why?"

"I suppose she thought you'd be interested."

"Oh, I'm sure she knew I'd be fascinated."

"They're a band, by the way; those people who were here before us. They're some sort of new Turkish pop group. I can't remember what she said they were called. But they're good pictures, aren't they?"

"I guess." I gave them back to you. "If you like that kind of thing."

You sighed. "What's wrong now?"

"Well, I'm not really sure they are a band," I said. "I saw one of them running down the hill before. The boy. The really skinny one."

"Right," you said in the way that means you don't give a fuck.

You glanced at the photograph on the top of the pile. It was the one with the half-revealed breast. Then you started rearranging the pictures, putting the suspect one back where it had originally been, toward the end of the sequence.

"And, OK," I said, "I mean, they're basically pictures of an extremely attractive woman who is thinner than me, prettier than me, younger than me. Why do you think Isabella wanted me to see them?"

You looked at me as if you couldn't believe how boring I was.

"Oh God, not this again. Why is everything always about how you look? Has it even occurred to you that Isabella might want you to see them because she took them? She might want you to actually like something she's created for a change? I think she wants you to approve of her."

"My God. Do you really? Then you're far, far madder than I am."

"Don't start twisting this situation even more."

"This 'situation' is not something I'm creating," I said.

"Really?" you said. "Are you sure about that?"

"I am one hundred percent sure," I said. "Look, you don't know how some women operate. I wish you could see that I really am not the one doing this."

"Well, I'm just not sure that's true," you said.

I exhaled slowly and sadly. "For God's sake."

I started making the bed. Whoever had come in to remove the tulip pictures had neglected to make up the room while they were here. A glass half full of water was still on my bedside table, with a lipstick mark from last night. The mark was in the shape of a dead bird.

"Anyway," you said. "I almost forgot. She wanted to borrow a screwdriver. Do you have it?"

"What?" I'm sure you can remember how I said that. I mean, really. What was wrong with you?

"Do you have it? I said we traveled with a screwdriver."

I travel with a screwdriver, yes. I travel with all sorts of useful things. The tool you had in mind is a large, comforting, multi-bit ratchet screwdriver that used to belong to my father. It has fifteen different bits that go with it—Phillips, flat-head, Torx—although I don't travel with all of them. They came in a box that makes them look like ammo, like something you'd take on safari.

I'm pretty sure you don't even know how to use a screwdriver. If ever something breaks, I fix it, not you. I travel with it because my suitcases are old, and the handle sometimes comes off one of them. But for can-do-no-wrong Isabella, you wanted to borrow my screwdriver now for the first time ever.

"Doesn't she have a screwdriver in the hotel?"

"Look, be difficult if you want, but I just said I'd help, all right?"

"Help what?"

"Fix a bed in one of the rooms. There are new guests coming today."

"In the storm?"

"I suppose so. Not everyone's afraid of a bit of wind and rain, you know."

I laughed then. This was becoming absurd. "So Isabella wants you to borrow my screwdriver to help her fix a bed? Can't Kostas do it?"

"There's a handyman, but he can't come during the storm. Since we're stuck here I offered to help. I'll be out of your way so you can get on with your writing."

"So she wants you to go and help her with a bed? With my screwdriver? Why doesn't she just lose the bullshit and take all her clothes off right now and give you what you really want? She's already dispensed with her bra, presumably in your honor."

"Evelyn," you said. "Please just stop this. Everything's completely normal and friendly. Why are you making it so difficult?"

I sighed.

"Evelyn?"

"This is not normal," I said.

"It is."

"OK, what about the tulip paintings?" I said.

"What?"

"The fucking tulip paintings," I said patiently. "That fucking disappeared."

"She probably overheard what you were saying about them and took them away. I think you are genuinely upsetting her."

"Right. The fucking tulip paintings that she fucking took away—along with my note, by the way, because she's fucking crazy—because she fucking overheard me talking privately, in our fucking private room when—" To be honest, at this point I was planning to go on and on and on. Hot tears were spilling down my cheeks like a cauldron boiling over and I couldn't stop the words bubbling out of my mouth. The whole thing was so unfair, so fucking—

Which I guess was why you slapped me.

Yep. And OK, I *know* it's never happened before. But you hit me. You said I was mad and then you hit me.

Again, I wanted to ring someone—Paul, my mother, your father, a taxi—but there was still no phone signal. I wanted to leave, to pack and go, but the room darkened and it was at that moment that the first flash of lightning came like a jagged machete. The pathetic fallacy. Excellent. I expect you don't know what that is, but it's bad writing. It's the kind of writing I do all the time. Maybe I'm doing it now.

You were still standing there, the lightning illuminating you like some kind of forsaken stag. The clouds outside darkened like ashes. Dogs howled in the distance. Amidst all this came the sound of a car engine, and then some doors slamming. The hurried footsteps of people trying to escape heavy rain. The new guests? But of course I didn't care about them, and barely heard anything outside our room.

It was as if we were inside a bubble of silence for a second or two.

I opened my case and took out the screwdriver.

Then the hail started. It beat against the windows like little bullets. I could see it piling up on the patio, too fast, like something unnatural.

"Well?" you said to me.

"What?" I said, holding the screwdriver. I wondered if it looked like a weapon.

"Oh, I see. You expect me to say sorry."

"You hit me."

"I did not hit you."

"Er, what the fuck do you call it, then?"

"I slapped you. Lightly. You were becoming hysterical."

"This is over," I said. "I'm leaving."

"Good luck," you said, looking out of the window.

"I'll leave when the storm ends."

"No, you won't," you said. "You'll apologize and everything will be fine."

"Me? Apologize? Fucking hell."

"Grow up, Evie," you said, and then you took my screwdriver, grabbed your waterproof running top and turned to leave the room.

I wonder what you'll think when you read this. Have I not told it properly? Were there tears in your eyes when you hit me? Did I fight back? Did I start punching you in the chest, harder and worse than your single slap? And did you hold my wrists to stop me? And did I then start kicking you? And then to stop that did you push me down onto the bed?

Imagine. It would have been like old times. We could have made up then, while the storm raged around us. But none of that happened. You put on your top, pulled up the hood, left the room and I was alone.

At least you didn't have all the screwdriver bits. That's what I thought at that exact moment. *You only have the Phillips.* It's odd what we choose to think, isn't it? In these defining moments I can never think thoughts that are big or important enough, and perhaps that's why I never made it.

When we got married, at the precise moment you put the ring on my finger, I was thinking about which one of the airport drivers would take us to Heathrow. I'm really sorry. Maybe I never was quite good enough for you.

I went to splash my face with water. Then I drank the two miniature bottles of vodka I still had in my bag from the minibar in the Athens airport hotel where we had our layover. Why do I carry vodka around with me? For the same reason I have a screwdriver. So I am prepared for situations like this.

The vodka made the storm seem quaintly dramatic and almost fun. Bang! Crash! Haha! The large hailstones built up on the patio and bounced joylessly off the walls. At one point it sounded like the hail might break all the windows. It grew darker and darker and then the rain began. It was like no rain I've ever experienced. It didn't seem to come in drops, but rather as one large waterfall, pouring out of the sky. I wondered briefly if it might wash away the hotel, and me, and you, and everything that had ever happened to us.

The vodka made me laugh at the treacherous rain, and that you'd decided to go and help Isabella with the bed. Did you not give a shit about me, stuck in this terrible storm? Were you naked at that moment? Was she? Or was it just a quickie, with neither of you properly undressing? But you'd never liked quickies, or any kind of "dirty" sex.

So, we'd got married and then we'd come on our honeymoon and now it was all over, just like that, like speed dating. You were fucking the glorified maid. Hilarious, really. And it wasn't even the first time, because I was a glorified maid too, as you'd pointed out. Maybe it was simply that we—the glorified maids—were your type? Or perhaps you preferred us less glorified and more maid. I'll never know.

The room had darkened so much by then that I went to put the light on, but as soon as I flicked the switch the whole place seemed to fuse. Things that had been humming stopped. The fans stilled. Everything in the house was dark and quiet. Even the rain became softer for a while. The dogs in the nearby yards suddenly seemed so much louder.

My hand hurts from all this writing.

Right now I can hear the ragged Alsatian, and the songs of all the caged birds, and the hiss of a long-ago hot-air balloon. A few moments ago I thought I heard a woman singing—or screaming. A high pitch, and then silence. The lightning just flashed again. It flashed inside me and outside me and I went over and unlocked all the doors and stood on the patio in the desperate weather, hail melting and soaking into my trainers.

This is it, I guess. The storm.

And as soon as it is over I am going to leave.

*

Now it's late in the night. You are sleeping awfully peacefully, lying in our hotel bed with that vaguely narcoleptic air you have whenever things have gone truly wrong. It's something I've always admired about you: the ability to go to sleep while all hell rages nearby. Arguments have always kept me up until the early hours, but you have always been like a candle, so easily snuffed out.

I'm sitting at this creaky little desk again, writing to you on the extra hotel notepaper I found, finishing this, because I feel compelled to. I am using the torch from your phone, because mine is gone, and also because I want to do little things to spite you. As soon as the sun comes up I'm going to leave, and hopefully never see you again.

You'd been gone a couple of hours when the rain stopped and the sun came out. You returned with my screwdriver and an apology and a dinner reservation for the place we should have gone to the night before.

"Can we start again?" you said, your cheeks flushed. "Please?"

I breathed in and then out, unsure.

"I just want us to be happy," you said, taking my limp hands in yours.

"I know," I replied.

"I've got a good story for you," you offered with a little playful smile.

You couldn't stop talking in the cab to the harbor. The driver was the same man as the night before. The same crackly Greek radio station was now playing Dinah Washington's "You Don't Know What Love Is," which he hummed along to, in a melancholy sort of way. I was intrigued to see that we were going to a completely different part of the island than the night before. How could the driver have got the restaurant so wrong?

You were talking about the new guests.

"It's a film producer and his wife," you said, clearly quite thrilled.

You gushed a little over the fact that they'd arrived on a private plane from Athens. Not their own jet, you'd established somehow, but one they'd hired that would still take off in the strong winds. A desperate bandana-ed pilot, maybe. A new type of front wheel. The wife had thrown up in the turbulence and the producer had drunk Scotch and soda and made a video call to LA in which he'd joked about "the bumps." They'd sheltered in the airport during the worst part of the hailstorm, having just landed before it began.

"They want to option Isabella's story," you said excitedly. "They're having a big dinner tonight."

"Isabella's story?" I said, trying to keep my tone light but interested.

I'd decided never to let you see me bothered by Isabella again. This was the role I was now playing, my new one-woman show: slightly stupid young wife who nevertheless understands the ancient wisdom that says you free something by letting it go. That you turn the other way when your husband's eye roams like a hungry stray, because he will always come back to you, because the law says he has to, and because ultimately he is a house pet who desires comfortable pillows and what is right.

"Well, the story of the sleepwalkers," you said, flushing a little. "The people who drowned in the storm last summer. You remember."

Of course. We'd been having dinner at the expensive fish restaurant in the harbor, the night before Paul and Beth arrived. That was when our Greek waiter told us about the husband and wife who'd walked into the sea together in the middle of the big storm and drowned, just the year before. He'd really got into the story, embellishing and waving his arms around like something from a guidebook, until Christos had come and told him off. We'd never seen him again after that. Marlena had talked about the sleepwalkers a lot too. Everyone— well, apart from Christos—seemed to like saying the word *ypnováadtes*. It was like *parakalo*, but perhaps even better.

The story was that the wife had loved her husband so much that she'd gone out into the storm to rescue him after he'd sleepwalked all the way to the sea. It was why there were no sun loungers in front of the motorcycle man's shop, just the withered floral wreath from when the couple's daughters had visited the island not long after it had happened. We'd both been quite taken with the story. Your interest in it had surprised me, but I'd gone along with it.

"They stayed at the Villa Rosa too," I said now, with a careful, neutral tone.

"How do you know?" Your voice turned suspicious for a second. "Are you sure?"

"Well, yes," I said. "I mean, that must be how it's 'Isabella's story,' right?"

You frowned at the finger quotes, then let it go.

"Their daughters wrote in the guest book," I said. "It's quite a moving entry."

In fact, I'd been looking at it just before we left for dinner. The guest book was in the hallway—where I'd been told to leave my bag when we first arrived. I was waiting for you to go and change your contact lenses, which had been bugging you ever since the dramatic drop in air pressure during the first part of the storm.

I'd been wearing sunglasses to mask my puffy eyes and I felt light and strange from the vodka, and from not eating all day, a balloon with an empty basket. The fan was revolving slowly overhead, making no impression on the close, sticky heat that had returned with the now clouded-over sun. I could hear the buzz of a trapped bluebottle, but I couldn't see where it was or I would have tried to set it free.

On the chiffonier were several of the little paper archives— bundles of notebooks and old letters tied with string—that I'd noticed before. One had a title that said *Les histoires d'amour finis mal*. Another appeared to be in Greek. One of them had no string tied around it, and another had patches of brown that looked like scorch marks.

Alongside them was the large leather-bound guest book, which I lazily flicked through while I waited for you. I was looking for the same thing I'd sought on Tripadvisor, of course. Bad reviews. I wanted to float away in them like a large dirigible. But there were none.

The entries were all written in that twee guest-book style I find so emotionally crushing. Remember the time we stayed in the New Forest and I tried to write in the guest book about what we'd done on our holiday and it went horribly wrong? Other people wrote in careful biro about eating fish and chips in the local pub, and I wrote in real ink about the exact red of the beetroot-pickled quail's eggs we'd eaten in the only Michelin-starred restaurant in the area.

The beautiful people had not written anything in Isabella's guest book, and nor had their managers. Only one entry in the guest book was at all interesting. It was dated almost exactly a year before, and began, "We stayed here in the worst possible circumstances, after losing our parents in the great storm just last week. Isabella could not have been kinder nor gone out of her way more." Such an awkward sentence, so full of negatives, and a lesson on why one should never write freestyle in guest books—you can end up lost in your own sentences, like pythons wrapping around you.

When did she start watching me? Was it before that? Or did she only appear when I started pulling open the string on one of the paper archives? The letters on it: υπνοβάτες. And then in English on a slip of flyweight paper that I saw properly only once I'd opened the bundle: *The Sleepwalkers*.

"Do not touch," Isabella hissed from behind me.

I jumped. I dropped the bundle back on the chiffonier and some of the papers came loose. A paper doily fluttered to the floor.

"Sorry," I said.

"You touch too much," she said, no need to feign sweetness when you weren't there.

Did I hear her accent slip then, just a little? I went to university with a girl who had grown up in both Glasgow and Texas after her parents got divorced. She would trip and stumble effortlessly into any accent she was near—she couldn't help it. But there was always that neutral space where no accent was, a peculiar hollow in her tones rather like the dips in your mother's lawn, and that was where Isabella strayed then, just for a moment. Was it that, or was it that I'd caught a faint trace of Texan? Something in the "too" was too long. A brief drawl. It suggested, for a tiny second, that maybe she wasn't the innocent European woman you were clearly so taken with.

I bent down to pick up the doily, and realized it had writing on it that had been crossed out.

You sweep me off of my feet, baby.

And then some large Cyrillic letters I didn't understand.

Isabella grabbed the doily and stuffed it back in the bundle, which she then tied up and pushed into the chiffonier before turning the little brass key.

"Please," she hissed. "Respect other people's privacy."

I bit back the obvious response about everything being open and free, because you then appeared from outside, a little smile on your lips as you saw Isabella and me in what you probably decided was light conversation.

I still had not taken off the sunglasses.

"Ready?" you said to me.

"Sure," I said.

"Have a wonderful evening," Isabella said, I thought slightly bitterly.

As we got in our cab, I saw the film producer and his wife going up the stone staircase toward the upper bedrooms.

He was a large man in a yellow two-piece linen suit and a Panama hat. She wore a floppy sun hat, which she was pressing against the top of her head lest the breeze take it. Its wide brim was slapping at the edges of her too-thin face. But as we traveled in the cab and you talked about their plane ride to the island, I didn't tell you I'd seen them. You didn't like it when I usurped one of your "discoveries."

The cab slowed as it reached the harbor where Paul and Beth had got their boat back to the mainland, just a few days before. How I wished they were still with us. Well, mainly Paul. He somehow functioned as a stop-loss on our relationship. Is that the right trading term? He was your friend, not mine, which I always thought made our closeness OK.

You would accept being teased by Paul in a way you never would from me. Sometimes you'd get in a huff about something ridiculous—being overcharged for socks, not having the right amount of air miles credited to your account or missing a train by one minute—and we'd both laugh at you and you'd take that too. But from me alone? Never. Occasionally we'd hit a nerve and you'd smile along but then let me have it when Paul had gone home. Always the same argument, with you asking why I needed to make you feel small in front of your friend, then escalating to bitter observations about me "throwing myself" at Paul in a desperate, hopeless, embarrassing frenzy. We both knew I was not Paul's sex-doll type, and you often found little ways to remind me that I was too fat for him, too old, too used.

Do you remember the time you and Paul got nits from a work colleague's niece and I washed your hair with medicated shampoo and then combed out the dead insects afterwards? You took it in turns: you first and Paul second. We must have been in Paul's ludicrous "bachelor flat" in Notting Hill, because I remember first you, then him, bent over his retro avocado bathroom sink, and me pouring water over your hair from a priceless antique vase, because there wasn't anything else. I collected the nits on a white linen napkin, because Paul didn't own anything like kitchen roll.

While you were watching cricket in the front room, Paul suggested he do my hair, just to be sure. All that humid chemistry between us, and then, finally, the electricity of his actual touch, as he massaged the awful medicated shampoo into my scalp. For some reason, possibly the size of my boobs, I couldn't bend over the sink as easily as you both had, and Paul had suggested I get on my knees in front of the bath instead.

He'd kneeled behind me so he could pour the water over my hair and rinse away the chemicals and the nits we knew I did not have. I don't think either of us could breathe properly. Paul had often talked about how he liked to choke his sex-doll girlfriends while fucking them. When he touched my neck, it was the barest little stroke as he flipped my hair over to rinse it. I don't know what would have happened if you hadn't walked in at that moment.

"What are you doing?" you'd said coldly. The tone of your voice meant you were speaking to me alone. You'd never have spoken to Paul that way.

"Yeah, we probably gave her nits so I thought I'd do her too," Paul said, without getting up. "Nearly finished."

Paul couldn't stand up because of his erection, which was

pressing into the back of my right thigh. It was the most real thing I've ever felt.

Why am I telling you this? I'm not sure. To even things up, after what happened before? Perhaps I'll never actually give you this letter. But Paul did want me, even if it was just for that ten minutes when he was washing my hair. And— perhaps most importantly—we never acted on our desire. Out of love for you, we never, ever consummated our flirta- tion. It would have been disappointing anyway, after all that build-up. Those things always are.

Like the first time I slept with your father.

It was before you and me, of course. Long before. I am surprisingly faithful, even if your father is not. Perhaps you get it from him, your faithlessness, and how easily you are distracted by glorified maids.

There'd been so much build-up with me and Peter, it was simply

　　　　　　　　　　　I knew he liked my innocence,
　　　　　　　　　　　　　　　and so I wore my

　　　　"Slut!" he said, pulling my hair and

The taxi dropped us off by the pizza place with all the mopeds parked outside. A sign for a nearby taverna advertised "finan- cial menus."

"Sounds like some part of your job description," I quipped.

"What does it mean?" you said, frowning.

"I guess someone just stuck a phrase in Google Translate," I said. "Maybe 'budget menus' or something."

You didn't look convinced, even though that was obviously the answer.

The restaurant was just beyond the taverna, in an old stone building with aged red gloss paint flaking off its doors. Inside, it had the same ruin-bar vibe as those places in Budapest, but with unmistakably Greek touches, including several gold-finches in cages. I shuddered at them, poor things.

The dapper little man was sitting there at a small Formica table, eating bright pink taramasalata from a white bowl, and drinking a frosted glass tumbler of liquid that was probably the lemon liqueur that we'd long ago begged George to stop giving us for free. There was something bird-like about the dapper little man, something hawkish and pensive.

As he spooned taramasalata from the white bowl he stared at one of the goldfinches as if he were about to swoop on it and rip its head off and then dip it in the bowl like some bloodied breadstick.

"Where do we know him from?" you asked, a touch loudly, smiling and ready for some pre-dinner banter. You'd relaxed a bit since we'd made up and agreed to "start again."

"Shhh," I said instinctively.

You have always hated me telling you to shush. You sighed and looked away.

"Come on," I said. "Let's not argue. Not again. Please."

"I'm not arguing," you said calmly.

I smiled and touched your arm. Dropped my voice.

"The curio shop, remember?"

"Um . . . ?"

I didn't want to remind you by saying it was the place you and Paul had begun your spectacular row, the one that had almost ended in a fight out in the street. I still have no idea what that was about. Ostensibly it was something to do with the way you'd betrayed the owner of the small start-up private equity firm you'd been working at. It had been Paul's idea to cut a better deal elsewhere, and he'd arranged for you to go with him. It was one of the reasons you were both available for our too-long honeymoon. A week for him and two for you. A break, before your new roles began.

But out on that dusty street with the whitewashed villas, you'd got him up against a stone wall, and you were hissing into his face.

"You fucking pervert," you were saying. "You fucking perverted cunt."

All that swearing was most unlike you.

"How long have you known?" you demanded. "Does she know everything, too?"

The argument seemed like something two friends would have trouble recovering from, but somehow you did recover; well, almost. Anyway, I certainly didn't want to remind you of the whole episode. So I tried to bring the curio shop to life in another way.

"You remember, with all the leather packing cases and riding crops and white nightdresses? And those little paper archives tied with string? They looked like they'd maybe been dipped in tea or set on fire?"

Your mother had a friend who used the tea method with curtains, I think, to make them look sepia-ish and old.

"Isabella has them too," I prompted. "Everywhere apart from our room."

You frowned. Was I complaining again? I tried to cover it, without success, by talking about the odd performativity of text that you're not supposed to read, displayed in bundles you're not meant to untie. I didn't tell you that I had untied one of the bundles earlier, nor what I'd found.

Am I boring you? Probably. You never let me talk at this length in real life. I really need to finish this letter and go. I'm not sure how many fountain pen cartridges I have left; I've gone through three already. I thought I saw a glimmer of red light outside, although I am still quite drunk, and the wind is howling like a starving wolf.

I'm trying to get my heartbeat and my breathing to settle down as well, because in the last couple of hours the storm has become so intense I almost cannot bear it, and I am a wretch who will never be saved. I wish I had some painkillers, a lot of painkillers, but I can't find any in my bag, or yours.

Do you remember the night we went to that exhibition in London that was entirely about Solpadeine? It started badly, but ended up being one of our happier recent times. It wasn't long before the wedding. You and your hedgie mates were buying art that week because that's what your boss wanted. Anything that would appreciate, and the more ridiculous the better. It was like a scene from that TV show Paul used to like, with the actor who previously played a king.

But you were never any good at that stuff. You didn't much like irony, or the spontaneous wacky madness that came with your industry. You were in it for the maths and the stability. The spreadsheets and the Amex points. On evenings like that your colleagues would do some coke and have a ball but you were always so careful and measured about everything. Maybe that's why you took me with you. I am the sort of person who has never needed a recipe to cook, and who can tell quite a convincing lie with no prior thought, whereas you would rehearse before a game of charades.

Is it embarrassing to recall that we were actually quite moved by the final piece in the exhibition? We'd traipsed around looking at sub-Warhol depictions of white pills. Pills on a wooden table. Pill fizzing in glass. Pill packaging. Two pills fizzing in a crystal tumbler. White pills stacked like poker chips. Pills like tiny moons in a twilit sky.

You'd eventually put a red dot on a packet of pills signed by the artist. It was unclear whether he'd made the pack, or just bought it from a pharmacy around the corner.

We queued for the final exhibit. Around us, the crackle and hiss of people who did not know what was behind the black velvet curtain but suspected something shocking, a skinned rabbit perhaps; a deranged artist in situ. Something daring. Difficult to be with.

People were let in one by one, alone. You could see them as they emerged, pale and overcome. A woman passed me, mascara running down her face.

"It's so beautiful," she said to me.

"Is it claustrophobic?" you asked her, even though she hadn't engaged with you at all. Bless your little cotton socks. Still scared of enclosed spaces after the bad trip you had on the ghost train in Deal back in nineteen-ninety-something.

"God no," she said. "It'll change you."

You balked, not wanting to be changed. So I went in first. I needed something unfathomable, if I'm honest. Some kind of skin-shedding ceremony. A mild flaying. A hard reset. Ayahuasca for bad girls who don't learn and don't try.

Please don't judge me for this, but I was still regularly texting your father at that point, in the lead-up to the wedding. What was I hoping for? That he'd leave your mother and we'd call it all off? But then what? I did love you at that point, Richard. It wasn't a lie. I just loved him more. I'm so sorry. Of course, the wedding cured me of loving your father once and for all—just not in the way I'd imagined. But perhaps you haven't put all that together yet.

I pulled the curtain aside tentatively, then felt the waft of air on my bare legs as it flopped shut behind me.

There was a dark passageway, like being reborn or converted. Black walls. Black floor. Eventually I got to a kind of central shrine and it was so quiet in there, the hum of the opening party a long way behind me. There was a black dais, and on it—

A white candle. A single candle, burning alone.

And I did cry a little. Does that shock you now, after everything? I hid it from you at the time but there's no point in hiding anything any longer. Even then I didn't want you to think I was at all unhinged—I'm not even sure why. You came out looking pale and moved yourself, though, which surprised me, and when we got home that evening we played Beethoven loud and you peeled up my bandage dress in the kitchen and lifted me onto the sink and penetrated me in a way you never have before.

The dapper little man left the restaurant after finishing his lemon liqueur. He looked at his watch, glanced at you and shuffled off. You were looking at the menu, so you didn't see him greet a young man outside. It was the glitter-boy, the one with the doilies on the hill, who had not gone back to Turkey to be in the new pop group you'd told me about. He was still wearing skinny shorts, now with a cropped and faded T-shirt with what seemed to be the face of a man on it. Around his neck was a thin turquoise scarf like something from the Saint Laurent spring 2015 women's collection. They seemed to be having some kind of argument at first, but then the boy gave the dapper little man a thin carrier bag with something small and heavy in it and this seemed to calm everything down.

I wondered whether to tell you what I'd seen. My new rule at that point was not to mention anything that could make me look remotely paranoid. In your world it seems there are no bushes or thickets or secrets or fat envelopes and no one ever lies or does anything underhanded at all. This was to be my new code. It's incredible how simple suspicion of others can make a person seem utterly mad.

So I decided to suspect no longer.

I gently reminded you of the curio shop and then went

back to looking at the menu. You ordered fish of the day. I ordered a small prawn cocktail with no bread. The least calorific thing on the menu, as always. Not that it ever made any difference to my ballooning stomach and thighs and buttocks. Losing weight for the wedding had left me like a starved animal, and almost anything I ate now was converted directly into fat; I could feel it.

When we got back to the Villa Rosa, the rain had started again. The lights in the hotel had come back on—they twinkled uncertainly as the cab crunched up the driveway as if it were a pestle grinding something in a mortar. When we got out, I could hear the unmistakable sound of an electricity generator whirring from the back of the house.

The dapper little man was inside, in Isabella's private drawing room. I could see him through the stained-glass window beyond the pillars of the downstairs veranda. How had I not noticed this window before? I realized it was because the light had not been on inside when we'd returned from dinner on previous nights.

But this was clearly a special occasion. The dapper little man was sitting at a large oval dining table with Isabella, the film producer, the film producer's wife and a man I thought I'd never seen before, until I realized it was Christos, dressed up in a waiter's outfit with a black bow tie. The glitter-boy was there as well, standing in the corner with a white linen cloth over his arm like a small creature that had recently fainted. He was wearing a dinner jacket a couple of sizes too large over his shorts and crop top. Did he look upset, or was I imagining things again? This was the "big dinner" you'd said

Isabella was throwing in honor of her film option, or, more likely, to try to get it to solidify, like the vast jelly beneath an ambitious trifle.

I don't think you have ever really understood how bull-shitty and bogus the entertainment industry is. People pretending to be your best friend because you need intimacy to get any kind of show going, so everyone is fluffing each other all the time, like walruses at the circus. You pretend to be so close and tell each other secrets and then some of these secrets get turned into mirages and trompe l'œils with costumes and glitter and sometimes even gaudy fireworks and flamethrowers and clowns.

Everyone so hot for each other's dark mysteries. So horny.

I remember you being unconvinced when I told you how phony the production companies were when there was the big scramble for my first one-woman show.

But that was before you, and so it must have been your father, who was always just as unconvinced by me as you are.

Which perhaps means maybe it's me. Maybe I am simply unconvincing.

At the time, I was losing my own father. Every day I drove to the big hospice just outside the town where I grew up and parked in the same place by the bush with pink roses and gathered myself before going in. Years before, I used to drive past the hospice on the way to one of my holiday jobs. I couldn't ever properly take it in then, such a place of sadness and death and forced liminality. I couldn't believe anyone had to go there, what it would be like. And then, all of a sudden, it was my turn.

Mum couldn't get to visit Dad very easily because of her mobility issues, so I went every day of Dad's last fortnight with whatever he asked for. A caravan magazine, a bottle of Sussex Best Bitter, a vintage cheddar wrapped in wax. The hospice was a jolly place with few rules, it being too late for rules. People were wheeled into the garden in their beds with their whole families to look at their last sunsets. People laughed in their relatives' rooms and then came out and did jigsaws in silence. The whole atmosphere was a plane full of people waiting to jump.

Afterwards, people celebrated their dead relatives with large cigars or bottles of brandy. When it was my turn I toasted my dad with one of his undrunk bottles of real ale, and then I was told to take his things and leave as soon as possible, because of the waiting list. It was three in the morning, so I arranged to return the next day.

Overnight, the hospice had been rendered unimaginable again, but in a different way. I had a panic attack in the car and then crossed the threshold of this place that had become like a second home. The place in which one of the biggest moments of my life had come to pass.

The atmosphere that morning was suddenly that of a theatre after the show has moved on. Before, I'd barely noticed the receptionist gently asking the name of the patient I was visiting, and hardly felt the scratch of the pen as I signed in. But this time, when she'd said, "Who are you visiting, dear?" I'd stumbled. I couldn't say it, exactly. I couldn't say that Dad wasn't there anymore.

"Um, he's, er, he actually . . ."

"Sit down, dear. I'll fetch a nurse."

"It's fine, I'll just . . ." I went to walk down the hallway, and she held up a hand.

"Please wait there for the nurse to come."

I wasn't allowed in, because I had no one to visit.

The doors had closed on me, and on my dad. Five minutes later a hospice nurse brought me his things in two carrier bags.

But I've got ahead of myself again. I hope you're following this, with all my jumps in time? Perhaps not. Maybe it doesn't matter. I'm not even sure who I'm writing this for, or why. It soothes me to write things in some sort of order, even if it is one you'll probably deem wrong, when there is now such chaos outside. And our lives, in tatters.

I'd got into a routine that fortnight at the hospice. Each day I arrived just after ten, and stayed until four, when I'd go home and cook dinner for Mum. On the way back I took whatever class the cheap leisure center had that day. Yoga; Body Combat; Legs, Bums and Tums. I didn't care. The stupider the title the better. I was trying to lose weight for the auditions I still had back then.

I also had a lot of strange adrenaline I needed to process somehow, after the unnatural calm of those days. Is it odd to say that the hours in the hospice were some of the clearest and happiest I'd ever spent? Of course, it was partly because I was connecting with my dad properly for the first time. We talked about his school days up north and his coal-miner father who beat him and his brothers because that's what people did in those days.

My father was such a solid man. He'd go out in a blizzard if my mother wanted anything. With such a devoted wolf in her pack you'd think she'd ask for foie gras and truffles, but instead it was Black Forest gateaux from Iceland that she'd eat in one sitting while watching romantic comedies on DVD. Sometimes she didn't even defrost the cakes first, and I'd hear her crunching through them as if they were full of bones.

Dad looked after Mum, and she looked after me. That was the unspoken deal.

But I was so wayward that even Mum washed her hands of me for a while.

I suppose you have no idea of what a childhood like mine would have involved or how I became the person I am. You never really asked. You, with your big house and your plush, streamlined life. How could you possibly know? My mother liked to buy things from catalogues when she was sad, and my dad would work evenings and weekends to pay the overdue bills while the garage filled with dollhouse furniture, porcelain animals and supplies for crafting projects that Mum never started. Dad was a plumber—just imagine that— and so there was always work if he wanted it, unblocking other people's toilets and restarting their boilers.

When I was a teenager I'd skive off school and Mum and I would loll in the pink-and-purple nest of our small sitting room, where everything was soft, and we'd watch all her soaps, one by one: *Doctors*, *Home and Away*, *Neighbours*, *Emmerdale*, *Eastenders*, *Corrie*. Mum would give me whatever thick paperback she'd just finished, usually featuring a cleaner who doesn't know she's a princess, or an exploited actress who ends up marrying the CEO of the movie studio and then firing all the people who were ever mean to her. The meanness in these books was sometimes workplace bullying, but since the workplace was usually a movie set or Hollywood mansion, it would often turn into lurid sex: forced threesomes or violent blow jobs, and it sort of made me think that's how the world was.

Mum would go to bed early with her magazines, and if Dad was working late I'd take the bus into town and drink cheap cider in the Railway Tavern and play cribbage with the regulars. One of the younger ones, Gav, turned out to be a trainee of Dad's, and one day when they were unblocking someone's toilet Gav mentioned this eager little slut he knew who'd give you a blow job for a snakebite and a packet of salt-and-vinegar crisps. Whenever I script this nightmare scene I can't decide on the moment when Gav identifies me. Does he say my name, not noticing the surname is the same as Dad's? Or does he give a description of a vaguely emo girl in polka-dot tights, a Joy Division T-shirt and a too-short black velvet skirt? Anyway, Dad beat him to a bloody pulp and then came home and sat in silence drinking whiskey for hours. I don't think anything could have been more heartbreaking for Dad, really. Drugs would have been a lot better.

In the hospice, all those years later, it was all fixed. Everything.

It was the Tuesday of the first week when I learned I was to become a big success. Emails were followed by phone calls, all about my Edinburgh show, and how it might translate to a TV series. There were meetings booked in my agent's office for three weeks hence. I scheduled a haircut, and shopped online for silk tank tops and flattering jeans, late into those nights after cooking big fry-ups for Mum and watching old episodes of *Real Housewives* with her. My dad was so proud of me.

One of the producers, Tilda, had my phone number from a previous encounter (her company had got me into their office the previous year to pitch ideas). She rang me on my mobile on the Thursday morning, just before ten.

"I'm actually in a hospice car park," I said.

"Oh gosh, how fascinating," Tilda replied.

"It's my dad," I said.

Most people get unnerved when you say "hospice." It's almost a safe word in our society. It means "be gentle with me" and also "leave me alone." But for Tilda I realized that it was just another topic of conversation. She started telling me all about the time she'd been a volunteer hospice visitor when she was at school. I knew I should have hung up and gone in to see Dad, but I was craven and desperate and so I joined in with her happy banter, telling her about the awkward schoolboy who popped in every day at around three thirty to offer to read to Dad, even though he was quite capable of reading to himself.

"There's also someone with a zither," I said. "A music therapist."

"Oh my God. Wow."

"Yeah, my dad said he'd literally rather die than be visited by a zither-playing music therapist."

Which was true. It had been funny in context, but I resented Tilda when she guffawed. It didn't stop me, though.

"They bring a drinks trolley around twice a day," I told her. "Noon and after supper. It's the leftover booze from all the dead people, you can tell." It was true. Dusty bottles of Cointreau and Chartreuse, and the ancient Armagnac my dad always went for. "The woman who pushes it is hilarious," I said. "Blue rinse, slippers, the works."

Because of the phone call I was late in to visit Dad, and he seemed forlorn and expectant when I arrived. He'd been looking for me at ten, when I usually got there. I hadn't even realized he'd noticed my timing, but of course he had.

"I thought maybe you weren't coming, love," he said, with loneliness in his eyes.

I hated myself then.

Later, Tilda phoned again. She wanted to know how I might see a second season.

"I'm actually walking down the corridor of the hospice right now," I said, trying to sound cheery.

"I don't need much detail," she said. "Just something for the head of drama."

I burbled about using the same cast to create a different version of what the character thought had happened, and I could tell Tilda wasn't impressed. But she still wanted the rights to my original show because everyone else wanted them too. She was an obedient spaniel, and I was a dead pheasant she'd been instructed to bring back to the hunt.

Actually, I was right the first time. It was you I told about all this, but of course we talked about it later, once you and I were together. You knew Tilda's husband, it turned out, and we had drinks with them in London, remember?

We were in a bright new bar in King's Cross. Tilda twittered about this and that. Everything was "fascinating" to her. She was one of those types who makes other people talk much more than they want to about subjects that feel private.

"That's right!" she said to me, after her husband had said something about their Iranian cleaner, who apparently didn't iron his shirts very well. "Weren't you once Richard's maid?"

She literally said that.

Or maybe she didn't. Later, when we were arguing about it, you claimed it had been more innocently meant, more delicately phrased.

"You were like a housekeeper, for his family?"

I agreed, she'd said that too. She kept pressing the point, how *interesting* it was that I'd used this as inspiration for my show, until I'd stopped giving what I thought were obvious social cues to change the subject and simply said, "Can you drop it, please? It's not something we really like to talk about."

And so you and I argued, as usual, when we got home. I'd been "rude" to her, when she'd simply meant well. She just wanted to know about me, you said. She was *interested*. You wondered why I couldn't be as interested in other people as they were in me. Was I perhaps a little self-obsessed? Was I a narcissist?

I tried to tell you about the hospice, and how fake and desperate Tilda had been then, and how she'd only cared about trying to get the option her boss must have sent her for, and not at all about my dad, but you thought I was "reading too much into it." Just like you always do.

*

We paid the taxi driver, and the cab turned and ground its way down the driveway, back toward the sea.

We hurried inside the Villa Rosa, to avoid the worst of the rain. We just meant to shelter in the reception hall before making our way up the stone staircase. It had been an OK evening, and I think you were in the mood for some makeup sex. We certainly had no intention of disturbing Isabella's big dinner party.

At the back of the house the whirring stopped, gasped and then started again. Lights flickered. I thought I could hear the sound of something like swearing in Greek, and a thump that I imagined was Kostas kicking the generator.

"You are here." It was Isabella, in a long, wine-colored gown, flushed and slightly vampiric.

We were standing by the chiffonier. The bundles of paper were now all gone, but the guest book was still there, its leather cover lit by flickering candlelight.

I realized there were candles everywhere.

"The rain," you said, with a sweet smile and a little shrug.

"Sorry," I added.

"Come," she said, a grin slicing her face. "Have brandy with us."

"I mean, we should really—" I began.

"Thank you," you said. "That sounds nice."

She took you by both hands and sort of danced you through the doors and into her private dining room. I followed, leaving wet footprints behind me.

A lavish, fetid smell hit me as soon as I entered the room. It wasn't wholly unpleasant, but it was very strong.

The dapper little man was sitting at the table doing something with a ball of string. He looked up sharply, as if we were a couple of small insects he might like to lash with his tongue and then swallow whole.

"*Kalispera*," he said, I thought slightly sarcastically, in an accent that sounded more French than Greek.

"Oh my God, Marcus, it's *them*!"

It was the film producer's wife, the one you'd said had been sick on the plane. Her accent was American, New York-ish. She sounded like someone who might be described as a "broad," who would probably cackle when she laughed. Well, that's what someone would think if they spoke to her on the phone. In appearance, she was more like a rare bird waiting to be put in the oven. Her body had clearly been well cared for, perhaps a little too much, and she sat with an aristocratic, haughty air. As she craned forward in her seat to stare at us I saw there was something carcass-like about her, as if she'd been starved and electrocuted and plucked. Over the carcass, she wore a delicate golden gown with a pearl choker and large diamond earrings.

"The sleepwalkers!" she said, clutching her throat, staring at us.

"Oh Debbie, don't be such a drunk," said her husband.

Isabella bit her lip and slightly rolled her eyes, as if she might laugh, or, possibly, cry.

"We've been having such a fun evening," Isabella said, a little too fast, more to you than me. "Please, I would like you to meet Mr. Marcus Drake and his wife, Debbie."

"Oh honey, we're not married!" declared Debbie. "No prenup in the world is ever gonna make that happen."

"Yeah," said Marcus, grasping her bony shoulder. "We're just fuck buddies."

"For the last twenty years," added Debbie.

Marcus was standing by the table, still in his yellow linen suit. I wondered what you were seeing, how much you were taking in. The impression the room was making on me was equally singular and kaleidoscopic, with its various pieces all swirling around.

There was Marcus's large cigar, sticking out of his face like Pinocchio's nose, creating some of the fetid smell. The cigar looked like a dick, as all cigars do, but there was no need for an objective correlative for Marcus's penis, because it was completely visible through the thin fabric of his trousers. Did he know? The penis was semi-erect, like a small snake asleep in a thicket. Had I developed X-ray vision somehow? I could see it all. The stitched outline of his white y-fronts around his sleeping viper, a few fronds of pubic hair escaping here and there, even a tiny splatter of something that could have been mineral water or rain, but could equally have been semen.

I looked away.

The room was a mess. Remnants of a large meal lay everywhere. A gravy boat sat in the center of the oval dining table, still almost full, with a congealed layer of fat on the top. Underneath it was a white paper doily. There were grapes, cherries and blueberries strewn around the pale tablecloth as if they'd been part of some sort of game. Almost all of them were squashed and bleeding their juices into the fabric. There was a half-eaten bowl of pâté next to a large and lavish cheeseboard, which was the main source of the fetid smell. A Camembert had a cigar stub in it and only a blue cheese remained untouched.

Half-eaten rare steaks sat wetly on plates decorated with yellow flowers. On the table just in front of where Marcus was standing was an empty plate with small smears of blood on it.

In the center of the table was a large plastic cool-box, of the sort you'd take on a picnic. Marcus now gestured at it.

"Wanna steak, kiddoes? Brought 'em all the way from Milan."

"There's no fridge here due to the storm," said Debbie. "Right, Isabella? We gotta eat them all before they go bad."

Isabella shrugged charmingly. So much for her "vegetarian" hotel.

"Please," she said, pushing a plate in front of you. On it was an untouched rare steak. "I will fetch a salad."

"We've already eaten," I said.

You glared at me.

"We ate quite lightly," you said, picking up a knife and fork. "This looks amazing. Thank you."

Isabella hissed at Christos to run and get a salad. Then she brought over a bottle of cognac and poured some in a crystal glass for you. She seemed to look around for someone who was not there—perhaps the glitter-boy, whom I had not seen since we'd entered the villa.

I picked up the only intact blueberry and rolled it in my fingers like a nipple. Isabella continued to fuss over you, producing a clean napkin in a silver ring and a small side-salad. No one offered me anything.

Isabella then went to the dapper little man and refreshed his glass.

"Monsieur," she said, with an odd curtsey. He nodded coldly at her.

"Would you like another steak, Mr. Marcus?" Isabella offered next.

"*Another* steak?" you said, with a little laugh, sounding impressed.

"We're carnivores," Marcus explained.

"No, baby, it's called the Carnivore *Diet*. Saying we're carnivores makes us sound like a pair of wild beasts."

"It's changed our lives," said Marcus, this time to the whole table. "In so many ways. Better blood work, blood pressure, yadda yadda. All the blood things. Blood for blood. And our love has grown too. Right, honey?"

"Sure," said Debbie, sipping what looked like port.

"I feel so masculine," Marcus added. "More virile."

He squeezed her shoulder tighter, and I looked away as his viper began to stir.

Isabella could hardly take her eyes off you, the brazen hussy, as you ate your steak in little bites. Were you really enjoying it, or simply doing it out of politeness? It was impossible to tell. Isabella stood behind you, still watching.

"You do seem very happy," you appeared to be saying, to Marcus and Debbie.

"Our love can't match the love of the sleepwalkers," boomed Marcus. "It's such an incredible tale, Issy. And amazing that the wife happened to tell her entire life story to you on the day before she drowned."

Isabella looked pleased.

"Do you two know all about it?" Marcus asked.

"The people who drowned?" you said. "I'm not sure."

"We actually first heard about it in Milan," said Debbie. "We were in our hotel bar, weren't we, honey, literally surrounded by these gorgeous young Italians all dressed from head to toe in fur, or feathers, or wearing leather socks with shoes made out of wax, and it was all a little overwhelming and so we got talking with the only other American in the bar and he'd just come from here and he told us the whole story."

"Baby, he barely told us anything, you know that!"

"I guess that's true, honey. I think you just heard 'Lovers drowned while sleepwalking' and booked the plane immediately."

They were laughing and I could tell you'd lost interest.

Your hair was slightly ruffled, and you looked beautiful and insouciant in the dim candlelight. Don't take this the wrong way, but I always felt more attracted to your father than I ever did to you. He is properly handsome, with his defined jaw and high cheekbones. Once I even thought he was the love of my life. You inherited a softness from your mother and so your good looks have always been less rugged than his. But right then you looked glorious. Was it something about eating rare steak? But I've seen you do that before. As I write this, you are sleeping like a mythical animal, fronds of your thick hair splayed on the pillow. But at the dinner table you were awake, so awake.

Suddenly, I wanted to be alone with you. I wanted to wipe everything awful from our lives and start again, you with your flushed cheeks and me having somehow washed it all away. I'd be wearing pearls like Debbie's and something white—but not my wedding dress.

"Which room did they stay in?" Marcus asked Isabella.

"Well, in fact, they stayed in Richard's room," she said.

Would it have killed her to say "Richard and Evelyn's room"?

"Can we see it, Richard?" Marcus boomed.

"Oh my God, we can block it out," said Debbie. "What fun! You can pretend you're them, and we can see how it must have happened."

Isabella giggled then, and I could see how drunk she was.

"Oh no," she said. "But we couldn't possibly—"

"*Avanti!*" cried Marcus. "Eat up, Richard, and we'll begin."

Everyone was looking the other way when lightning flashed, bright and fierce, and lit up the stained-glass window. There was the biggest crash of thunder I've ever heard, and the ground seemed to shake with it. Another flash of lightning came. And there, in the window, was a face.

It was

Dear Evie,

So you've gone without even leaving a note, as usual. Something short would have done. Isabella is out searching for you now, with Kostas. You stupid girl. You don't even have your phone. I know that, because I have it. It's beside me here, now. The battery is on twenty percent and it's still recording, because I can't switch it off without your password.

I am locked in our room at the Villa Rosa, for my own good, apparently.

It's a little quarantine; a minor lockdown. Basically so I don't go running after you. If the door was unlocked, what would I do? I don't know. Perhaps let you go, because maybe it's time. Would you be happier without me? Probably.

The fear, of course, is that we really will reenact the sleepwalkers. Amazing that they were still so in love after all those years, and we never even made it to one year. No paper anniversary for us.

But Evie, I do miss you, and I am sorry.

I haven't ever written you a letter before. Perhaps it can be our non-anniversary present? But I don't know if I can do this at all. There's simply too much to confess. You once asked why I never wrote you any love letters. What if I was killed, suddenly, and you didn't have enough tokens of adoration by which to remember me? How had I been so selfish not to think of you in this eventuality? Never mind that I'm dead, what about *you*? My school report as usual: must do better. I did try. And I'm sorry that in the end I failed. (Or should that say "in the beginning"? In the beginning, I failed.)

You're extremely hard to talk to, by the way. Has anyone ever told you that? You never listen to the ends of things. I have so much to say to you that I could never dream of getting through in person. If I'd ever tried to tell you any of this you'd no doubt have started shouting and breaking crockery and then eventually flounced out. You don't realize what hard work you are, how high maintenance. Perhaps that's why all your old lovers actually did write you letters. Maybe they caught on faster than I have.

I found the letters, by the way, stuffed into an old raspberry-ripple ice-cream tub, when you moved into my London flat. They spoke, in several European languages, of your slim legs and pert breasts, your heady philosophies, your love of danger, your sexual stamina, your obsession with the absurdists and in particular something called *Zoo Story*, your fondness for eating passionfruit in a highly mineralized bath, your ability to extend a metaphor over months, and something I didn't understand about Napoleon brandy. They were quite disgusting.

You might remember that you went through a phase of telling jokes about a narcissist obsessed with her own narcissism? I can't remember how any of them went. That was around the time you were possessed by the idea, probably true, that everyone at the TV production company thought you were a dreadful prima donna. All your obsessions and fads and issues and melodramas. You sometimes complained that I was quiet, but it was impossible to get a word in most of the time.

So much of my life you simply don't know.

I may as well have been a ghost.

I started writing a novel once, which I never showed you, or even told you about. It was inspired by an unnerving Anita Brookner novel my mother gave me one Christmas. I did have my work professionally analyzed, which is how I learned that I have several insurmountable shortcomings as a writer. You've never understood how someone could be secretive. You always let all your own insides spill out, like feathers in a pillow fight.

Since I was a teenager I've learned to control myself, like a well-constructed train set. There's no use expending energy for no reason, is there? It's why I stopped listening to opera on all but my most intense runs. Opera—all music, really—asks for more of your attention, and more of your adrenaline, than you can spare. It's like you in that respect, always demanding more. Didn't you once say Nietzsche had an interesting theory about opera? I should have asked you before you went.

La Traviata works very well for a marathon, though. I wonder if he knew that.

OK, look, I know that this whole thing is not your fault. And I'm sorry I've been such a beast, but I just kept asking myself if you'd known for a lot longer than I had. If you knew before the wedding. Were you toying with me? Of course, it wouldn't have made sense. Would you actually have married me if you'd known? Would you have gone through all those minute preparations for the wedding, counting all your food points and drinking three liters of water a day and throwing up your last few spare calories on our final night as simply lovers?

I find myself thinking about cortisol, suddenly, and how it affects insulin, and the fat we store on our bodies. This isn't meant to anger you, but you've always found it so difficult to not boil over and you've also found it so much more difficult to shed the fat that came after you hit thirty. I'm not sure how much we'll speak after this, or if I'll even still be alive, but if you want a diet to work, try being calm instead of throwing tantrums. Or maybe just learn to live on steak and grapefruit like all your ridiculous idols did. Maybe even go back to eating passionfruit in the bath. That obviously worked for the eye-watering number of men you were with before me.

So. The wedding. Incredible how two people can manage to avoid the elephant in the room, isn't it? I always thought that was a stupid expression made up by *Guardian* journalists until this happened. I never realized that people could avoid talking about something so big. Here's how: I'm too reticent and you're too sulky. Yes, sulky. God, how you'd erupt if you were here. But you're not.

Look, I'm a disappointment. I know that.

And you. Always so touchy about people thinking you once did a bit of cleaning and meal prep for my parents. Why is it so unspeakable to you that you should have worked? I have always worked too. Even when I was a kid I worked—there was my paper round, and then some odd-job work later on.

I've worked for you just as you once worked—tangentially—for me. I've been your accountant (for free) and your fund manager (at a reduced price). I wonder how our funds are doing. I can't find my phone, and I can't open yours.

Anything could be happening out there in the storm. The effect of the shutters is oddly comforting as the winds lift and then fall, lift and then fall. How many eyes can one storm have? To recollect the short joke-telling phase of my youth: How is a storm like a potato? But maybe now is not the time for childish jokes. I do miss that time of my life though, before it was ruined forever.

I wish I were writing this on a laptop, but I've never been allowed to touch yours, and I don't know the password. Why do you always lock me out of everything? Always with your little cordoned-off areas and setting your phone to make sure it doesn't ever preview any of your messages on the home screen. Anyway, already I want to scrub what I've said and start again. What do I need to tell you? It's over? Is it? Of course, in another way, it's just beginning. And I have to confess now, I realize that.

You've already left me, anyway, I know, like all those other men—the ones who wrote actual letters begging you to come back. Did you make them do that so you could keep the trophies? The letters were a lot more poetic than any text message or email I've ever composed or received. You certainly seem to have had the most torrid gap year of anyone I've ever met, breaking hearts across the Euro rail network, leaving your own tragic goodbye letters on pillows across Prague and Budapest and Barcelona.

So, yes, fine, I hesitated earlier. Since our wedding day I've been a condemned man anyway. You probably don't know I've spent over half our honeymoon researching ways I can kill myself. It's harder than you might think. I'm sure you'll eventually forgive me my half-night with her, with Isabella. Should I admit that she wasn't "as good at" sex as you are? I'm not sure what would make you feel better. For you, of course, everything is a performance. Sex, conversation, living, lying. Because you did lie. It wasn't just me.

<u>PLEASE</u> don't just screw this letter up and throw it away at this point. I am trying to <u>BE HONEST FOR ONCE</u>. I'm going to say it quickly and then we are going to move on, OK?

She came in just before dawn broke this morning because she was so worried about your idiotic phone recording, and it was actually all rather magical. I awoke to the sound of something like rustling paper, which was oddly Christmassy, like the frosty nights when my father used to deliver my stocking. I felt the sensation of her warm flesh on mine. There was a liminal sleepy period where I promise I tried to believe it was you, but you do not smell so strongly of almond and vanilla and your breasts are plumper than the tight little buds I found lowered into my mouth. I was inside her before I knew what I was doing.

I wish you'd tried harder to like Isabella. I suppose you'll never be friends now. You probably don't know that she's Spanish, not Greek. She used to be poor, and worked her way here via Morocco and Istanbul. She inherited the hotel from her cruel husband, who tricked her into marrying him many years ago. You disliked her from the beginning, but I never really understood why—were you jealous of her? Or was it something else?

And yes, of course the first words out of my mouth were "Where's Evelyn?" You know how disorientated I can get when I've just woken up. It took me a while to fathom what had gone on.

You know most of what happened, but I'm trying to get it straight in my mind, so here it is again from the top. Or, actually, should that be from the bottom? That sounds wrong, sorry. Perhaps I should remind you what happened after you stormed out and see if I can fill in some of the blanks. And then I'll try and explain everything.

You'll remember the dinner party of course. Isabella kindly invited us to join her and her guests, and you threw a sulk as usual, refusing to eat anything and instead imposing yourself on the man from the curio shop as he worked on his craft project. Earlier that evening we'd been at the harbor trying to resurrect our flagging, doomed relationship, remembering some of our more glorious times. We'd talked about the year I came with you on tour for your one-woman show, when we became obsessed with pinot gris and ate oysters every night in Sydney. But of course talking about that brought back memories of the show itself and the feminist themes and . . .

We ate in silence for a while after that.

You were always afraid we'd turn into one of those couples who sit in the Liberty tea room or the Eurostar champagne bar not speaking. Ostensibly having a good time, but unable to have a conversation. I knew what you meant. That couple was everywhere, like a real-world meme. The woman in an unflattering top and the man bursting out of his dad-jeans. Even the nicer restaurants we frequented often had a couple like this in their fifties or sixties, not saying anything.

My personal fear was in fact that we'd never turn into a couple like that, that our small flame would be extinguished long before we could grow so old and comfortable together. And so it is, and we are now in darkness.

I'm sure it was right of Isabella to confine me for my own safety when I wanted to go after you. She angrily reminded me of the sleepwalkers, not that she really needed to after you and I had spent the evening acting out their story, and how they'd both died because one had gone in the sea after the other. The *ypnováteès*—a word with which you became quite fascinated, pronouncing it *hypno-vatees*: those who walk while hypnotized, or asleep. And I'd briefly imagined exactly that, two people, hand in hand and with their eyes shut, traipsing into oblivion, into the sea.

I could even imagine why two people might want to do that, together.

Of course you were delighted to put me right, as usual.

"It was him," you'd said, I thought a little pointedly.

It must have been when we'd gone for dinner that first night at the Villa Rosa. How had you found out the sleep-walkers had stayed there too? Maybe we always knew and I'd forgotten. Maybe the owner of the other hotel had told you. Anyway, you were eating a feta salad, and I was trying to debone a fish of the sort I'd been swimming with only that afternoon. I was concentrating on doing it gently—I'd recently acquired the knack of being able to lift out the entire backbone.

"What was him?" I said.

"The man wandered out into the storm in his sleep, and then she tried to rescue him."

I laughed. "Rubbish."

"It's the story they all tell," you said, with a flirty smile.

"Right. So this, as you would say, 'dude,' gets out of bed in the middle of a hurricane, and, still in his pajamas, and still asleep, just toddles off, down the stone stairs and the long driveway, and the road, in complete darkness, wind howling around him, probably being rained on and lashed by, I don't know, leaves and debris, never once waking up, until he gets to the sea and simply walks in?"

"Yes!" Your eyes were bright.

"And the woman?"

"Realizing her husband was gone, she . . ."

"Arose from the bed . . ."

"Got up."

"Got up from the bed and espied . . ."

"*Saw* . . ."

I sipped some of my wine. Your cheeks were aflame.

". . . him from the window, so she struggled into her robe, as there was nothing else to cover her, because who takes a massive anorak on their summer holiday? She ran after him in only her dressing gown but she was too late and he was already in the turbulent water so she threw herself in after him, hoping to save him, but also knowing with total clarity that if it was too late she couldn't live without him anyway."

You'd pressed your hand over your heart and put on a tortured Greek accent for the last part of the story. You sounded more like Dracula. Then you laughed and popped a cube of feta in your mouth.

I probably frowned.

"Like I said, utter rubbish."

"OK, well, how else do you account for the fact that they were found in the sea in their nightclothes? Well, he in his pajamas and she in her hotel robe?"

I shrugged. "Well, I—"

"And in the middle of a hurricane!"

What had I been about to say? That maybe it was she—the female "sleepwalker," the *ypnováta*—who'd gone out into the storm, full of bile and womanly hysteria, and he'd followed behind (which I can now picture so vividly of course—there but for the grace of Isabella went I). When I first heard the story I had no idea what would make someone go out into weather like that, and even less of what would make someone follow.

But now I do know.

Isabella was probably right. No—she was definitely right.

What would I have said even if I had caught up with you? "Don't go?" I wouldn't have meant it. When something is as tainted and tragic as our relationship, eventually it will die. You need someone who knows what *Zoo Story* is, and who can read lines with you. I'm too easily embarrassed to be part of your life. And you do deserve someone far better than me, even if you are, by your own admission (and on the evidence of your gap-year letters), a bit of a slut.

None of it was your fault of course. But you already know that. Maybe if we'd realized much earlier, things could have been different. I sincerely treasure so much of the time we had together. You've probably already called the police. I can't stop you. I'll just have to take my punishment—or die here.

I have a theory about hot places that would no doubt have me canceled if I were to share it back home. Yet it is an obvious truth, or at least it seems to be. People don't like to work in the heat. In the heat, one wishes to loll around in sandals and shorts, to mooch slowly, to think very few thoughts.

On a previous holiday in Dubrovnik with my parents, I remember thinking that if I lived there I would do nothing. I would do nothing except lie in the sun, and stroll very short distances, and never work a day again. Perhaps I'd even change my name, or my identity, like the protagonist in the Ripley novels, and start again. Perhaps I'd even forget my terrible secret.

And yet.

In Greece they invented tragedy, such a cold-climate sport, don't you think?

That night of the dinner party, the film producer, Marcus,

suggested we act out the story of the sleepwalkers. You didn't want to. Being a professional actress meant you never felt you should have to perform for free. I didn't want to because I am shy, and not a natural performer. But somehow Marcus's enthusiasm got us out in the rain and up the stone staircase and into our rooms. By then I wasn't unexcited; you were not entirely reluctant.

I've never minded people popping round, never been upset about my space being invaded by others. As I've said before, I feel that my soul is contained inside me, in a tiny tight ball that I protect at all costs. And I don't care about anything beyond that—my flesh, my blood, my clothes, my surroundings. But you always particularly hated anyone seeing into your private space without prior arrangement, as if your soul was diffused into the environs of wherever you happened to be.

You insisted on us having a couple of minutes in the room alone first, to "straighten the bed."

"Hiding the stains, honey?" slurred Debbie. "Don't mind us, we've seen worse."

Indeed. You also swept your pack of contraceptive pills into the bedside drawer. I'd noticed you begin taking them again on the plane here, after the wedding. So you no longer wanted to try for a baby? It hadn't come as a huge surprise, although you'd been very keen before.

"Right, kids, into bed!" said Marcus, as he, Debbie and Isabella entered the room.

"Seriously?" you said, a touch huffy. "I'm not sure what we're going to actually learn from that."

"I wanna see how it all looks," said Marcus, shaking the rain out of his hair.

"Please," said Isabella. "Let us try this."

"Hey, we should film it," said Debbie. "Who has a phone with battery? Ours are flat."

You and I were in the process of getting into our hotel bed, fully clothed. It was hot, but we were game. At least, I was. You kicked me a couple of times, and seemed to shake your head, but I ignored you.

"Yeah, and there's nowhere to charge them," said Marcus.

"You've got battery, presumably?" I said to you. "Where's your phone?"

You kicked me again. "I don't know," you said.

"You don't know?" I said, perhaps a touch mockingly. "Don't you video yourself every hour anymore to check your hair and your outfit?"

"Richard," you hissed. "For God's sake, shut up!"

"This is great!" said Marcus. "Maybe this is how it started, with an argument."

I lay down as instructed, but you kept wriggling and sighing and generally making a spectacle of yourself.

The rain beat against the window with its incessant little fists.

"So the couple were asleep up here," said Debbie. "With the howling wind outside, just like now. And she was a journalist, right, Issy?"

"Yes," said Isabella shyly. "She had been a famous travel journalist but then stopped when her husband become ill. She tell me all about it."

"Wait, I thought she'd been fired," said Marcus. "I googled her, I think?"

"Yeah, wasn't she some kinda TERF?" asked Debbie.

"No, baby, that wasn't it at all," said Marcus.

"She got canceled for something, though, right?"

"They were so in love," said Isabella, clasping her small hands together. "But he was so ill—so, so ill."

"I thought you'd know more about them, since you've come all this way for the film option," you said, intemperately, from under the covers.

"We were only in Milan," said Debbie. "Not far."

"It is this image of the two in love, standing in the sea, about to drown," said Isabella. "Right, Signor Marcus?"

"That's right," said Marcus. "Sometimes, it's all we need. One great shot. The movie poster. Once you got the poster, you can create the movie around it."

"Yeah, just look at *Titanic*," Debbie said.

I have to say they were right. We'd been taken with the story on the basic information too. But you would not play along.

"OK, *Titanic* existed long before the movie poster," you huffed.

"Ah, but did it?" said Marcus. "Did it really?"

That shut you up. It was the kind of thing you were so fond of saying.

"So what was wrong with the guy?" asked Debbie. "The husband-sleepwalker?"

"Maybe dementia?" said Marcus. "But I'm not sure I like dementia."

"The wife, Claire, she tell me all about it," said Isabella.

I could feel you rolling your eyes next to me.

"He have schizophrenia," said Isabella. "It come on late in life."

"I don't like schizophrenia," said Marcus.

"But if that's what he had, honey . . . ?" said Debbie.

"Yeah, I don't like it," Marcus said again.

"He believed God was speaking to him directly," you said, as if you knew anything about it. "Maybe he was. How are we to know?"

Now it was my turn to kick you. Why do you always have to weigh in on everything? You can't ever shut up or not have an opinion. But my kicking didn't work.

"You can't ever really be certain what someone else feels or knows," you said.

Which, can I just say, is utterly wrong. But it is just like you to think that everyone is a unique snowflake when in fact humans are completely predictable—more so if they have a recognized disorder. How do you think hedge funds and insurance companies make money if we can't predict what people are likely to do?

If you ask people whether they'd prefer a ninety percent chance of getting £1,000, or getting £900 for sure, they choose the second option. But when you offer them the choice between losing £900 for sure, or a ninety percent chance of losing £1,000, they go for the gamble. The question is the same, and yet people choose different answers depending on how you frame it. It is a fact of life that people gamble more when they are faced with significant loss. People grasp any chance to minimize their failure, their despair. Offer them something good, on the other hand, and they bite your arm off.

"It start in Rome," said Isabella. "A sort of, how you say, Jerusalem Syndrome?"

"Pretty sure you can't get Jerusalem Syndrome in Rome," you said.

"I actually like Jerusalem Syndrome," said Marcus. "And I like it even more if it's in Rome. Doesn't seem so anti-Semitic. Can it be called Rome Syndrome?"

"Can you rename a known disorder?" said Debbie. "Hey, what about that thing you get in Florence, baby? Where you faint because you've seen too much great art?"

"Yeah, I can't remember what that's called."

"Florence Syndrome?" you offered. "Sounds like a psychotic nurse, though."

"Or an emo rock group from 2002," I added.

And we both giggled then, which was nice.

My hand hurts, writing this. When did I last handwrite so many words? I've never been a keeper of journals, like you are. I've never felt the need to document my innermost thoughts. I read somewhere that there's only a point to keeping a diary if you regularly read it back to yourself and learn from it. If you use it as a way of gathering intelligence on yourself—only then is it at all worthwhile.

Do you remember our Scrabble game, the night we arrived on the island? I don't recall the name of the woman who ran the cheap beach place you booked for our pre-honeymoon, but she had dusty old board games piled up in the breakfast area, behind the stack of cups and saucers with the dead flies in them. I have to say you were right about the breakfast there—it was indescribably awful, particularly the gray hard-boiled eggs and the jellied meats—but I never understood why you objected to the breakfast here at the Villa Rosa, over which Isabella took such care.

Why you can't just be more polite, I've never been able to fathom.

We'd spent the afternoon of our arrival exploring the area around our hotel, and then you'd gone for a swim. You'd complained about the tendrilous sea-plants that licked your legs under the water. We'd drunk large glasses of cheap cold wine on our whitewashed balcony and then gone for dinner at George's Taverna.

It was clear that this was the first moment we could possibly talk about what had happened at the wedding, and so instead we played Scrabble. It was incredible how we just silently agreed never to speak of what we'd learned, to squash it down like silk blouses in a suitcase, as my mother always did quite firmly, almost violently.

One would think you might have beaten me, it being a word game after all. But Scrabble is more of a maths game, like everything, really. You always played Scrabble the way my father had apparently taught you: get the big letters and do something flashy with them. But my strategy is more mathematical. I've never much cared for the big difficult letters. Give me a rack of Ns and Ls and a few vowels. An S and a blank and—bingo—literally.

You preferred "nice words" to big scores. But what is the point of nice words, really? So often true beauty is made from simple words, in any case. Like those of Hemingway or Murakami.

Did the sleepwalkers ever play Scrabble? I tried to imagine what it would have been like to be them as we lay fully clothed in the hot bed with you kicking me and Isabella telling Marcus how the sleepwalkers had been married for forty years before James, the husband, had started dropping to his knees and praying, wherever he happened to be.

"That's right, honey," said Debbie, suddenly remembering. "Claire Kearney, the wife, she wrote a long piece in a newspaper about the power of religion to heal. That was how she got canceled. She said her husband had actual healing powers."

"People don't like religion," said Marcus.

"Don't they?" I said. "People act as if they do."

"It's true," you said. "All ethics in society come from a religious foundation. If it wasn't for religion everyone would be killing each other and coveting their neighbors' wives—well, way more than they do already."

"Feel like the humanists would disagree with you there," said Marcus.

"In secret, people do the right thing," I said, instantly feeling this wasn't entirely true. Where had I read it? Perhaps I was just expressing it badly.

I thought it was nice that we were agreeing, for one of the first times in recent memory, but no one else seemed at all interested in what we were saying.

"You gotta think of China now," said Marcus. "No one

wants God in China. They want that other stuff. Like, what's it called, cheese?"

"Qi, baby."

"And the type of people who buy tickets to movie theaters in the west aren't so godly either. All the god-fearing folks stay in and watch network TV and read self-help books on their Kindles."

"People think religion starts wars," said Debbie.

Marcus started pacing slowly, and scratching his head.

"So if our guy, the husband-sleepwalker, is super religious? I might be cooling on this idea. I'm not sure I can see it. I'm losing the poster. It's fading outta my mind. If the guy's now standing in the sea with his hands clasped in prayer? No one wants to see that movie."

"I guess if there were any photos of the sleepwalkers they'd be on some electronic device that doesn't have any power right now?" Debbie said to Isabella.

"Of course!" Isabella clapped her hands together. "The photos!"

While she was downstairs looking for them, Debbie directed us to get up and walk to the door a couple of times so Marcus could see what the sleepwalking would have looked like. Me first, pretending to be in a trance, and then you following. You kept moaning about being too hot in the hotel robe Debbie made you put on over your clothes.

"This doesn't make sense," you said grumpily. "There's no way the woman would follow him all the way to the sea from the room. She'd wake him up way before that."

"You're not meant to wake sleepwalkers," I said, breaking kayfabe for a moment.

"Right, so instead you let them go out into a storm and then walk for half a mile before getting fully clothed into the sea?"

You had a point.

"If you wake a sleepwalker, can you kill them?" asked Debbie. "Honey, do you remember hearing that? A sleepwalker might go into a coma, or have a heart attack?"

"Yeah, much better to let them drown," you said.

Isabella returned, flushed and damp from running up the steps in the rain.

I could tell you were suspicious when she showed the photographs to us. She'd taken them on her Polaroid camera, like the ones of the Turkish band, the ones you'd objected to for your own unfathomable reasons. They showed the sleepwalkers having breakfast, walking up and down the stairs, and in bed (although even I admit she moved on from that one pretty fast).

They actually did bring to mind the couple you never wanted us to be. Potato-ish faces. Wattlish necks. The wife looked like an aging heiress who travels as an excuse to skip meals and miss the parts of life she doesn't like. The kind of person who plays at being a socialist but forgets to take off her pearls. The husband looked like a vicar whose dog collar had been misplaced. The sort of man who'd buy special port at Christmas and then forget to finish it.

"Wait!" you said, instantly mistrustful. "What was that?"

You grabbed the photo of the sleepwalkers in bed.

"Why do you have a picture of them in bed?" you demanded.

"This one they ask me to take for their children," Isabella said. "It was for a joke, for them to laugh."

I could tell you didn't believe her.

"Quite convenient, given everything," you said, rudely.

"Wow, he's actually praying in this one," said Marcus.

In the next photo, James Border, as I learned he was called, was indeed on his knees. It was in the courtyard garden of the Villa Rosa. It was hard to tell whether he was in fact praying, or just looking for something under the table.

"Ah," said Isabella. "Here they have just arrived—a day early actually, because of husband illness. They get the date wrong. Oh, how we all laugh at this!"

You'd already discarded the previous photo onto the bed, and Isabella had carefully slipped it back into the correct place in her set. You now clawed the current one out of Isabella's hands and studied it intently. You didn't have your glasses on, so who knows what you were actually seeing.

"Hang on," you said. "What's that young guy doing there?"

"This is just Hamza," Isabella said, snatching the photo back. "He is from Turkey. He help me sometimes. Ignore him."

"So was this husband ill, or just super religious?" mused Marcus, still pacing.

"He have schizophrenia," said Isabella.

"But the wife believed her husband could cure the sick?"

"That was earlier," you said. "Before he was actually diagnosed."

"How do you know any of this?" I asked you, adding, for the benefit of our audience, "She always thinks she's an expert in everything, by the way. It's because she's an actress."

"It's all in the guest book," you said. "Downstairs."

"Why would someone write all that in a guest book?" I said.

"Because they wanted to leave a record of their brave and wonderful parents wherever they went, but especially here, where they died," you said. You paused. "And yes, they wrote that down too. Well, something like that. Go and look for yourself if you don't believe me."

I could tell the way we were talking was upsetting Isabella. There was something fragile and troubled about her that night that I couldn't quite understand. Yes, she was drunk and flushed and giggling and excited, but I had a strange fancy that she was afraid as well.

"I don't like schizophrenia," said Marcus once again. "And I don't like religion."

He paced up and down a while longer, and then left the room.

Debbie looked hard at us and frowned. "I feel like this might actually be a story about you two," she said, and then she left as well.

It seemed that the reenactment, such as it was, was over.

Once they'd all gone I found I was in the mood for some alone time. I traced the outline of your breasts with my finger. You sighed softly. I am sorry to confess this, but I closed my eyes and pretended you were Isabella in her white dress, and you'd never seen a naked man before.

It will make me sound like a complete creep if I say that I sometimes wanted you to resist my advances. I wanted you to be modest and shy, to find sex dirty and unwholesome, and treat me like an animal, a Neanderthal, trying to force himself on you. I wanted you to lie still, taking me unwillingly, because you were better, purer than this base thing we felt compelled to do because of raw biology. It's hard to say this now, and you probably won't understand, but I always wanted to be the opposite of Paul. Alas, I've always been just as perverted as him, really. Perhaps even more so.

Remember when we both had Covid? It was a sort of literal fever dream. We'd been together for almost five years when the pandemic struck, but our relationship had always had a temporary, airport-lounge feel, as if we were both waiting to take flights to different destinations. We always had our secrets, didn't we? Our own lives.

You'd kept the terraced house you'd bought in Canterbury, on the same side of town as my parents' village. Before the pandemic you would teach at the university all day on a Tuesday, and so you stayed in your house from Monday to Wednesday. The rest of the time you lived in my flat in Clerkenwell. Our relationship was a little passionless, but it felt solid. Were we both getting our real kicks elsewhere? I certainly was, and I never established whether or not you knew.

After you'd got the teaching job in Canterbury I'd fallen into a routine that I rather liked. My mother was always in London at the beginning of the week and so I took her to lunch every Monday. On Tuesdays I treated myself to a gram of cocaine and a prostitute, and then I did a juice cleanse and a long run on a Wednesday. Does this surprise you? I know you always thought you were the only one who ever dabbled in illegal or unusual things.

There was no possibility of any of that in the pandemic, and certainly not when we were both ill. For what seemed like days I'd be quivering on the floor of the shower cubicle while you almost drowned in the bath. We slid around in bed, all twisted in our damp sheets. We'd try to have sex and fall asleep halfway through. We coughed on each other and brought each other glasses of iced water and then my breathing went wrong and you looked after me so tenderly. I'm still so grateful for that, Evie. You may have saved my life.

You ordered exotic remedies from the internet. Herbs, potions.

You ordered me to stop eating wheat and dairy.

You consulted a homeopath for me.

You made me drink about four liters of water a day and you brought me bone broth in porcelain bowls. You made it yourself in the new slow cooker you'd somehow managed to obtain, in those strange days when you couldn't even buy pasta, or toilet rolls.

You fellated me so very tenderly while I wheezed and spluttered.

And that's when I asked you to marry me. You were tracing your tongue around my foreskin with such love and care. The sensation could not have been more perfect, and you were simply the most gentle nurse. I had to repay you somehow. You'd just come upstairs from taking a delivery of a batch of beef shin bones you'd managed to get hold of. You'd already put them on to cook with some thyme and celery and carrots. You still had your apron on over your short silk pajamas.

You were ravishing that day.

And so I said it. "Evelyn Masters, will you do me the honor of becoming my wife?"

You nodded, my penis still in your mouth. Later, in bed, you said you wanted the wedding to be as soon as possible, and you intended to try for a baby immediately. You particularly wanted a son, you said. You wanted to make sure you never lost me and my beautiful genes.

I think that might be the nicest thing anyone's ever said to me.

You were certainly the warmest girlfriend I'd ever had. The ones from the past all had a certain haughtiness and loft. You were earthy, substantial. You'd have a great baby, I thought. Women like you were made to have babies. Even when you commissioned our astrological chart and it was so horrific, I never thought there was anything fundamentally wrong with us. "A hopeless relationship" is one of the lines I particularly remember. "May quarrel often" is another. Apparently our sex life would "lack tenderness" (you'd already disproved this with your gentle fellatio) and we would continually try to dominate each other. We would also be extremely secretive, the commentary had predicted. We laughed it off, of course.

Had you known about the Tuesday prostitutes? I'd wondered if you were toying with me that evening when you showed me that model online. Do you remember? You were "writing" on your laptop on one of our leather sofas; I was reading the newspaper on the other. It wasn't that long after we'd got engaged, and I felt that we suddenly meant so much more to each other. It was as if you were an antique I'd just had valued and realized I'd need to insure. We were exchanging little smiles and enjoying the comfortable quiet we'd established despite the stupid horoscope.

You weren't really writing. I could see page after page of expensive short dresses and silk underwear reflected in your glasses. They were scrolling fast, like the titles at the end of an old film. I would have preferred it if you could have spent your evenings poring over full-length gowns and designer blazers with large gold buttons. It annoyed me that you still liked clothes that showed so much flesh. I hoped you'd become more modest after we were married. I mean, you couldn't go about like that if you were pregnant, surely! But you always laughed away my concerns and said you were worried you were having an early menopause anyway, because you were hot all the time.

Paul was the one who shared your taste for slutty clothing. You never quite had the body of his tiny young girlfriends, but you favored similar outfits. Skimpy skirts with vests and boots, cropped tank tops with shorts, little backless dresses. Personally, I have always liked you in white if possible. Cotton, ideally. Most women don't realize the erotic power of a pair of simple clean white cotton panties. Only real animals get off on the idea of a thong, surely? And I prefer nipples bare, not covered in black lace.

But that didn't stop you browsing for outfits you knew I wouldn't like.

"What are you doing?" I asked you.

"Research," you lied. Well, it could almost have been true, I suppose. You found so many ways to revel in your own glory, even though you were supposed to be working on your next show. In those days you made endless mood boards, all about yourself. Your perfect outfit for a red carpet, your ideal weekend capsule wardrobe, your teaching ensembles. It was around that time that you started claiming to be a minimalist, and telling me you didn't buy the outfits but simply saved them to Pinterest.

I liked the teaching ensembles best, incidentally. Black cigarette trousers with crisp white shirts and black-rimmed glasses. I relished the lingerie you wore under white shirts, but you rarely wore white shirts when you were with me.

On a different evening I may have breathed in and out and rolled my eyes as you scrolled through bralets, cut-out tops and designer running shorts you would never run in. Instead, I said, "Liar."

You let a little smile play over your lips, but didn't look up.

"Just like Danny," I went on, leaning into the playfulness in my voice.

"Who?"

"Nerdy guy on the law desk?"

"Um ... ?"

"With online poker or football reflecting on his glasses during team Zooms."

You carried on scrolling.

"I mean," you said, but didn't add anything. Perhaps some awful zebra-print suede skirt had caught your eye. Or those skinny jeans that cost £600.

There was an extremely long pause.

"This girl," you said lightly, "is your type."

I felt as if someone had tipped a bucket of too-warm water over me.

"What?"

Was this your way of telling me you knew about the Tuesday prostitutes?

You turned your laptop around. On it was a video, oddly jerky like a GIF, but perhaps the strange jerkiness was created by the movements of the model? You were right. The model *was* my type. Looking back now, I realize she resembled Isabella. The same little pout. Long sun-bleached hair. A jauntiness. Spirit. Exactly the kind of girl I'd pick on a Tuesday. The one who looked youngest and least used. Freckles. A slight smile at all times. Fresh and clean.

Was it an accident? Did you know? If so, how did you know? How did you know it was innocence I longed for most of all? That I paid the prostitutes to act like women who are shy and humble—a type that barely exists in the real world nowadays.

"Oh God," you said. "Your face." You laughed and then stopped. "Wow."

I could feel my heart thumping, like at the end of a long run, or the beginning of a fever.

"She really is," you said. "You're bright red!"

After that, the evening went wrong, as so many did, in one of the myriad ways predicted in the astrological chart. You apparently found something attractive in my embarrassment. You came and sat on my lap and suggested you might dress up as the girl: use eyeliner for the freckles, apply some pink lipstick and so on. I pushed you off and said I didn't understand why you would fail to grasp that I didn't want that. I never wanted that, Evie.

And now you're out there somewhere, in the cursed wind and the Turkish rain.

Evie, I do miss you. And I'm glad we made love before you left, even if it was disappointing for both of us.

Marcus, Debbie and Isabella had finally gone downstairs and we almost went with them for a nightcap, but we'd both had enough of the sleepwalkers for one night—or so I thought. I stroked your breasts, as I've already mentioned. We undressed fast, giggling a little as we did. I actually always found clothed sex more arousing, because it spoke of spontaneity and accident and youth. The time before I was ruined forever. But normal adults undress for sex and so that's what we did. You lay back on the bed, the one in which we'd so recently been playing the sleepwalkers. You opened your legs. I entered you.

"Fuck me," you said. "Fuck me hard."

You clawed at my back like some kind of cheap prostitute.

"Fuck me like we're about to get murdered," you breathed.

I wished you'd be quieter so I could think of you as Isabella, her long hair flowing down her straight back. Her prim little curtseys.

You said my name and I imagined it with that slight accent of hers which I thought was Greek but now know is Spanish. Your trained voice, with all its hidden husk and hysteria, doesn't arouse me quite as much as it used to. I'm sorry to admit that. It did in the beginning, though. That summer, years ago, after we'd both finished university, when you were going to start your theatre studies master's, and I was off to the US for my MBA at Harvard. You were the virtuous house-keeper and I hated myself a touch less than normal because I'd got a first, and because I felt I was growing up and leaving my shameful youth behind me.

I couldn't have you, and that made it OK to want you.

There was no way in this world I could get involved with my father's housekeeper.

You were very much his, which was odd. You'd think a housekeeper would more properly "belong" to the wife, yet it was my father who gave you your instructions. But then he was the one who'd found you, wretched and needy, in some unspecified trouble, and he'd rescued you. He did that sort of thing, my saintly father.

I suppose now I know what the trouble was.

You never seemed to require very much instruction any-way. You seemed mainly to spend your time in bed in your plush attic room, or reading in the summer house. You did two loads of laundry a week: one white, one mixed. You took my mother and father's dry cleaning to Master John and picked it up again. As far as I could make out, you were allowed to put your own clothes in as well. Once I saw you coming back from Master John with three garment bags. I thought a shirt of mine had gone in and so I went looking while you were making lunch. Almost all the clothes were yours: those dark floral silk minidresses you liked back then, and several lacy chemises, all black.

When I masturbated later, I pretended they'd been white, with much less lace.

I imagined you saying my name with your filthy accent: Rich-id. Rich-id.

I never thought one day you'd be mine.

God, I feel so grubby writing like this. It's probably best if I destroy this letter once it's finished. I think it's important for me to get my thoughts in order, but I can't possibly ever give this to you. You'd likely turn it into a one-woman show anyway. Have you ever seen the irony in that, by the way? You, oh great prima donna, so me-me-me, and what you do for a living is create one-woman shows, as if your whole life were not a one-woman show. It is quite funny when you think about it.

I was supposed to see the premiere of the London run of your first one-woman show, *The Chambermaid*, with my parents, but they couldn't come for some reason, and so I attended alone. I have always felt most captivated by shy women, and you were not shy at all. But there was something in the character you were portraying that I found compelling. Or maybe I was just starstruck.

I took you for dinner afterwards in a tiny French restaurant. We ate *moules marinière*, do you remember? You were always a little frightened of seafood in those days, and you clutched at your white napkin under the table when you thought I wasn't watching. It wasn't that far for me to go home, but we went back to your hotel room and drank Cointreau with ice and you seemed so pure in the candlelight, and then splayed and naked on the white hotel bed.

That was our first time together. Did we both decide the next morning that it had been a one-off? Perhaps. But then it happened again, after a trip to Tate Britain. Each time we fucked I'd make a mental note to try not to do it again, but then we would. Perhaps it was the same for you. We drifted together like two mild weather fronts.

Your show was about a maid who gets involved with her employer. I'm not sure what I thought at the time—I'm not even sure what I think now. Of course it couldn't have been literally true. No one thought that. It would have been too outré even for you. And it wasn't even meant to be a realist piece exactly. Your maid was deliberately flirty, and the show portrayed her grinding down the male employer, behaving, I now realize, just as you believed Isabella was acting with me. The maid in the show cleverly sidelines the wife and manipulates the husband. Finally, she marries him and then one night she stabs him with a massive kitchen knife and burns down the house and goes to the Caribbean and lives happily ever after.

I thought it was quite clever the way you created the show from the male POV. Excuse me sounding like the *TLS* for a moment, but I thought it was daring and original that you leaned into the male gaze and told the story the way he would have told it. The over-sexualization of the maid, her revealing uniform, and the employer's belief that she "wanted" his advances—or even that she was the one responsible for them. And then all his greatest fears realized. The maid is super sexy, but then also prone to violence. Sex leads to death. And look at who triumphs in the end. It's all about the power that a certain type of man believes belongs to a certain type of woman. The man as poor, seduced victim. But in fact the power has been his all along.

And the stupid left-wing press, and all the idiots on Twitter, couldn't see that this was what you'd done. Once it was on TV they decided to take it at face value. And, OK, I know I'm not the greatest feminist in the world, but I was so angry on your behalf then. All those centuries of male artists being given the benefit of the doubt. *Lolita*, for heaven's sake! My English master at school was still recommending it as a literary classic in 2009. And that novella that won the Booker Prize which was brilliant but essentially a warning to men not to have sex with women over forty because they could end up with a disabled child. (I forget its title, and I still don't have my phone.) All of the complex, layered, disgusting—and frankly *great*—works of literature by men that have stood so proudly on bookshelves for centuries. When women were finally allowed into this world they were basically given about five minutes before they were told to shut up and behave and never write anything with nuance.

I don't think you ever realized how much I understood your show. I knew what you were portraying, and I'm grateful for it.

I wish I could have told you that. Now you're gone.

Yesterday evening, though, you were still here. The wind was howling, and the window rattled in its frame. The rain continued to pour.

We were post-coital in the Villa Rosa after our reenactment-night sex and we should have been happy, but we were not.

"Do you think we are going to get murdered?" you asked.

"What?" I said, irritated.

"OK, why are you saying it like that?" you demanded.

"I'm not saying it like anything. I just have no idea what you're talking about."

You sighed and wriggled around in bed. You looked for your glass of water and drank from it.

"Ugh," you said. "This glass still hasn't been changed. This water's been sitting here for two days."

"Well, maybe Isabella has better things to do than run around after you?"

"Right, but that's basically her job. What we're—well, your mother—is paying for."

"And I expect she's busy with those producers here."

You gulped your substandard water. "Yeah, that's all bullshit."

"What?"

"Marcus and Debbie. They'll be going all over the world doing this number on people. I bet they're not even paying to stay here. They get their snazzy dinner and a free suite and an evening's entertainment—better than a murder mystery weekend. If only there was Wi-Fi, I'd look them up on IMDb. Feel like I'd definitely find that they made one film in 1980. An uptight businessman has his world turned upside down by a kind-hearted prostitute. That sort of thing."

I sighed. I didn't think it necessary to reply. But you wouldn't shut up.

"More efficient than your Hilton Honors reward scheme," you said.

Again, I didn't reply. You sighed.

"Don't you think Isabella is acting super suspiciously?"

"No. I really wish you'd—"

"That boy in the photograph. He's got something to do with the sleepwalkers."

"What boy?"

"Hamza, she said he was called? He was at the window earlier, outside the dining room. He looked totally fucking mental. We saw him at the harbor before. Oh, and I think he brought the doilies for the dinner party."

"Doilies?"

"*Right?*"

I rolled my eyes. "What's that got to do with the sleepwalkers?"

"That's what I'm going to find out."

You got up and put on the hotel dressing gown, just as you had earlier, in the shambolic reenactment.

"Evie," I said. "Don't."

"I just—"

"If you're so worried about getting murdered then why don't you just stay here quietly instead of blundering off 'to investigate'?"

"Like the sleepwalkers did."

"We don't know what they actually did!"

"Yeah, well, I've got some idea. I think they lay down and went to sleep and never woke up. Or maybe they woke up in the sea, wondering how the hell they got there."

"But—"

"Come on, even you must admit to seeing the way Isabella reacted to the photograph of the sleepwalkers that had Hamza in it. He's the key, I promise you."

You were determined to go downstairs, so naturally I followed you. I thought at least I could explain to Isabella, apologize for you or something.

The rain lashed against us as we walked down the stone stairs.

"You're mad," I said. "Really, Evie."

"And I need to get my phone back," you said, ignoring me.

"From where?"

"Where I left it recording. In the dining room."

And you really did look unhinged then, the rain gushing violently into your hair and face like some kind of extreme bukkake as you grinned at me in the darkness.

"You did *what*?" I said over the sound of a car crunching up to the house.

On the driveway below, Marcus and Debbie were being helped into a large black car by a chauffeur holding an umbrella.

"See," you said. "I predicted this as well."

"Goodbye!" called Debbie happily.

"Take care!" said Marcus. "We'll be in touch."

There was the sound of more goodbyes and thank-yous and the *thunk* of the car door, and—

"I told you," you hissed through the rain. "Smash and grab."

"I have no idea what you're talking about," I said.

"They didn't even stay one night," you said.

"OK, but how exactly does that work with your theory that they were freeloading?"

"It's probably the storm. They're making a break for it while they can."

"They brought their own food too," I reminded you.

Isabella didn't see us as we stole into the reception area just after the car pulled away. But we saw her. She thumped the wall with her small hand and then traipsed sadly into the dining room. I felt so sorry for her then. You were probably right; I could see that. Her one dream was coming to an end.

You didn't care. You went straight for the guest book.

"I'm sure it was here," you said, flicking through the pages.

"What?" I asked, with slightly gritted teeth.

"Oh my God," you said, pointing inside the guest book. "Look."

"What?"

"Someone's ripped out the pages! The pages where the sleepwalkers' children wrote all about them."

"Really? This wouldn't just be in your fantasy world again, would it?"

"The rip marks are literally here, Richard."

I didn't look, deliberately, to spite you.

From the dining room there came a big crash.

"I'm not doing this anymore!" came a male American voice.

Then someone with a French accent said, "You don't have any choice, idiot."

The first voice continued: "If this is going to be made into a movie, we are all screwed."

"You wouldn't dare. You'd go to prison."

"Yeah? And so would you. All of you."

I didn't look at your face, but I bet it was smug.

Isabella appeared in the hallway, her face red. Behind her

came Christos, looking angry. The dapper little man hovered in the background, holding a Polaroid camera.

"You are here," Isabella said to us. "Why? And what is the meaning of this?"

She held up your phone. The lock screen appeared, with the old photo in the background of the stage from the original Fringe version of *The Chambermaid*. In the top left-hand corner was a little yellow microphone graphic, pulsing on and off. It was the app you use to record yourself practicing for auditions, or to transcribe your ideas. It transcribed unknown voices laughably badly—as you loved to point out whenever you used it. Whenever someone said your name, it would come out as "a violin." You always secretly recorded the meetings you had with casting directors and producers, which I'm not sure was totally ethical.

"You have been recording us. Why?" Isabella approached you. "Please, you must tell me how to switch off and delete."

"Why?" you said. "I thought you had no secrets here. I thought everything was public and open?"

"Please," said Isabella.

You reached out your hand to take the phone, but Isabella didn't want to give it to you.

"That's mine," you said.

"Tell me how and I do it," she said. "Then you have back."

I mean, she had a point. Isn't it illegal to record someone against their will?

"No," you said. "Keep it. I have the recording online anyway."

"This is an invasion of privacy," she said, biting her lip. "You have accidentally recorded very private things."

"Yeah? I bet I'm not the only one," you said bitterly. "You've been listening to us since we arrived. Do you get off on it somehow? And what have you done with the notebook I left in my room?"

Isabella made a complex face then that you might have described as "sneering." But you really were trying her patience. And mine.

The next thing Isabella said startled everyone, especially me.

She took a step forward and touched my arm. She looked into my eyes.

"Are you coming to bed, Richard?" she said, with a crisp smile.

I should have said no immediately, but I didn't. I hesitated.

I may have taken just one small step toward her.

The dapper little man raised his camera, pointed it at you and clicked.

You screamed and ran out of the hallway into the storm.

So, OK, I admit it. I did want her. It had been brewing since our first day at the Villa Rosa, if I'm honest, when I'd gone into the wrong room for breakfast. I'd seen Isabella naked then for the first time, and I'm afraid the image rather took hold of me. She'd been pale and trembling on a chaise longue, stretched out like a hairless cat.

The dapper little man had also been there that first morning, by the way, sketching Isabella in charcoal. I possibly should have told you, but you'd already decided you didn't like her and I didn't want to make things worse.

Anyway, I hesitated, because I am human. I fear I'll be dead or in prison within the month, so why not at least think about indulging my final desire? Some men want KFC or a rib-eye steak. I just wanted Isabella. I'm so sorry, for that, and for everything.

I hesitated only a moment longer, and then I chased after you.

I ran up the stairs through the thick wet rain and into our suite. You'd locked yourself in the bathroom. I lay on the bed and waited for you to calm down. I must have dropped off, because the next thing I remember is Isabella's flesh on mine, and then waking to find you gone.

Actually, no. Maybe there was something else? A huge crash of thunder in the very dead of night, and the room all lit up bright yellow for a second, and you—sitting at the desk writing something. Yes! What were you writing, Evie?

And then, even deeper into the night. You seemed to be shaking me.

"He's out there, Richard! He's bleeding!"

But maybe I dreamed that second one? Maybe both?

The second time, I thought I could see your suitcase in the background, and you had your Gucci belt-bag on, the one my father bought you as a honeymoon gift.

I wish you hadn't left. But you did. You left me, Evie.

So maybe it's time to tell you my terrible secret? How it all started.

You can't interrupt now, or explode when

The hotel is rather charming. It sits like a plump little king at the end of a dusty driveway, all pomp and hauteur, as if it's just ordered a bowl of peeled grapes and is waiting for them to arrive. It has a quaint majesty, so out of place on this small island. You almost want to pat it on the head and say, *There there, your highness, the grapes will come soon.* The owner is called Isabella. She has the same baffled look of everyone here. Is it something to do with the light? Isabella apparently inherited the whole place from her dead husband, a much older man who for some reason I picture wearing a ragged vest and drinking bottled beer every night on the veranda. Although if he had been elegant and white-shirted that would perhaps have chimed more with the place. In fact yesterday I saw a picture of him, and he loomed moodily out of a too-small chair with a broken nose and gold watch, but when I tried to press Isabella for more details she pretended not to have understood me and said she had to go and boil some eggs.

"I will lend you a boy," she says to me today, after breakfast.

"I'm sorry?" I say. But then I realize she means she has found me a guide to go to the refugee camp, which I'd asked her about yesterday.

She is a woman of few words, but she has been kind to James, who has not been feeling so well these last weeks. It's difficult to know what to do when your husband has found God, and you haven't. It's not that I didn't try. But our long quest across the US, with all the big trees and big egos and big gurus—for me it was about travel, movement, escape, and for James it was about finding stillness. But such is the case with so many marriages of our vintage, of course.

James says that God gives you sickness or troubles when he knows you can handle them, when you are strong enough. He persists in seeing his own weakness as a strength. But this is not about James. And I will write no more about James, after the last time.

The boy arrives late. I want to call him something else—a man, a bloke, a guy—but he is a slip of a thing in his high-waisted shorts and cut-off Lou Reed T-shirt. Where does one buy clothes like that around here? I have found only one acceptable shop on the island, but you would not be able to buy anything genuinely stylish there, or proper moisturizer, or good makeup. Yet the boy has traces of makeup on his face. Scrubbed black eyeliner that has not quite gone from the corners, something electric blue. He reminds me a little of the fa'afafine I encountered in the Pacific all those years ago, with his slender wrists and the way he walks. The dark pink of his full lips.

"My English is not so good," he says, in remarkably good English, with a trace of an American accent. "I apologize."

"Well, I have no Greek," I say. "But we'll muddle through, I expect."

He doesn't tell me then that he is actually Turkish; I discover that later. They are not fond of Turks here, it seems. They like the English, and the French. They dislike Muslims and Arabs. They believe their closest neighbors to be bad tourists: dirty and cheap.

The taxi driver is gruff and taciturn, and seems to mistrust my guide. He does not want to take us to the camp. So much for my useful helper. Yet the boy is persistent. He wriggles through the smallest gaps in conversation, and negotiates with a ratlike persistence. He has been to the camp before, of course, like everyone on the island. How they put us to shame on these small islands where they are eager to help refugees, not leave them to drown or starve. They may not like Muslim tourists, but refugees are a different matter. And perhaps the people here have learned from their Islamic neighbors that when someone is hungry, you must give them food, or God will be displeased. I have to say, although I don't believe in God-God, like James suddenly does, I do rather cling to that universal principle of goodness that makes people want to care for one other.

The camp itself reminds me of Glastonbury, except for all the crying babies. Who brings a baby to a place like this? But then I realize they have probably been born here, poor little wretches. Everything is so flimsy. There are sad washing lines with hoodies and hijabs hanging limply on them. Rubbish is piled high in black plastic sacks and old carrier bags bearing the logo of the nearby shop. It's less Glastonbury and more Christiania, perhaps, with that feeling of a long-term encampment. Although the sweet pungent fumes here are not hashish and lentil burgers, and this is no happy play-utopia. The tents are worn out and threadbare. People's coughs sound frightening. Everyone wears a mask.

"Not so many people come to help now," says the boy, contradicting what he told me before, and what other islanders have said. "The residents are angry with the rubbish, and they say there is crime and disease."

The boy's name is Hamza. He seems to be a general helpmeet and fixer around the camp. Everyone knows him. People want to see him, touch him. A teenage girl in a turquoise hoodie has been waiting for him, it seems, wearing what appears to be all the makeup on the island that isn't in Hamza's own possession. He hands her two gaudy packages—sim cards for her friends. She has some English and they converse greedily, like birds in the early spring. He promises to come back next week with news of a photo shoot and even a movie. I hear the phrase "Your dream will come true," and she looks as if she wants to believe it, but doesn't quite. He hastily snaps portraits of her with his beaten-up phone and promises to show the pictures to the "lady who decides." The girl reminds me of someone, but I'm not sure who it is. She seems to carry her important things in a fabric bag that bears the legend *Istanbul is Contemporary*.

I feel like a voyeur here, and so we don't stay long. Not for the first time I wish I had James's first-aid skills, and his ability to genuinely care. He would find the right things to say and do, while I can't wait to leave the miasma of depression and desperation that envelops the camp in its thick fug. I imagine every resident of this place feels exactly the same way. But while I can leave this afternoon, their claims for asylum can take a year, two years, or may never be processed at all.

On the way back Hamza evades my questions about the girl, and instead tells me about a new camp the authorities are building in the mountains. Many concrete structures, apparently, with basketball courts and flushing toilets. Walls. Better hygiene. But there are terrible rumors about similar camps on other islands, camps from which you may only leave twice a week, or not at all; camps with immense fortifications built around them, with moats and drawbridges; camps that are essentially prisons, or awful reminders of the Second World War.

Is this his way of talking about the girl after all? It's obvious he wants to help her, to save her from this fate, and I realize I do too, although it's not at all clear how one might do this. I suppose James would now simply pray.

As we travel back across the island, Hamza becomes fascinated by Google Lens, which he has never heard of, and the way I use it to read the tatty flyer the girl gave me, which is written in Arabic.

"Look." I show him. "It makes in English."

(I have no idea why I can't stop myself speaking a kind of pidgin when talking to someone foreign. And all I can say in my defense is that yes, I am aware of it.)

He peers at my screen, eyes wide like he's watching a conjuring trick. The flyer is not that exciting. It tells of an exercise class, "dance fitness," which will take place on the beach near the camp at nine a.m. every Thursday.

"You can do this with any language?" Hamza says, astonished.

When we arrive back at the Villa Rosa I pay him more than double the going rate, and add a large tip. Then Isabella comes out and says something about a tablecloth, and Hamza darts off like the rabbit in a greyhound race.

The tablecloth is perhaps for the dinner party Isabella is insisting on throwing for James and me later this evening. James is keen and I am not. I feel tired and arthritic, and I still need to finish the piece that will pay for all this. There is something troubling about Isabella that I can't completely fathom. There is gossip about the mean husband having been murdered, and some ripe chemistry between Isabella and the French man from the harbor. Isabella seems to believe that James and I are a celebrity couple, but it is not at all clear why she would want to woo us. She has a dream too, it seems, but what it might be remains mysterious.

Late in the afternoon, Isabella

y who decides"?

so very sleepy, perhaps

because of all the wine? I hope James will come up soon. I expect he will be cross because I ventured too many questions about the girl in the camp, and Hamza, and why exactly

Dear Richard,

I've just gone for a walk up the hill.

See you later.

E xxx

~~You sweep me off of my feet, baby.~~

Бізге көмектес!

AUDIO TRANSCRIPT 1/1

21:03

SPEAKER 1
Of auntie! Eat up Richard and will begin.

SPEAKER 2
Yes come on kids this'll be fun.

SPEAKER 3
I'm not sure. This plan has a little
Magnus in it.

SPEAKER 2
I Jess think Marcus needs to see a doll.

SPEAKER 1
Yes baby that's sad funny I can see it.

EVIE MASTERS
Yes, well, eat up, Richard!

SPEAKER 1
Of auntie!

EVIE MASTERS
Yes, Avanti!

RICHARD LAWSON
That was a delicious steak, Isabella.
Thank you.

SPEAKER 3
It was enough for me it was from
senior Marcus.

Sound of plates being cleared away.
Silence.
Footsteps.
21:34

SPEAKER 4
Para Carlo.

SPEAKER 5
Okay.

SPEAKER 4

Get your key.

Sound of footsteps.

SPEAKER 3

We live photo?

SPEAKER 5

You're not fucking serious?

SPEAKER 4

Crystals, silver plate!

SPEAKER 5

This is a fucked-up miss! This cycle path
sister tying all the evidence in string because
it amuses him and Gibson are hard on.

SPEAKER 4

Family la bush, Christos.

SPEAKER 5

No! Not anymore. Yeah make it more give
sleepy walkers a slipping peels and then
dumpy down the sea.

SPEAKER 3

Scuzzy! You mess never Mercedes.
Mustard Mercedes.

SPEAKER 4

Shut your mouth, Crystals.

SPEAKER 5

You are a traffic cone, it's a Bella. This is
what the world is now discovering. It is not
Claire knew.

SPEAKER 4

Crystals, for God's sake.

SPEAKER 3

If I could get out of this I would I'm just as
chat as you I'm still be paying my own debt.

SPEAKER 5

All because of this goddamn little vampire.

Footsteps.
22:01
The door creaks.
Footsteps.

SPEAKER 4

Be more careful what you say.

SPEAKER 5

I'm not doing this anymore!

SPEAKER 4

Do you have a good choice, idiot.

SPEAKER 5

If this is going to be made into a movie we are
all screwed.

SPEAKER 4

You would not dare you'd go to please on.

SPEAKER 5

Yeah? And so with you. All of you.

SPEAKER 3

You are here. Why? And what is the meaning
of this? You have been recording us. Why?
Please, you must tell me how to switch off
and delete.

EVIE MASTERS

Why? I thought you had no secrets here. I
thought everything was public and open?

SPEAKER 3

Please.

EVIE MASTERS

That's mine.

SPEAKER 3

Tell me how can I do it. Then you have back.

EVIE MASTERS

No. Keep it. I have the recording
online anyway.

SPEAKER 3

This is an invasion of privacy. You have
accidentally recorded very private things.

EVIE MASTERS

Yeah? I bet I'm not the only one. You've been
listening to us since we arrived. Do you get
off on it somehow? And what have you done
with a notebook I left in my womb?

SPEAKER 3

Are you coming to bed, Richard?

05:30

SPEAKER 3

You do want me. I do not imagine?

RICHARD LAWSON
You do not imagine.

SPEAKER 3
Please. You would like water?

RICHARD LAWSON
Yes. Thank you.

05:43

SPEAKER 3
You like?

RICHARD LAWSON
Yes I never.

SPEAKER 3
Like this more?

RICHARD LAWSON
Oh yes.

SPEAKER 3
Oh Richard.

RICHARD LAWSON
Where is EV?

SPEAKER 3

I should put this pho somewhere.

RICHARD LAWSON

Is it still the recording?

06:01

Knocking at door.

SPEAKER 3

Yes please wait there.

06:03

SPEAKER 3

Richard. Wake up!

RICHARD LAWSON

What's happened?

SPEAKER 3

It is your wife. A violin.

RICHARD LAWSON

Oh my God. Is she OK?

SPEAKER 3

They have not found her. I Moscow.

06:07

SPEAKER 3
You will stay here, for only good.

RICHARD LAWSON
Sorry?

SPEAKER 3
Darling Richard I am going to lock you in
because you must not go after the storm
it is still so bad. EV hasn't been seen since
the airport.

RICHARD LAWSON
I don't understand.

SPEAKER 3
I will come back with a violin soon.

RICHARD LAWSON
But what about you? What about us?

SPEAKER 3
The patient, darling.

06:12
Sounds of paper rustling.
Sounds of pen on paper.

11:15

Knocking sound.

                    RICHARD LAWSON
        Hello? Who's there?

11:18

Knocking sound.

                    EVIE MASTERS
        Richard? Richard?

11:22

Knocking sound.

                    EVIE MASTERS
        Richard!

                    RICHARD LAWSON
        Evie? Where are you?

                    EVIE MASTERS
        I'm in the store cupboard next to you. I'm
        locked on. What the fuck's happening?

                    RICHARD LAWSON
        What store cubby. Where?

EVIE MASTERS
It's like some kind of drum cover or
something. I've been banging on trying to get
attention for ages. The door's locked. What the
fuck's going in?

RICHARD LAWSON
I really don't know. It's a Bella said she went
to rescue.

EVIE MASTERS
You have to speak up Richard I can't hear you
properly through the war.

RICHARD LAWSON
Well are you rescued where did you go why
didn't you leave a note why are you locked in?

EVIE MASTERS
What? Seriously?

RICHARD LAWSON
What's that supposed to mean?

EVIE MASTERS
I left you a long letter.

RICHARD LAWSON
Well where is it?

EVIE MASTERS

Maybe you should ask for a bell and. I
inspect she got all of my notes by now or
oh my God the dapple little man I bet he got
them somehow.

RICHARD LAWSON

The dapple little man why would he
have them?

EVIE MASTERS

Because he's a collector he collects everything
that's what he gets so fun.

RICHARD LAWSON

I've been I've been writing your
letter actually.

EVIE MASTERS

What is it say?

RICHARD LAWSON

It says I'm sorry I'm kind of a long winded
way and I suppose it kind of concludes that I
do love you.

EVIE MASTERS

How is it possible that I've only just realized
that I actually do love you too what we
done Richard?

RICHARD LAWSON

Is this bad?

EVIE MASTERS

You know how much I hate you as well?

RICHARD LAWSON

I'm sorry.

EVIE MASTERS

And you want to go to her after everything he
went to her why Richard?

RICHARD LAWSON

I'm sorry.

EVIE MASTERS

I suppose it's because she doesn't know who
you really are why are you really are your
dog secrets.

RICHARD LAWSON

It's not like I've got anything left to lose.

EVIE MASTERS

Oh for God's sake when are you going to stop
running away?

RICHARD LAWSON

What happened to our CV is it too late could
we maybe start again completely from scratch
this time?

EVIE MASTERS

I can't tell you how much I love that I just
don't know how far back would have to go if
there even is a time when you're okay you
know I'm not even sure there was ever a
time when I was okay I don't know when I
got broke but I don't know why I thought you
could put me back together.

RICHARD LAWSON

It was sort of fun earlier before. Acting the
sleepy walkers.

EVIE MASTERS

Why can't it be like that more often why are
we so spiky all the time?

RICHARD LAWSON

Because we've always been tragic.

EVIE MASTERS

Utterly doomed yes. Just like heretic his
horoscope.

RICHARD LAWSON

Did you know before the wedding I mean
that's what I keep asking myself if you knew
and somehow even punishing me.

EVIE MASTERS

What? Of course not. I had no idea. I mean
I'll be mad if I fucking hell is this you still
thinking that I'm mad?

RICHARD LAWSON

I mean maybe we can have some therapy
and talk about it all you know my father
especially and.

EVIE MASTERS

I think they're gonna kill us.

RICHARD LAWSON

No.

EVIE MASTERS

Yes. It's too late.

RICHARD LAWSON

Why?

EVIE MASTERS

Because we know what they did.

RICHARD LAWSON

I don't know anything.

EVIE MASTERS

Are you sure?

RICHARD LAWSON

I mean maybe the story of the sleepy walkers
there's a little suspicious.

EVIE MASTERS

You wreck on?

RICHARD LAWSON

I heard something earlier about a traffic king?

EVIE MASTERS

What? I can't hear you properly.

RICHARD LAWSON

A traffic cone? With those young people.

EVIE MASTERS

I still can't hear what you're saying. I just
took hands up to the airport.

RICHARD LAWSON

Who? Hamza? That Arab boy? How?

EVIE MASTERS

We used Christos's car Hamza is in trouble.

RICHARD LAWSON

Because of the traffic?

EVIE MASTERS

And I gave Crystals the password for my
audio transcription but he

It began

£25 book token that my aunt Sylvia bought for my twelfth birthday.

Paul was already my friend—we took the same bus to our secondary school in Canterbury, and sometimes into town on a Saturday. I wanted to go to WHSmith to buy military magazines with my book token, but Paul thought we should go to "Mike's Emporium," just off the Ring Road. He'd heard you could look at dirty books there. I'd already found some thrilling passages in my father's favorite series of spy novels. But the books in Mike's shop weren't like normal adult books. They were mostly secondhand, and sometimes quite old. They'd been loosely arranged into sections called things like "Alternative," "Horror" and "Speculative."

The section we most liked was labeled "Counter-culture," but it may as well just have been called "Porn." The books were dog-eared and smelled of cigarettes. The first time we went there, Paul found a book about an alien race that kidnapped Earth women to keep as pets. He flicked through the yellowed pages until he found a particularly ripe section, and then passed it to me like a hookah, eagerly watching for my delight and shame as I read about a woman mewling in her cage with desperation to be tamed, and then being fitted with a tail and then paraded naked in front of all the other aliens, who then took turns with her.

It blew my mind. What kind of person would write such explicit, bizarre material? Who bought these books? I wasn't as keen to go back as Paul was. But every Saturday we'd eventually end up at Mike's Emporium, in the Counter-culture section. Paul was obsessed. I'm not going to pretend it had no effect on me. It did. But while Paul hoovered up graphic novels about Japanese schoolgirls being spanked by their teachers, I awkwardly searched for more tender volumes that might tell me, for example, how to kiss a girl. There were none.

The owner, Mike, was about forty or so. He had slicked-back gray hair and wore gold flesh tunnels in his stretched earlobes. He had a tiny tattoo of an upturned cross just under his left eye, and his arms were festooned with colorful scenes involving swords, flowers and big-breasted women. He wore Nirvana T-shirts and thick, black-rimmed glasses. He sometimes sat tuning his electric guitar while we browsed. Sometimes he played complex solos. Other times he sat with an unlit cigarette in his mouth, counting money from his till. I can't remember any other customers, but there must have been some.

For the first few weeks we went in there, he didn't approach us. He'd nod a "hello" sometimes, or give us a tight smile and a shrug that I wasn't sure how to read.

But then one day he put down his guitar and sauntered over to us.

"You kids ever gonna buy something?" he said. "You're bankrupting me here."

Of course, we'd never actually bought any books from his shop. How could we? Where would we have hidden them?

"Sorry," I stammered.

"Ain't a library, you know," said Mike. "And I don't want stains on my merchandise."

He laughed after he said that, and his laugh was croaky, as if there was something wrong with him.

"You boys wanna help me with some boxes?" he asked. "I'll pay you a fiver each. And I won't throw you out for not buying anything."

It sounded like a fair enough deal.

The boxes were heavy. I tried not to notice that they were full of old-fashioned shiny porno magazines. Some of them had terrible titles: *Asian Babes*; *Big and Busty*; *Cockade*. This last featured topless women on its cover. I tried not to look as I piled up the boxes in Mike's store-room. But Paul couldn't wait to start flicking through the magazines, laughing at the men with their blond mullets and the women with their shiny leotards and acid-wash miniskirts. There was something dirty about the pictures that I didn't like. Everyone had a lot of pubic hair and wore clothes like my grandparents. But Paul was so enthralled he didn't notice Mike watching him from the top of the dark staircase.

"Sampling the merchandise again are you, boys?" he said, smiling.

At first a lot of it seemed funny. Back up in the Counterculture section of the shop, Paul became particularly amused by a series of thin dystopian novels where naughty teens would be discovered out after curfew and spanked with regulation paddles. Perhaps it was to his credit that he preferred his thrills to come in prose or line drawings rather than photographs. Or maybe it was simply that what he liked was too explicit to be photographed very easily.

Paul loved spanking. He was obsessed with the film *Secretary*. He used his dad's Blockbuster card to rent it one weekend when we were about fourteen. Suddenly all his jokes and references were about that film, or the stupid dystopian novels. He was always giggling about "The Enforcer" or getting "paddled." You more than anyone know what Paul's like with an in-joke. Back then he was just as merciless and obsessive. The only difference is that I was his special compadre then, not you. I was probably slower and less fun though, even then.

Were you ever frightened of Paul? Perhaps you should have been more careful around him. He was repulsive toward most people, but if he liked a person he allowed them to believe he was a creature they'd tamed, that only they understood. He was always like that with you. And I know you had your little secrets that didn't include me, your shared references, your dark wit I never quite got. I just never understood what was so funny about the word barnyard, I suppose. Or what you both found so hilarious about Mr. Ed the Talking Horse. You were so comfortable with Paul, though, and I never understood why. Especially since our terrible wedding.

Did he ever tell you that his mother left him and his father when he was fifteen? Perhaps a therapist would connect that with his objectification of women, and his need to think of them as sluts, but as you can see, his tastes and peccadillos had begun to develop long before she went.

One rainy Saturday in Mike's Emporium, Paul discovered a series of graphic novels—all in French, for some reason—with very explicit drawings.

"Enjoying the stock again, boys?" Mike asked, sauntering over. He was swinging his shop keys on a long chain.

"Oh yeah," said Paul enthusiastically, with a wet little grin.

"Your parents know you come in here?" Mike asked.

"No," I said. "Well, not really."

"You wanna make some more pocket money?" Mike said.

"How much?" asked Paul.

"Wow, good question. The wrong question, but a good one. Let's say two hundred?"

"*Pounds?*" I said, incredulous.

"Sure," said Mike. "Always better than dollars. Worse than euros, though."

"Doing what?" said Paul. "Moving more boxes?"

"You should've asked that first," said Mike. "Now you can't say no when I tell you what it is."

"Why not?" I asked.

He narrowed his eyes. "Because now you know what it's worth."

This made no sense, but Mike had this aura about him and it sounded plausible at the time. It was the first time—not the last—that Mike really scared me. Something in the way he said it. His thin smile.

"Do you go to school with girls?" he asked, still playing with his keys.

"No," I said, at the same time Paul said, "Yes," and glared at me.

Mike chuckled. "So one of you tells the truth and one of you is a liar. Like the Barber of Seville."

This made no sense to either of us. As everyone knows, the Barber of Seville is a paradox in which the barber shaves those men who do not shave themselves.

"I've seen your school uniforms. I know you go to the boys' school."

"Why did you ask, then?" said Paul, crossly.

"Wanted to know if I could trust you. And I can't, so."

Mike shrugged, sighed unhappily and made to walk away. If only he had, and if only we'd left then and never come back. My life would have been—would be—completely different. Yours too.

"Wait," said Paul. "What about our two hundred pounds?"

He was always sharper than me about business and finance, even then. Sharper, or more desperate? Some people would say it was the same thing. But too much desperation can blunt you. I discovered that a lot later.

The following Saturday, Mike gave us a disposable camera.

It was bright pink, and looked as if it had been ripped off the front of a magazine for teenage girls. Those were the days before anyone worried about plastic, when every new magazine and comic came with a bulky "free gift," the bigger the better.

When I say he gave it to us, it actually wasn't that straight-forward. Every transaction with Mike left me feeling as if I'd suggested whatever terrible thing it was he wanted me to do. That it had all been my idea, somehow.

Instead of giving us the camera, he simply showed it to us. He wondered out loud how it might work. Turned it over in his hands. Looked confused.

Paul took it from him, and just like that it was "ours."

"Take some good shots for me," Mike said. "You'll prob-ably know how. Bring the camera back, and I'll give you the money. That's right, isn't it, Paul? I take the camera to a shop and they develop the photographs for me?"

"Sure," said Paul, sounding grown up. "Exactly."

"Or maybe if the pictures are good enough I'll have to take them to my friend who has a darkroom," Mike said.

"How do we know what a good shot is?" I asked.

Call me stupid, but at the time I thought he meant artisti-cally good, like something in a photography class. I'd misin-terpreted the idea of the "darkroom."

Mike picked up one of the graphic novels and flicked through it until he came to a picture of a schoolgirl with a short skirt, the wind blowing it upward to reveal she was not wearing underwear. He gave me the book and raised an eyebrow.

"Maybe something like this," he said. "But of course it's up to you."

I felt like I was being drowned in warm water.

The term "upskirting" didn't exist then. Even the word "creepshot," which I discovered a lot later on a horrific subreddit, wasn't in common usage in 2004.

Paul's father worked long hours and so we spent a lot of time alone in Paul's large house in Wingham. He had fast broadband—quite a rarity then—and there were no parental controls. In those days, you could search for anything, but we hadn't realized that until the day we entered terms like "camera," "schoolgirl," "short skirt" and so on. You can imagine the kinds of images and sites we discovered.

In fact, I know you can, because you've looked at plenty of porn yourself. Anyway, it was almost ironic, because all of a sudden Paul and I no longer needed Mike and his shop. All the porn was right there on Paul's computer for us to enjoy without ever leaving the house—for free too. All the stuff Paul dreamed of, but in videos, not words and fantasy drawings.

But Mike was never going to let us escape.

The following Saturday, we didn't go to Mike's Emporium. Instead, we drifted around town looking for opportunities to take pictures of girls we thought Mike would like. But it wasn't so easy.

We tried going up and down the escalators in the big department store, but you couldn't really see anything, and hardly any girls wore skirts back then. There were a few emo teenagers who hung out in the park wearing tiny plaid kilts but we couldn't get anywhere near them. They would have thought we were posh, nerdy brats.

We tried the local swimming pool with the unisex changing rooms but the large "No Photography" signs were quite off-putting, and made me feel like a criminal.

I felt sick the whole time. Bizarrely, what we were trying to do didn't even become illegal until 2018. Mike had strongly implied that we should make sure the girls were over sixteen. But it still felt so horribly wrong. If my parents found out . . . If the headmaster was told . . . I could taste hot bile in the back of my throat all day. I'd never even stolen anything, and I barely swore. This task felt impossible.

And it was impossible. We were geeky little boys who had no idea how to get anywhere near girls, especially not ones who were, or looked, over sixteen.

That day we didn't click the camera once, and I was so relieved.

It looked as if we were just going to park the idea and move on with our lives. Paul had a couple of other money-making schemes and I had my paper round. We didn't want two hundred quid that badly. My heart jerked and fluttered when I thought about how close I'd come to doing something I knew was a huge mistake.

Yet the pink camera sat there on Paul's desk, its lens pushing forward like a snout.

"We should give that stupid thing back," I said one day.

But neither of us wanted to return to Mike's Emporium and we silently agreed never to mention it again. I know you understand that process. Even you, so keen to say everything, to put it all on the table; even you keep quiet sometimes.

It was maybe two weeks later when Mike managed to get me alone.

Why me? Well, I was the weaker of the two cubs. I still am.

It was an autumn afternoon, already dark. I was coming out of school by myself. Paul must have had clarinet, or Japanese, or detention.

"Wanna lift?" Mike said to me, pulling up in his estate car.

"Oh, no thanks," I said. "I'm good."

"You look like you wanna lift," he said.

He never threatened me. Not directly. He found indirect ways of making me do what he wanted.

"I've got a book for you," he said, his tone ninety per-cent friendly. "One I know you'll like. I could just drop it at your house though if you're busy. Leave it with your mum and dad?"

So I got in his car.

Grooming is basically a strategy game in which the groomer always remains on dry land with access to an escape route—sometimes several—while making the subject of their grooming feel unsafe, imprisoned on an island far out at sea, with less and less hope of ever being rescued.

I would have done anything to prevent my parents seeing the kinds of books I'd read in Mike's shop. Anything. And that was how it all started. That was how my island appeared.

For some reason—because it is not a complete analogy—I find myself thinking of the card game Cheat, which we used to play in the school common room. Paul was a master at it—I'm sure you can picture him, with his victorious fuck-you-all expression. The best strategy in Cheat is to play a set of fake cards that are the same as a set you actually have in your hand. "Four kings," you might say, while playing a two, a four and whatever other crap you're trying to offload. But no one can confidently challenge you because you actually do have the four kings. You just didn't play them when you said you did.

Groomers also frequently use the same strategies Paul and I learned in our first finance jobs. The concept of hedging is also about minimizing risk and exposure. You sell something you don't have in the knowledge you can buy it back cheaper in the future. (Which I know you promised me you'd never understand, no matter how hard I tried to explain, so maybe I won't go into it now.)

Mike made us culpable for everything.

"How old do you think these girls are?" he'd asked when he first gave us the pink camera. He showed us a page from one of Paul's favorite graphic novels. It was Japanese. Truthfully, the girls in it looked about twelve.

Paul frowned. "I'd say—"

Mike put up his hand to stop him.

"Before you answer," he said, "I should tell you that if you even *think* they're younger than sixteen, that makes you, well . . ."

He never said the word.

"A pedophile," Paul said to me later, sounding worried, even for him. "But I'm not a pedophile, am I?"

Wasn't he? He did love those pictures. But in the sense you

or I would understand it, of course he wasn't a pedophile. He'd completely accidentally found books of a sort with barbs that had got hold of his brain and hooked into it. Would he have hung around school gates waiting to abduct little girls? Of course not. But did he like getting his girlfriends to dress up in school uniforms when they and he were old enough to consent to it? Sure. And so what if he liked drawings of monsters keeping schoolgirls in dungeons? Monsters don't exist. The girls were never real girls. The dungeons were never actually there.

At the time, though, we knew Mike had something on us. Perhaps to underline the point, he started talking about opium laws in the US and how if you grow opium poppies in your garden you can be arrested and imprisoned, with all your assets seized—unless you can prove you didn't know what the plants were.

Another axiom from the financial world: always look at who can afford to lose the most. They are the ones with the power.

"So," Mike said, when I got in his car that day after school. "You never brought me back that camera you borrowed."

"Sorry," I said. "We will. We can drop it off next—"

"I think to replace it would cost around a hundred pounds," he said. "And then there's the kill fee you'd owe me."

"What's a kill fee?" I asked.

"Where you pay to break a contract." He laughed. "No actual killing involved. Well, not usually, anyway."

We were driving past the old Odeon cinema, its neon lights pointlessly advertising a film I'd probably never see.

My parents were more likely to rent something highbrow from the Blockbuster across the street.

"What contract?" I said, the car lights splashing through the gloom as we headed out of town.

"The one you and your friend made with me," said Mike. "You promised to supply me with some photographs. I gave you boys that contract—no one else. If I were to have to replace the camera now, and—"

"We can give you back the camera," I said urgently. "We can give it back and then we're square."

"The time it'll take me to get a new camera and brief someone else ..." He shook his head. "We're looking at around three hundred."

"Three hundred *pounds*?"

"Yup. That's the kill fee."

After that, he wordlessly drove to my village and pulled up outside my house. He knew exactly where I lived. He touched my leg just before I got out of the car, and a horrible jolt went through me, like lightning.

So naturally we joined a local dance class. It was Paul's idea.

My parents thought I was gay. Is that almost funny? I never had your sense of humour, so I just don't know. They arranged for me to see a male therapist who was almost as bad as Mike, asking if I masturbated, and what I thought about. Perhaps we'll gloss over him. He wanted me to do some kind of drumming workshop, and go along to a weekend class where you make your own axe and engrave the handle with ritualistic symbols.

I couldn't dance, but Paul could. He had that lack of shame

that dancers need, especially male ones. It didn't matter that he was a little overweight, and always wore unusual clothes. All the girls wanted to dance with him. The teacher loved him. He'd goof around in a straw hat, or some ragged grass skirt from the props cupboard. People just wanted to be near him—a bit like you always have.

If only it had been fifteen years later. My ex-boss bought into a company that makes spycams, and although I disapproved of them, I still knew they were genius. The spycams were disguised as smoke alarms, air fresheners, radios—all the normal devices you'd never think were in any way sinister. You could put these things anywhere, connect them to Wi-Fi and, bang. An air freshener in the girls' loo for example—Mike wouldn't even have needed us if those devices had been on the market then. But he did need us. He needed us more and more.

But at that point all he seemed to want were a few photos on the pink camera.

So we took them. Well, Paul did, one evening at the end of ballet class. We always got changed in the same lobby as the girls, and they seemed to trust us. When Paul took out the camera and started mucking about with it, the girls squealed and pretended to hide, and shouted at him that they were hardly wearing clothes. In the confusion he managed to get a few of one of the smaller girls, Chloe, in her pink leotard. Paul made such a big deal of messing around with the camera and not hiding it that he was able to take some very compromising shots just by pretending he was threatening, rather than actually doing it. But he was doing it. No one would have believed it.

Mike liked the pictures a lot. He liked Chloe.

He made us introduce her to him.

We were all getting on for fifteen by that point. Chloe came to my house a couple of times for some maths tutoring, and then she and Paul went on a handful of dates. There was a photo shoot I never knew anything about. Then, once Chloe turned sixteen, Mike offered her a job in his shop. I wanted to tell her to turn it down, to run, as fast as she could, in the other direction. But she took the job and completely changed. Over the next two years she got tattoos and piercings and dyed her hair purple. She developed a haunted look. She broke up with Paul, saying she wanted someone older. She dropped out of her sixth-form college.

There was a rumour she'd had her nipples pierced.

Then she disappeared.

I felt sick when I saw the story in the local paper. I knew it was because she'd got mixed up with Mike. I'm certain there was something genuinely evil about him. But I couldn't tell anyone. There was appeal after appeal on the local news, and even at school. I wonder what you would have done in a similar situation. But perhaps you would not have let yourself be imprisoned on the island in the same way Paul and I were. And at that point, we were still imprisoned without even knowing it.

We saw Mike only occasionally around the time it happened. We always understood that he had the photos of Chloe from ballet class as a sort of insurance, but for years it didn't seem as if he was going to collect. Giving him Chloe in real life (God forgive us) seemed to have temporarily settled our strange long-term debt. We'd pointed at something more brightly colored than us, and he'd looked, and we'd run away. Or so I thought.

He would sometimes ask one of us for a "simple" favor. To take a package across town or, as we got older, to lug boxes of books or magazines from auctions or house clearances. We never said no. Paul and Chloe still had a complex relationship, and he always wanted an excuse to see her. Mostly, she was "busy," but they sometimes locked themselves in Paul's basement for a whole weekend, listening only to the Pixies, eating only sweets and doing God knows what else.

And then she was gone.

The panicked, vomit-y feeling when I heard about Chloe's disappearance has only ever been matched by the feeling I had when I found out the awful truth about us.

Did you know? You can't have done. You must have been as in the dark as I was.

My most shameful secret.

And I was suddenly faced with it, with its true horror, at our wedding reception of all places. Luciana. Dad's star student from the olden days, drunk, not understanding what she was telling us. Did she know what I'd done? Of course she did. And she'd covered it up and forgot it until that moment, so many years later, when it came out almost as a charming anecdote.

It was not charming at all.

It was horrible.

It happened not long after Chloe came back. Yes—she did come back. She'd been in Europe, doing something mysterious that no one ever found out. She hadn't been abducted, as the local news reports had said; she'd gone of her own free will with a man called "Tiger," who later disappeared, leaving her to try and work her way home.

Anyway, the point is that I felt free. For about forty-eight hours of my life, I tasted freedom. Mike hadn't been in touch for a while. And all the guilt I felt about Chloe possibly being murdered at Mike's behest—it had gone. I started thinking about my future, and going to university. Leaving my peculiar childhood behind.

People assume they can know about someone else's past because of their gender, or their social class, or their parents. Try asking them instead about the secret alliances they made, and who was blackmailing them, and the secrets they'd rather die than own. Ask them about their shame, and their darkness.

That was what I thought I saw in Isabella, by the way. Her darkness; the things she'd agreed to without realizing she would become stranded on her own island—simultaneously real and figurative—from which she could never escape.

Now she's gone to join the search and I am locked in. She didn't need to lock the door, I said. Really. I said I'd be able to stop myself going after you, and that is almost true.

Perhaps you don't realize that I have not always been as I am now. This control I have, my self-discipline, has been hard won, believe me. I can barely stand to think of the child I once was, smeared with jam and mud, obsessed with worms and insects, and how that boy turned into the teenager who agreed to go to the Freshers' Ball at the local university with his friend the weekend before they both left for their own universities, because it could be a laugh, because there would be girls.

A girl and

A boy and

The other boy

Will you believe me if I say it is the one thing in my life I would take back if I could? And I don't know exactly what happened, even now. I've searched on Quora many times. If a boy and a girl have sex and they have both been drugged, is it rape? If a boy has sex with a girl but can't remember who she is, is it rape? If a boy is seventeen and a girl is eighteen and the boy's friend is eighteen and his friend slips them all ketamine for a laugh, then is the friend a rapist? If two boys and one girl have sex at the same time and no one remembers it the next morning, did it even happen? If everyone was a virgin, does it count? Was everyone a virgin? I certainly was.

Which perhaps explains some of the intimacy issues I had later.

For years afterwards I dreaded the knock on the door, like on TV.

Prison. The thought of it. That hot and stifling feeling of a guilt that cannot be changed or removed, as in the early pages of *Crime and Punishment*.

A stain on my soul.

For the first year afterwards, when I was at Durham studying maths and economics, if anything came on the radio about date-rape I'd turn it up and sometimes even take notes and then burn them. Later, though, I would simply turn it

off. TV shows too. Podcasts. Chats in the student union bar.
I'd feign migraines or even panic attacks. I couldn't have sex
with any more girls for months, actually years, in case it was
revealed that I was a monster. The prostitutes later became a
way for me to regain innocence—but I can't fully explain this
now. I'm not sure you could ever understand. On so many
deep levels, we were never right for each other, you and me.
We could never absolve one another. I think the astrological
chart said that, too, actually.

I'm still almost certain that it was Mike who gave Paul the
ketamine, although later when I confronted Paul about it he
said it had come from his dad. Paul's dad had been having
another midlife crisis and did K with women he met in chat-
rooms online. Paul stole some—or so he said—and brought it
to the Freshers' Ball, where he thought we'd pass for a couple
of years older than we were, and get lucky with the new students so far from home. Was it his idea, or Mike's? Did he take
pictures that night? Did he make a video? Maybe the drug
wasn't even K. I never knew. I certainly didn't agree to take it.

Maybe it was Rohypnol—that was the big date-rape drug
back then.

But we'd all taken it, for "fun" apparently. So it probably
was ketamine.

One minute I was dancing with a girl I liked while necking
subsidized Budweiser and ignoring Paul's whispers about
low-life sluts and threesomes and the next minute I was
walking on the ceiling. Then I was in some kind of oblivion
that wasn't unpleasant. But.

Paul's hand up the girl's skirt when he knew I liked her.

My dad's star student Luciana seeing me so off my face.

Paul deliberately shaming the girl in public. Pulling her breasts out of her cheap sequinned dress in the passageway behind the campus nightclub. Walking her back to her hall of residence like that.

"You wanna three-way?" he slurred at her.

"Yeah," she said. "If you boys can handle me."

At least, that's what I think she said. I have no image of her in my memory. None at all. Or at least, perhaps I do now, but it's wrong, wrong.

She was completely off her face too. We were so anesthetized that all we could do was act out the fictional scenarios we knew.

"Beg us for it, you whore," Paul said, and then stuck his tongue in her ear.

And then it all goes blank. Such a convenient phrase, but it's true. There's the odd moment where I see her passed out and Paul's fucking her anyway and I think I'm only watching but then I realize I'm doing it too.

The glint of a camera lens.

I still have nightmares about it.

Until recently, the girl in the nightmares had no face.

I'd love to say I looked for the nameless and faceless girl back then and tried to make it right, but I had no idea who she was. I sometimes imagined being interviewed by the police, and an artist with a drawing pad asking me for hair color and eye color and shape of nose and I would have nothing to say. Long hair, maybe brown or blond or black? Possibly auburn? Eager eyes.

Oh, Evie, I am admitting to something terrible I cannot name. You know what I am, who I am, what I can never undo. But I did not know what I was doing, I swear, and in some sense I was raped too. I have no idea how to talk about it, because I am so terribly ashamed and afraid. I have never told anyone this before, and I certainly wouldn't be telling you unless I was sure you already knew.

Much later I asked Paul about it. We'd fallen out of touch—I found him so distasteful after that night—but he was back in town because his father was ill. And so we went out for lunch and we talked. He said I'd remembered it all wrong. That it really had been OK, and "the girl" had wanted it, and it was a rite of passage and we should not feel ashamed and neither should she. But I have always felt ashamed.

And somehow we became friends once more. It was as if every minute I spent with Paul when he wasn't drugging someone or suggesting a threesome made him one percent less likely to be the kind of person who'd do that. After many harmless encounters with him I stopped believing it had ever happened—until the wedding, when it was too late anyway.

He was my best man, somewhat ironically.

You and he always got along so well, with your in-jokes and your shared references.

I am pausing for a second. My fingers hurt from writing.

The wind is gasping and screaming through the shutters.

Isabella said she'd go to you, and bring you back. She knows the island, and its winds, and where you might shelter.

I half don't want her to find you, but I find it hard to admit that.

But if she does—

Could we just start again, my darling? And can you wear your white dress every day? We could pretend to be ghosts of ourselves forever.

Isabella went in her Land Rover, with Kostas. I think she was sorry for taking me from you in the underhanded way she did. I shouldn't have let her get into bed with me; I realize that now.

I am all alone here, locked in for my own good. The sounds are layering over themselves now: scraping, scuffling, clawing. Is there a bird trapped somewhere? I hope you're being careful out there. I hope you're not too wet, or cold. I'm so sorry, sorry for everything.

September 29, 2021

We stayed here in the worst possible circumstances, after losing our parents in the great storm just last week. Isabella could not have been kinder, nor

       and her breakfasts—not that we could taste anything much—have been incredible. So much delicious fresh fruit! Her house is a tranquil and calm
       wish we'd been able to come here in a happier time.

The island is, as our mother told us, exquisite, despite the refugee camp and the squalor around the edges. We can only imagine our parents' last days here. Our mother was researching a travel article and our father was

       so troubled.

scientific studies showing that prayer works, and that plants know when they are loved.

Our father, James Border, was "awoken" on the 15th March, 2021, while on a retreat in California. As part of the retreat he attended a healing session led by Byron Katie, who had herself awoken back in February 1986. After completing one of her "worksheets," our father went from being a tired academic with a heart problem to becoming a spiritual healer in less than a month. He claimed his power came from prayer, and said he knew how to speak to God. Many of his friends mocked or challenged him. Even those who were happy to receive the power he suddenly seemed to have to cure their migraines or their cat.

lunches became theological

would not enter Satan's world himself.

So it's not as simple as asking for miracles and gifts. The point is to awaken everyone, so that we can live in Heaven, and not inside an illusion. How do we awaken? With kindness, trust, love—and faith in something beyond. With knowledge of what the dream is.

It was our father's faith in this "beyond" that gave him his power. He told us that it's the same place Jesus

can move a mountain into the ocean. You can wither a fig tree if you're in a bad mood. You can do all Jesus did, because the only thing that really made Jesus different from us was his total, unequivocal faith in his

trapped into implying that homosexuality is a sin—but only because literally everything in our world is a sin, because to sin is to fall short of the glory of God, which yes, includes gay sex, and hetero sex, but also eating a piece of toast and Marmite or driving a car.

Satan was ruling over capitalism, and

weak victims who need products to fix them. It bizarrely gets people to believe that they can have   by becoming a slave in a generic culture factory.

God's actual name,

like a transcendent version of recalling the smell of one's old school-room, or a lost lover's perfume, or the phrase *je ne parle pas Français* from the Katherine Mansfield story he loved so much. But Dad couldn't tell us God's name himself. He couldn't put it into words, and anyway, he said, they'd be different words for us.

Eventually, someone suggested a holiday, and our mother brought Dad here, to this wonderful place. We wish we could have seen him here, enjoying his last days on earth in peace and tranquillity. We hope our parents were able to reestablish

in this beautiful setting. Our father never sleepwalked before taking the new medication recommended by

known side effects. And our mother was an incredible hero, trying to save him, staying with him, never leaving his side, even as they were both washed out to sea.

Polly and Olivia Border-Kearney,
Devon, UK

Plan/synopsis/something for play #3

A girl and an older man. He is married (of course—but isn't everyone?). A law professor. She goes and sees him after she does the rape kit. Or. It doesn't happen that fast? There's a bit of drifting around and thinking first? But it's definitely the next day.

Freshers' Week. The fucking bacchanals.

Smooth down your skirt, you fucking slag.

Always such a fucking slag. And now this.

We'll call you "She" for now, as in *He said, she said.*

She's the first person in her family to go to university but ofc we will learn this in a subtle way and not just be told it. She feels older than the others. More jaded. She is not a virgin and is shocked that some of them are. She's brought some bud in an old silver tin that maybe belonged to her father. He might have kept washers in it? Her hair is dyed red and she has a patchwork handbag and high-rise jeans. It's normal to dress up as your favorite characters from fiction, right? But she wasn't going to dress up for the Freshers' Ball—like, why would she? And she can't really be bothered anyway after so much spliff, but that girl across the hall comes out in a short skirt and she knows she can go shorter with that turquoise sequinned dress but does she dare?

And then she's at the sticky bar buying cider because it tastes like apple juice and the barman is young and cute in a pale blue shirt only he doesn't have a face and she looks around and no one has a face and—

That really is it.

The next morning in her tiny room, with stains on the sheets.

Three roaches in the frosted peach ashtray.

How when she stands up she knows she's had sex. It hurts when she pees. There's blood in the toilet. The brief thrill of still being a character in a story. And then she thinks. She can't remember consenting, and so she can't have done. She realizes that future-her wants options and so.

She goes to the police station and fills in a form and pees in a thingy and they take some swabs. Then she goes to the greasy spoon café near Westgate and eats fried eggs and mushrooms, which have been undercooked and look pale and watery on the plate, like things not quite dead. Her legs feel heavy and numb. She walks back up to the university and goes to the student union where.

The volunteer is a girl with a buzzcut.

The girl says there's someone more qualified to help. A law professor.

And that's when she meets the professor for the first time.

He's wearing a white linen shirt with the sleeves rolled up and his forearms are strong and darkly hairy. She goes to his office in the law building and sits on the gray institutional chair and he closes the door.

"So you remember barely anything?" the professor says after she tells him her story.

She shrugs. "I guess it was a date-rape drug?"

"Rohypnol. Ketamine. GHB. Sure. And you'd been taking drugs before that? And drinking?"

She nods.

He puts down his notebook and sighs.

"I'm going to go off the record now for a moment if that's OK."

"Yeah."

"I recently had a rectal examination." He holds up his hands. "Sorry, too much information, I know. It was a bowel-cancer screening. I was given the all-clear. They gave me sedation before the procedure. Do you know what that means? It's basically a date-rape drug but given in the proper context, to make sure you have no memory of something that would have been traumatic had you experienced it consciously." He rolls his pen in his fingers. "It turned something unbearable into quite a pleasant experience, if I'm honest. There was a study recently that said that people would much rather have a traumatic experience lasting for one hour that drugs caused them to forget completely, than be conscious for five minutes of terrible pain. Do you understand what I am beginning to say here?"

"I was lucky to have been drugged? But—"

"Do you feel traumatized?"

"No. But I know that something terrible happened to me."

"As it would have done if you had been to the dentist, or for cataract surgery, as my wife's sister recently did. They essentially sliced out some of her eyeball while she was awake. In that case there was not even any sedation—the patient must be fully conscious to move the eyes for the surgeon. But there was no pain. Her eyeball was sliced with a scalpel, but she felt no pain, because it had been anesthesized. Should she be upset? Should this experience ruin her life? Of course not. She was grateful for the procedure. She'd been on a waiting list for some time."

"OK, but that's hardly ..." She shrugs. "It's hardly."

The professor leaning forward ... His muscular forearms, etc.

"What's your goal in life?"

"Um ..."

"Short term and long term."

"Short term I think I might sue the university. I need to get a job too, because my loan doesn't cover everything, but maybe not if I get a good settlement. Long term I want to be an actor."

"You're doing ...?"

"Theatre studies."

The professor sighs and leans back again. He puffs his lips like they are little bellows.

"You won't be able to sue the university, I'm afraid."

"Then the guy. I could find him. There must have been witnesses."

All the people with no faces and no eyes. Can you still see if you have no eyes? If you do not have a face?

"No," says the professor. "You need to move on. I've seen this before in these 'he-said-she-said' cases. It destroys everyone. And in this case you don't even have a 'he,' so it will no doubt only destroy you. Something happened to you but it didn't hurt and you don't remember, so move on. That's my advice."

"It hurts now."

"On a scale of one to ten?"

She thinks about it. "Maybe three?"

"Move on." He pauses for a second. Puts down his pen and picks it up again. "Since you're here. Um. You say you need a job?"

So she becomes his housekeeper, just like that. It's a live-in position, so she gets to leave her shoebox-room in the strange concrete fairy-tale tower that looks more like a prison block. She gets a charming attic conversion in a large house convenient for the A2 and with good light in the afternoons. Instead of going deeper into debt, she actually saves. She pairs the family's socks. She folds the wife's microfiber underwear with holes in the sides from where the wife yanks it up and down because she's always in such a fucking hurry. She cooks the basic foods they prefer. Lamb chops with new potatoes. Shepherd's pie. Wild salmon fillets with basmati rice.

She doesn't meet the son for a while. Well, she glimpses him briefly and then he's off to university in Durham. She pairs his socks too. She irons his shirts. His white ones. His striped ones. She'll meet him properly a lot later of course.

She has sex with the professor in the mornings, when his wife is in London.

He phones his wife's secretary to check she's actually there, which he does in a number of unconvincing ways, and only then does he pull down his organic white Y-fronts.

It was probably she who started it—let's not make this the kind of story about a maiden who is used by many merry men. She is no Fanny Hill. All those evenings staring at his arms, and the wife insisting she eats with them, treating her like a daughter almost. A daughter who cleans. A daughter who fucks. Maybe not so much a daughter then. But they took such an interest. Such an interest.

The wife who both does know and doesn't know, giving her career advice and later helping her invest money when she suddenly earns a lot of it. Talks her into buying property and putting it in a trust run by the family.

And the professor, whose full name she never puts into her phone.

His bright blue eyes.

His sculpted eyebrows.

His thigh muscles on the rowing machine.

So pathetic too that she falls in love with him. It would have been such a good arrangement otherwise. They pay her well and she saves even more. She gets a first. She gets a first and a scholarship for the MA. She travels in the summer. She gets a distinction for the MA and one night she goes to a talk and the talk is from an actors' agent and the tutor invites her for dinner with them and she pitches her one-woman show and suddenly her show is in Edinburgh and then London and then on TV.

All those FaceTimes from hotel rooms. The sexting.

The messages of love before her planes take off.

But the professor won't leave his wife. He doesn't even know how to get his cock in the frame. She sees up his nose a lot. Her love should fade but instead she just loves him more because he seems so awkward and fragile in this new world of shiny screens and buttons that are too small.

All the hundreds of little theatres. Then the big ones. All that pizazz. And then she ends up teaching at the same university she'd gone to, all those years before. Back in Canterbury—in the terraced house that had been one of her better investments. And the rise of #MeToo makes her wonder about that dark weird night from Freshers' Week and what really happened to her, and she asks the professor if he can remember what she told him and he says it will only hurt if she rakes it up and so she doesn't.

But so many years on she suddenly remembers one new detail. The girl with the buzzcut standing at the bar when she bought the cider, just before. Staring at her and the boy she was with. The boy with no face, and his friend with no head.

The buzzcut girl, Luciana, who became the professor's star student.

The one she went to for help at the student union the next morning.

The buzzcut girl's own version of scholarships and glory and travel and tenure somewhere.

So much glory everywhere. Some kind of montage?

And the buzzcut girl with her hair grown long coming to the wedding and saying how nice it was that these two finally married, after dancing together so much at the Freshers' Ball all those years ago.

Can do a lot with the early scene when the professor fucks her in his sunlit en suite, and then his son comes home from Durham unexpectedly and she makes lunch for them both and serves it in the summer house.

"I'm Richard," the son says. "Nice to meet you at last, Evelyn."

October 1st, 2022

Dear Peter,

Here are some sandwiches for your journey, and a flask of the Moroccan mint tea you enjoyed so much last night. I do not have the words to say how sorry I am for what happened to your son and daughter-in-law. If you would like to come back after you have been to Patmos, or if you would like me to arrange further help in finding their bodies, it would be my pleasure. Also, if you would just like to talk some more, you know where I am—I now understand why memories and reflections are so important to you.

As I said to you last night, your son and his wife were such a delightful couple, obviously so close. We had been together that evening—all my beautiful guests sheltering from the storm, laughing and talking. But late that night Richard and Evelyn began to quarrel—just a minor lovers' tiff, I thought. But Evelyn ran out into the storm, and, although I tried to stop him, Richard followed her. I have asked everyone on the island what they saw that night, and several people did see a beautiful couple on the beach, kissing as lightning flashed so close to them, overhead.

The lightning was particularly fierce that night, Peter, I'm sorry to say. I do hope that the bodies you are going to identify are Richard's and Evelyn's, so that you are finally able to bury them and achieve closure.

Love and best wishes,
Isabella

Dear Mister James Border,

You ask me to write secretly about my dream, and to give you in private. I have tried, but I do not like to write—writings disappear here too easy.

You talk to me of love, and how one man can love another, and this I do want.

I will wait for you in the garden tonight as you suggest.

Yours,
Hamza :)

List of images

1. A young woman, clothed and unclothed
2. Four young people with ping-pong table, playing
3. A man and woman having breakfast
4. A man and woman walking up a staircase
5. A man and woman asleep in bed
6. A man wearing running shorts, putting on running shoes
7. A woman naked on a chaise longue
8. A man in a bathroom looking at his smartphone. He is naked from the waist down.
9. A woman looking at her reflection in a freestanding mirror
10. A man and a woman in mid-argument. She is pointing at the wall.
11. A man and a woman in bed, naked. A screwdriver rests on the floor.
12. A woman, shocked, in a hallway

13. A woman writing a letter at a desk
14. A man in a shuttered room
15. A generator with detachable cables
16. A woman sitting with her back against a wall
17. Cables in moonlight
18. A woman, running

December 22nd, 2023

Dear Annabelle,

I'm writing, somewhat belatedly, to thank you for your wedding present. As you can see, I did manage to do some writing in the time that you gifted me, and indeed Richard did some too. So your offering had the desired effect. I'm very grateful. I do hope you read the enclosed documents before you read this letter, because then I think you will understand exactly what happened and why I was not to blame for any of it.

As I type this, the sea outside is hushing and pulling at the sand, and the pohutukawa tree is still in blossom, its gash-pink flowers full of thirsty bees, and its branches home to the brutal mosquitoes that nip at my legs if I sit on the balcony too late in the evening. There's so much to look at here; I can barely write a sentence before someone walks past with an interesting tattoo or well-worn rucksack, or a tui lands in the branches in front of me and starts performing.

Have you ever heard a tui? They are not subtle birds. The tui's throat appears to have one small white pompom, like a clown's collar, until it starts to sing; then the little collar opens and it's more like two fat blobs of whipped cream on a shiny Black Forest gateau. The song is a joyful mess of notes that are too high or too sharp or have too much warble. One moment it sounds like a broken clock, then a cat in heat, then a songbird, then a honking ship. The tui somehow barks out what I feel, all my absurd confusion and muted rage—but also my joy at being released from your awful, awful family.

The tui sings, and then it flies away, just like I did.

So I am not dead; at least, I don't think so. You have recently declared Richard to be dead, and you even had a funeral for him. Was the body they found really his? You buried it anyway. But I am alive, Annabelle. Perhaps only just, after everything that happened, but I am alive. Although, of course, you've known that for a long time now.

We won't pretend you don't know where I am. That's not my reason for writing. I wanted a chance to communicate with you, woman to woman, in the hope that we can come to some peaceful agreement. I don't even need my whole inheritance at this point. All I want is my share of the joint bank account and the freedom to tell my story without you hounding me forever.

The lawyer I spoke to (just a friend, nothing official) recommended that I not write this letter, but here it is. I want to get the facts down, so you understand my perspective on what happened, and why I, as you put it, "ran away." I should point out that the main reason for my running away was because I was about to be killed. And I'm sorry, but I can't explain why I didn't send help for Richard, except to say that I knew it was too late, and I was scared.

I mean, I heard the actual buzz, Annabelle. It was the most sickening, terrible sound you could possibly imagine. I heard them do it to him—or I was as certain as I could have been at the time—and I couldn't let them do it to me too, however much you would have preferred that they did.

I'd just finished writing my letter to Richard when Hamza appeared outside the window of our honeymoon suite, the thin white curtain fluttering and making him slighter and more spectral than he already was. He was clutching his arm, which was bleeding. I tried to wake Richard with no success, and then I went after Hamza to try to get him to come inside, but he'd already disappeared into the storm. I'd been soaked through in about ten seconds as I pelted down the stone steps, hissing his name, saying I could only help him if he came to me. Rain was pouring down my face like hysterical tears.

At first it seemed I had no hope of finding him in the dark. I'd run out holding Richard's phone and I'd managed to switch on the torch, but it barely showed anything except raindrops. But then, through the whooshing and the rush of the downpour, I heard an engine start, and I then saw Hamza running down the driveway and getting into Christos's car, which was parked near a dripping pomegranate tree. I ran over and banged on the car window. Christos rolled it open.

"Go away," he yelled into the rain and the wind.

"What's going on?" I asked. "Why is Hamza bleeding?"

"Go away," said Christos again. "Haven't you caused enough trouble, with your fucking snooping, and your recording?"

"He wanted me to do it!" I said.

It was true. Hamza had seen what I was doing with the phone and had given me a tiny nod and then covered it with the napkin he'd been holding like a fainted creature.

"Right, and look what happened to him as a result," said Christos.

Sounds of shouting and slamming suddenly came from the house.

"Get in!" hissed Christos, so I did.

He drove too fast on the narrow roads, with the rain and the wind slapping the car like it was a little child. Hamza was shivering in the front seat, blood dripping from the wound on his arm. Christos was shouting at him, calling him fucking stupid, and a fucking waste of space, and soon Hamza started crying. Eventually, Christos pulled off the road and got a first-aid kit out of the glove box. He threw a bandage at Hamza and then drove on, just as manically as before.

"What's going on?" I asked Christos.

He didn't say anything; he just accelerated.

I was surprised when we arrived at the airport. If only I'd brought my bags, I thought then, I could have saved myself the very long walk I'd been planning. I had my passport in my belt-bag from where I'd been getting ready to leave after finishing my letter to Richard, and I was still holding Richard's phone with all his credit cards on it. I probably should have tried to make a run for it then. But I didn't.

"Happy now?" Christos yelled at Hamza. "Now you can go suck another American dick and maybe get what you really want this time."

Hamza tried to open the passenger door, but it was locked.

"Let me out," he said. "For God's sake, Christos."

Christos grimaced. "Sure, after I get the password for that file you both recorded."

"I don't know it," said Hamza. "Only she knows."

"Well, unless she tells me what it is, you're not going anywhere."

"I don't understand what's happening right now," I said, suddenly afraid. I thought I'd ended up on this bizarre road trip by accident, not on purpose.

"Give me the password," Christos said to me, "and he can go."

"Please," said Hamza, turning to look at me. "They will kill me."

"Who'll kill you? What are you talking about?"

"Shut up," said Christos to Hamza. "One more word and you're not going anywhere. What's the name of the app?" he asked me.

I told him, and he immediately started thumbing letters on his phone screen.

"But I can't just give you my password," I said. "All my important files are on there."

"Fine," said Christos, turning and staring at me. "Then

we're all going back to the Villa Rosa, and I'm going to tell Isabella that you're both planning to go to the police about her. Then we'll see what happens."

"So I'm meant to be scared of *Isabella*?" I said incredulously. "Um, OK."

Christos then punched the steering wheel and let out a sort of scream. He reversed the car at speed and did a terrifying three-point turn.

"If you don't give me the password, I'm a dead man," he said, wrenching the gearstick back into first. "And if I have to die, I don't see why I shouldn't take you both with me."

He started accelerating toward a tree a few hundred yards away.

I have to say, as a move designed to make someone do what a person wants, I have never seen it equalled.

The tree seemed to be racing toward us, like it was being pushed from the beyond.

"OK!" I shouted, over the horrific sound of the engine. "Fucking hell—stop!"

The car stopped with a loud screech and skidded, just missing the tree.

Everything smelled of burning rubber and carbon monoxide.

So I gave Christos my username and my password.

"But please," I said after I told him. "Please leave my other files alone, OK? I have so much work on there."

Christos didn't reply. He typed the password into his phone.

"Why can't I log in?" he said. "It's a fake password. I knew it!"

"The 4G is not good here," said Hamza. "Please, if you don't let me go now—"

"You'll do what?" said Christos.

But neither of them said anything else. Christos turned the car around in silence.

"Are you sure they'll take you?" said Christos when he'd parked outside the terminal. He suddenly seemed pathetic and deflated. "You look fucking awful."

"I know the story of the sleepwalkers more than anyone. And not because of what you think."

"Right." Christos looked sad. "Just make sure you leave me out of it."

"You know I will. I said already."

"How will you pay?"

"It's a private plane. There is no ticket."

"Are you sure?"

For someone who'd seemingly just been trying to kill Hamza, Christos was now speaking surprisingly tenderly to him.

"Wait, when exactly is the plane leaving?" I asked Hamza.

He was still trembling. "Soon, they said. Before the storm gets worse."

"Go," said Christos, while holding on to Hamza's arm, so he couldn't actually move.

Hamza leaned over and gave Christos a kiss, on the lips.

"Goodbye," he said.

Hamza got out of the car and ran into the tiny terminal building.

"I'll probably never see him again," said Christos unhappily.

He started the car. Then he turned off the engine once more.

"God," he said. "My fucking brain. I still need to delete that file before he downloads it himself. You did give me the right password?"

"I did, yes. Actually," I said, "I need to nip in to the loo if that's OK."

He laughed humorlessly. "Right, so you gave me the wrong password, and now you're running away? I don't fucking think so."

"I don't have my passport, or any luggage," I pointed out.

I was lying about the passport of course.

Christos hunched his shoulders. "Well, can you check he's OK? If he needs cash ..." Christos pulled a battered yellow nylon wallet out of his jeans and handed me a wad of euros. "Please. I'm sorry I'm acting so nuts."

I took the money and went into the terminal. It was eerie and quiet, and appeared to be closed for business. There were no staff; no machines switched on. Debbie and Marcus were sitting there in their coats, playing cards. Debbie was balancing an old-looking tea tray on her lap, and Marcus was putting a four of diamonds onto it.

I walked over to them.

"Room for one more?" I said, jauntier than I felt.

"You wanna get out of here too, doll, huh?" said Debbie unenthusiastically.

That was when I realized that I needed something of a killer line.

"Yeah, well, ever since that bitch tried to screw my

husband," I said, with a complicated smile. "And then the waiter tried to kill me."

Marcus looked startled, then guffawed.

"You got yourself a seat on the plane," he said. "I wanna hear all about this."

"When does it go?" I said.

"Not till tomorrow, sweetie," said Debbie. "We shoulda stayed longer at Heartbreak Hotel. Thought it'd be good to go tonight. But, you know, *weather*."

"None of the other planes'll even try," said Marcus. "Good job we brought our own guy."

"OK, right," I said. "I just need to go back and get my bags."

"Why don't you have your bags?" said Marcus suspiciously. "You were just passing or something?"

"Yeah, kind of. And, um, him?" I said, pointing at Hamza. He was perched on a chair on the other side of the small terminal, hunched over his phone. "He can come too?"

"Oh sweetheart, we've already told him no," said Debbie. She dropped her voice. "We think he might be illegal? He said something about asylum, for goodness' sake."

"I think he's Turkish, though," I said.

This made no impression on them.

"You're only going to Athens, right?" I tried. "He's already in Greece."

"That's true, baby," said Debbie to Marcus. "It is just an internal flight."

"I can pay for him," I said. "And me, of course. However much you want."

I showed them Christos's cash.

"No, sugar," said Debbie. "You're our guest."

"Well, I really need him to come too," I said.

"Well . . ." said Debbie, taking the cash. "OK."

"Where's your luggage, though?" asked Marcus.

"Just at the hotel," I said. "I'll be back in an hour or so."

And then I left before they could say anything else.

Back at the car, Christos was more relaxed.

"OK, I've deleted the file," he said, putting his phone down. "Thank you."

"They'll take him," I said. "But I have to go too. They think he's a refugee. You need to drive me to the hotel and then bring me back with my luggage."

"Sure," said Christos, starting the car. "Let's go."

At that point it was all surprisingly civilized. I didn't believe he was actually dangerous.

"Did you listen to the recording?" Christos asked me as he drove back down toward the road to the Villa Rosa.

"Nope," I said. "Isabella never gave me back my phone."

"Oh."

"What would I have heard?"

He sighed loudly. "You would have heard a lot about a turd on a stick."

"Sorry?"

"Couple of rich travelers disembark on an island and all the locals go crazy trying to sell them whatever they've got, even if it's only a turd on a stick."

"Right," I said.

We pulled up outside the Villa Rosa. The rain was getting worse again, but somewhere beyond the torrents, dawn was beginning to break.

"I'll be five minutes," I said.

I hurried up the wet stone steps as fast as I could, hoping Richard was still asleep.

At the top of the stairs, I went through the fire door, which had been hooked open. I walked quickly down the corridor toward the entrance to the honeymoon suite. I just wanted to grab my stuff and get out of there while I had the chance, before I changed my mind.

Isabella was coming out of the room—MY room—wearing a silk dressing gown, and holding an envelope. She seemed to say something to me, but her eyes were in the wrong place. Too late I realized she was speaking to the figure behind me.

"They know, Christos. They know *everything*."

I always thought that if something really bad happened to me, I'd have time to get away, like in films. I thought there'd be due warning, and then it would be like a game, or a performance. I didn't really understand the concept of being cornered, or there being no way out.

But there was no warning, and no way out. Isabella opened the storeroom door, and Christos bundled me into it. Then they locked it behind me.

And there I stayed for some hours, banging on the wall, trying to get Richard's attention. We talked, as you will have seen in the transcript, and then Isabella brought us cups of coffee. She did it so smoothly and silently that the cup of coffee was sitting there inside the door before I realized what was going on and the lock clicked once more. I thumped on the wall to alert Richard, but it clearly had no effect. I willed him not to drink the coffee. But evidently he did drink it. Perhaps we should be grateful for that, because it would have meant he didn't suffer.

I poured my coffee into a small gap in the skirting board. I left about a third of it, thinking that would seem authentic. Then I feigned unconsciousness. I've been trying to remember what we called the exercise back in drama school. I feel like it should have been "corpsing," but in fact that means to spoil a piece of theatre by forgetting one's lines or laughing uncontrollably. Perhaps we just called it "playing dead," which is what I did. I let them—I guessed it was Kostas and Christos—carry me by my arms and legs into the secluded back garden of the Villa Rosa, where they laid me down by the whirring generator. By some miracle no one noticed I still had my passport strapped to me. I'd let Richard's phone fall on the floor of the storeroom as a distraction—it must have worked. After they put me on the ground I opened my eyes a tiny crack. Ahead of me was a pomegranate tree, the one on the approach to the main house, where Christos had parked his car the night before. The large red fruits bobbed heavily in front of a churning khaki sky. I chose my moment with focused precision, then jumped up and ran as fast as I possibly could, while Isabella executed my husband. My rapist husband.

As I've said, I heard it. It was so awful, Annabelle.

And before you say that I'm not upset, I am upset. I am at least as troubled by the idea of electrocution as Sylvia Plath was. But how much worse a lethal injection would be, don't you think? I often wonder if drowning would be the better death. Perhaps even more if you were so drugged you knew hardly anything about it. Drowning after taking sleeping pills would probably be fine, don't you think? Anyway, I'm almost certain Richard knew nothing about what happened to him, and I hope that will be of some comfort to you. And although I know you think I should have gone back to save him, all I can say is that I warned him again and again and he chose to ignore me.

It was Kostas who ran after me. A bad pursuant, thank God. I'm not a great runner like Richard was, but I did pick up some tips from him. Keep your pelvis tilted slightly back; breathe in a waltz pattern; use your natural "gears." Of course I did none of those things. I ran like a ragged, hunted woman; like a bad dog with its muzzle full of stolen mutton. I sprinted enough to put a small distance between Kostas and me, and then I held my threshold pace while he wheezed and spluttered behind me. "Running away" sounded like the coward's way out when you accused me of it on the phone, but it was not easy. There were times when I just couldn't make my body move any farther, and my lungs felt like they'd been on the barbecue, and Kostas caught up almost enough to touch me. I couldn't believe I outran him, but I did.

I was in quite a state when I arrived at Kathos airport. There were still no staff—the place had the atmosphere of a dystopian mini-series. I heaved myself through the doors, breathless and shaking, and it was Hamza who ran over and helped me to a chair, his small hands barely touching my arms but somehow fluttering me along. I had finally managed to lose Kostas, or maybe he'd given up on me. Had he gone back to get the others? I still felt like a dead woman. My only priority at that moment was to get out of there and keep on running.

"Where's your luggage?" said Debbie when she saw me. Then, "Oh honey, what's wrong?"

"Please help me," I started saying, but when I saw the frightened look that crossed her face, I instinctively tried to lighten the atmosphere. "I don't suppose you have a mascara I can borrow?" I said it like a joke, because I didn't want her to think I was going to be any kind of burden. I just needed them to take me on their plane.

She and Marcus were still sheltering in the corner of the waiting area where they'd been playing cards late into the night before.

"What a godforsaken place," said Marcus now, thankfully no longer bothered by my lack of luggage. He was sipping a vending machine coffee and peering outside into the stormy morning.

I was still trying to get my breath back. One of my calves was cramping badly and I tried to stretch it out without drawing any more attention to myself.

"I feel like Meryl Streep in *The Devil Wears Prada*," said Debbie.

Outside the window was a small propeller plane with some metal steps next to it. Rain was pouring off its wings in ragged waterfalls. Little windscreen wipers flapped back and forth over the front window a few times and then stopped. A light went off inside. A figure in a large raincoat appeared and began wheeling the steps away from the plane.

"What on earth?" said Debbie. "Honey, why are they doing that?"

"I'll deal with this," said Marcus.

He walked over to the window and banged on it.

"Hey!" he called. "Hey!"

The figure gesticulated. Waved his arms at the sky. Whatever he was trying to mime was objectively incomprehensible. But it seemed to be something along the lines of, "You'd be mad to try to fly in this weather."

Marcus was wearing a cream trench coat over his yellow linen suit. He now took a bulging wallet from it.

"Let's figure this out," he said.

While he did that I went into the toilets and tried to clean myself up, but after my best efforts I still looked like something from one of my own deleted scenes, like a picnicker after the vampires have hurtled through the forest.

When I came out, Hamza was waiting for me. He was pale and trembling.

"You OK?" I asked him.

"I am afraid," he said simply. "Do you think we will crash?"

I thought of all the terrible flights I'd had in my life. Taking off from Venice in a lightning storm. Returning from Cape Town with food poisoning. Hitting the worst turbulence of my life somewhere over the Australian Outback, with one of the cabin crew cheerfully saying that if we did come down here, no one would ever find us.

"I don't know," I said.

The flight wasn't quite as bad as I'd feared, but we all threw up—even Marcus. Hamza clearly felt it the worst. The peak of the turbulence seemed to come when we were past the storm clouds and flying into the clear blue sky over Athens. Landing was like bumping a heavy case down an escalator. When we finally hit the ground there was a feeling in the cabin of joie de vivre, of being unexpectedly reborn. The sun had come out at last.

Still, my legs felt shaky as we disembarked.

"We're going clothes shopping," declared Debbie, taking my arm as we walked toward check-in for international flights. "We'll catch you boys up!"

"Don't you just want to get to the lounge, honey?" Marcus said, sounding annoyed.

"We just need ten minutes, baby. Wait here with the luggage."

Marcus looked displeased to be left with Hamza. He sat stiffly in a plastic chair outside a pastry shop drinking an espresso, while Hamza talked urgently to him. Hamza looked a wreck, although no one offered to take him clothes shopping. He was still wearing his odd little shorts and his thin turquoise scarf, but the ensemble looked ragged and dirty in the harsh light of the airport, and blood was beginning to seep through the bandage on his arm. I didn't know what he was talking to Marcus about then, but I suppose I do now.

God bless Debbie Goldstein. I didn't know what her motivation was at that moment, but she hoicked me into one of the designer stores and quickly picked me out a new outfit—a simple day-dress and cashmere cardigan—and she winked when she gave me the paper bag tied with the ribbon.

"I'll wait here," she said. "Go change." She pointed at the toilets.

She gave me her makeup bag too, all neatly packed for her flight.

"I know what it's like, sweetie," she said. "I've been there."

I went into the loos in a daze, blinking stupidly at all the bright lights.

When I came out, Marcus was talking to Debbie while Hamza sat there on the plastic chair with his tiny fists balled, looking as if he might be about to cry.

"Is there a Turkish Netflix, honey? I don't remember where they have all their outposts."

"Sure, baby. In Istanbul probably."

Marcus turned to Hamza.

"See, kid, the first step in a career like this is you go and intern somewhere. Learn how to pitch your ideas. Make coffee. Network."

"He could come back to us maybe in the spring, baby?"

"Yeah, we could have our PA squeeze you in for a ten-minute call."

"I'm sure we could do a half hour, honey."

"Eight to ten slides, like I said. No more. Save them as a PDF. All in English."

I must have looked a lot fresher in my normcore clothes, like a girl about to go to her first gymkhana or bat mitzvah, pure and almost virginal. Hamza flashed me a look, but I wasn't sure what it meant.

Marcus stood up and briefly appraised me before looking back at Hamza.

"And make it interesting. Funny, even!"

Debbie drained her espresso cup and then stood up as well.

"Oh, maybe like *The Death of Stalin!*"

"I didn't like that movie," said Marcus. "I didn't like that movie at all."

Hamza began to shake.

"But—" he began.

Marcus grasped Hamza's tiny shoulder, quite forcefully.

"And focus on the sleepwalkers, not all that other stuff."

"But you said—"

"OK, kid, you've had your five minutes," said Marcus. "We're going to find our lounge now. You gotta know when to stop, you know what I mean?"

Hamza stood up, let out a desperate sob, turned, and ran away.

Perhaps I should have gone after him, but I didn't. Frankly, at that moment I felt like I was going to pass out, from the shock of everything that had happened, and from lack of food and water. Hamza's skinny body weaved in and out of the chairs and tables belonging to the pastry café and then he turned just before a line of trolleys and he was gone.

Marcus looked at me. "Now, your story, sweetheart? That we *do* wanna option."

"Yeah," said Debbie. "Come with us up to the lounge, doll. We'll talk about it."

They started pushing their heavily laden trolley toward the check-in desks.

I began following them but then realized I didn't have a valid ticket. Richard and I were not supposed to be flying back to Heathrow for a few days yet.

"I might have to hang around here for a while," I said. "Change my ticket and stuff."

I felt dazed. So incredibly dazed. Everything was so loud around me.

"We'll be in the Emirates lounge, doll," said Debbie.

I had no cash and no purse. However, I did have an emergency credit card tucked in the back of my passport wallet. I checked it and by some amazing good fortune it hadn't expired. I went and used it to buy a large Mulberry handbag, so I didn't look so suspicious boarding a plane with no luggage.

I chose the farthest place Emirates flew, and paid for the 4,500-euro one-way ticket with the credit card, and then I checked in and walked through the terminal with my new bag, feeling like someone else's shadow, not even my own.

All I wanted was to keep on running. You do understand that, Annabelle? I couldn't fly back to London and face you and Peter. I'd just escaped from my husband's murder scene, for God's sake. I didn't know when I'd be able to stop.

I sat in the Emirates lounge shivering while Marcus stuffed his face with cold meats and told me what a great story he thought I could write, all about my toxic relationship and my doomed honeymoon, and the mystery of the sleepwalkers. But I didn't want to write at that point; I wanted to keep on moving.

At Auckland, I emerged into the spring sunshine, still

feeling I hadn't gone far enough. A loud and happy family seemed to be following signs to the domestic terminal, so I followed them, thinking how simple life would be if I could join their little flock. But they peeled off into a car hire place, and I was alone again, following the line on the ground. I went into the terminal and bought a ticket to Kerikeri, because I liked the name, and the flight was leaving soon.

At Kerikeri airport I got a bus into the town. Its main street was lined with garish takeaways, and the public toilets were full of mosquitoes. I asked a man in a car park where he'd recommend taking a honeymoon nearby. He said to go to Paihia, or better yet, to take the ferry from Paihia to Russell, in the Bay of Islands near where Captain Cook harbored on his first voyage on the *Endeavour*. Richard loved Captain Cook—did you ever know that? He once spent over a thousand pounds on a leather-bound set of Cook's journals that sat in one of our cabinets in the Clerkenwell flat, looking ancient and out of place amidst the rest of the minimalist décor. Perhaps you already know that. Perhaps you've already been and cleared them out. Have you sold the flat too? I can't believe you sold my house, Annabelle, less than a year after I went missing— but I have promised myself I won't get angry in this letter, and so I will breathe instead, and look at the sea, and try to calm myself.

It was when I returned to London last April that I first thought about coming to see you, to tell you I was still alive and to plead with you to not do anything drastic with anything that belonged to me that was still in the family trusts, but I couldn't face it, so I sat in a café and rang you instead. You were surprised to hear my voice. I possibly should have warned you first that I was going to be calling.

"Where is my son?" was the first thing you said. "Where is my fucking son?"

The body you'd later decide was Richard's had not yet been found.

I tried to tell you something of what had happened, but it came out all wrong.

"Then why did you run away?" you demanded.

I attempted to explain, but I knew it didn't make any sense.

"Murderer!" you screamed at me. "You're deranged, you're fucking—"

So I put the phone down.

I hadn't been able to tell you just how bizarre it had been arriving in Russell the previous September. I'm still not quite sure how to describe it, except to say that for a few moments I was certain that I was landing back on Kathos. It seemed either that Russell was Kathos's exact strange mirror, or that I'd accidentally traveled back to where I started—or simply never left, as in one of those nightmares where you can't move, no matter how hard you try. The sensation had made me feel faint, and I think I passed out for a few seconds because a German man had to help me to disembark from the Paihia ferry.

As I walked up the jetty, I wondered if I had actually died back in Greece along with Richard. I mean, it is so heavenly here: the light is warm and there is good food and wine and cheap oysters and so many pleasant tourists. But the restaurants may as well be tavernas, and the bees could yet be lazy hornets. Perhaps you won't believe me or even care, but the little town here really is reminiscent of the one I left so far behind. The white villas are made from wood, rather than stone, though, and everything is milder. Monarch butterflies flap lazily like orange sarongs lifted from washing lines by the gentle breeze. Elderly people loll in hammocks with thick paperbacks. Kingfishers bow slowly from power lines. Overfed ducks waddle around eating scraps the tourists feed them, and then float on the pondlike sea in the evenings like they're posing above my childhood fireplace.

As I write this a small boat has arrived at the jetty and some young men have got off. They've walked up to the highest platform and they're jumping into the sea, one by one. I thought for a moment that the last one reminded me of Richard, because he seemed to be lagging behind, moody and anxious, not wanting to do these pathetically bro-ish stunts. But then he put on a pair of large sunglasses, lit a cigarette, handed it to his friend, vaulted onto the highest wooden post at the end of the platform and backflipped into the sea. And Richard was gone again.

Dear Richard. I love him so much more now he's dead. I see him here often, although it's always only his ghost, of course. Some days I see him more than once, and it's comforting to think his spirit is still so strong. Yesterday there was a pale British man looking awkward in a new Panama hat; the day before, it was a good runner pounding up Telegraph Hill. Even now I can see a hesitant swimmer in slightly too-short bathers, and again I am transported back to Kathos.

I remember a queer day on our honeymoon, perhaps the penultimate time I swam on Kathos, before I knew that's what it was going to be. I went out beyond the unnerving stroke of the sea plants, a little too far from shore for my liking. There was a strange foam in that part of the water, and then I noticed hundreds of small fish, maybe sprats or anchovies. I was going to call out to Richard to come and see them, but then I realized they were dead. The whole sea in front of me was sprinkled with tiny dead fish, flip-flopping in the froth, like some terribly themed Frappuccino. I can still see their thousands of eyes, flat and glossy, as their corpses bobbled on the water.

After Richard and Paul raped me, I signed up for an optional module in "Self as Performance." I got a distinction for my work that term. I constructed a new persona for myself—Hannah Kayak, a mute mime artist inspired by Harpo Marx—but I went further than the other students and got my persona a bank account. It's not that hard. Perhaps that's why your lawyer had trouble finding me at first—I haven't spent any traceable money since I left Kathos last September, not that I officially have any money now anyway. I'm not exactly sure why I did it, but at the height of the success of *The Chambermaid* I put £10,000 in Hannah's account and never told anyone. I suppose even back then I felt I might need to escape one day. It was Hannah's card I'd used to buy my plane ticket in Athens, and again at Auckland. I'd had to travel under my own name, of course, and I guess that was how you eventually found me.

Back in the days of Hannah Kayak, Peter liked to fuck me

as soon as you left for London on a Sunday evening. He'd do it desperately sometimes, like a slavering hound, bending me over your white porcelain sink, or pushing me down onto my hands and knees in front of the cream enamel Aga.

"Why do you make me do this?" he panted one cold Sunday evening.

"Because I'm a disgusting whore," I said back obediently.

"You fucking bitch," he breathed raggedly into my ear.

Afterwards he was usually more gentle, but later, in the lead-up to the wedding, he became colder and rougher. He'd barely speak to me once he'd cleaned his jizz off my lower back with a Kleenex. But I think he loved me, in his own way, and I know he feared losing me. In fact, if it hadn't been for Luciana, and your poorly chosen honeymoon gift, things would likely have carried on as usual, with Peter being serviced by his daughter-in-law. There are much worse forms of incest, I expect.

I always thought you knew and never said anything. It can't have been such a bad deal. I soaked up Peter's rage and his spunk (it only went on my back if my app said I was fertile) and handed him back showered and in a pressed shirt ready for your dinner parties and family events. I was like a dog-grooming service. Not that you ever had a real dog. You didn't really need one.

But how much else did you know? I wondered if you were aware when you booked the Villa Rosa that terrible things had happened there, but I don't believe you were. I think you simply saw the reviews and didn't look into it any further. For a while I wondered if one of your well-connected friends had told you of the horrors of the island, and that was what inspired your choice, but it makes no sense. You wouldn't want to harm your precious son, would you? But then how precious was he really? When I finally read the letter he wrote me, I couldn't help wondering where you'd been when he'd needed you. But you know I don't like blame-the-mother narratives, so we won't dwell there.

It dwindled fast, Hannah's money. New Zealand isn't a cheap country. Still, I lived in the motel easily enough for almost a month. You'd be horrified by what I ate. Grimy, gritty strawberries from plastic punnets, thin processed ham, packet pastrami with a rainbow sheen, the most basic South Island brie and nothing organic. For the first week I lived on pure white Greek yogurt, because my stomach was recovering from all the vomiting. It had started on the propeller plane, but continued through my next flight, and then the one after that, until my bile turned pale green and then became a kind of foresty color, before drying up completely.

I don't eat carbs anymore. I've become a carnivore (well, almost—I also eat berries and yogurt) and I highly recommend it. Debbie explained it all to me at Athens airport, while I was trembling in the lounge. Humans should function as machines for turning earth into beauty, not sugar into fat, she'd said, stroking my arm softly with her manicured fingers. Cows and other beasts eat the inedible things of the world, things that sprout out of the mulch of the dead, and then we eat the animals and then we produce art and culture. Then we die and it all begins again. The miserable starvation diet you had me on for the wedding, all that oatmeal and dry Ryvita, that just creates disease and waste, according to Debbie. And it doesn't even stick, as you well know.

It certainly helped me go undetected, having little bird shoulders like Debbie's, and a skinny waist like on fitness magazines. In Russell I started wearing a khaki baseball cap all the time, and I got a few small tattoos. I bought cheap bracelets for my wrists and let the sun bleach my hair and grew out my fringe. You probably didn't notice me walking by your house last spring? Don't worry, I'm harmless. I was hardly going to knock on your door after our terrible phone call. But I did wonder for a while if you were harboring Richard, if by some miracle he was still alive. Anyway, I'm back on the other side of the world again now, where I belong, in the ghost version of Europe, all upside down like *Erewhon*.

One day, probably in the second or third week after I first arrived here, I was running up the hill from the sailing club, on my way to Long Beach. Beating Kostas had made me think maybe I should carry on running, and I'd picked up a second-hand sports watch of the type Richard always favored. I was looking out for the kingfisher I sometimes saw on the power lines, but instead I glimpsed a bright parrot lunging out of the bushes by the road. It was every color all at once: a red beak, a blue-and-yellow head and a green back, as if someone had given a primary school child too many crayons. I was moved by its ridiculously extravagant palette, its brash beauty. When I got back to the motel I used the Wi-Fi to look it up and I found it was a rainbow lorikeet—an "unwanted organism" in this country. You were supposed to call a number to report it, but of course I didn't. I realized how scared I was of being reported myself.

Another day I was on my way to Four Square to buy more yogurt and a plastic carton of blueberries when a police car cruised the main road. I ducked into a side street and in a slight panic ended up in the Russell museum—$12 entry, seriously. Inside, there was a shark's jaw, and a replica of Cook's boat, some military buttons and the tooth of a sea elephant. There were also samplers and tapestries done by the nineteenth-century women who lived the kind of life I think you always aspired to. One of the samplers had the phrase "A little pot is soon hot" stitched again and again. Just beyond that was a sad-looking taxidermized kiwi with an egg far too big for its body.

Until I finally read Richard's story, I thought he was so unworldly, that he didn't see the grime of life because he didn't know it was there. I recall a previous holiday in India, which I think you may even have booked as a birthday gift. We'd had a pleasant-enough time following all the other tourists from the city to the lake to the mountains to the tea plantation, before ending up back at sea level at a beach resort frequented by politicians from the UK and a celebrity chef I wouldn't have recognized if I hadn't overheard two other women talking about him in the pool.

Richard was such a good tourist, so compliant and cheerful. Like other good tourists, he wanted "authentic" experiences. The Indian beach hotel was contrived and fake, with its thatched huts and outdoor dining areas fringed with palm trees, and the brightly lit shop selling factor-50 sun cream and

T-shirts with the name of the resort on them. One morning Richard suggested going for a walk down the beach, even though the hotel and guidebook advised against leaving the official complex. As we walked, we noticed men squatting on the sand near some fishing lines, and we assumed that they were fishermen working. I felt uncomfortable watching them, and suggested to Richard that we turn back. I've never liked to think of other people's labor as a sideshow. But Richard wanted to carry on, and so we did. One man seemed to have caught something between his legs, some sort of seafood, and he was grappling with it, so Richard stopped to watch, full of enthusiasm. I realized before Richard did that the seafood was actually the man's penis, and that he and all the other men were squatting on the seashore because they were taking their morning shit.

Now I'm a good tourist too, now that I basically live on holiday.

But do you think I was happy when I arrived in Russell, so far from home and everything I'd ever known? It is a perfect, tranquil place, but I couldn't enjoy it then. Those first few nights I dreamed I was still in Kathos, locked in the store cupboard, or lying there by the generator, and then I'd wake too early in the shimmering waterfront town that looked so familiar, and wonder if I was quite mad. Eventually, I tried to write it all down; not for a film adaptation, but for myself—at least at first. My contacts in the film and TV world in the UK had long since dried up, and I wasn't there to take any meetings anyway. I wasn't even in the right time zone for a call. So when I realized my money was running out I did the only thing I could think of. I called Debbie on the number on the card she'd given me at Athens airport.

It took a few rings for her to pick up.

"It's Evelyn Masters," I said. "Evie. We met on Kathos, in that storm?"

"Um . . . ?"

"Last September," I said. "In Greece."

"Sorry, doll, not totally sure I can place you."

"You flew me out of Kathos on your private plane? I was running away from my husband? You were there because of the sleepwalkers, and—"

"Oh, *hi*, sweetie! How are you?"

"I'm good, how are you?"

"Honestly? About to go out for a mani-pedi, so . . ."

"Right, well, I'll be quick. Um, what you said about optioning my story."

"Yeah, what story was that?"

"About breaking up with my husband, and, you know, that weird hotel owner Isabella, and how controlling she was, and—" My pitch wasn't coming out the way I'd hoped. I remembered how mad I must have seemed that morning at the Athens airport, when Debbie had taken me to buy new clothes. But it had been Marcus's idea to option my story. He was the one who'd brought it up.

"I just wondered if I could send some material?"

"Oh, doll, I'm sorry but you're too late."

"What do you mean?"

"The Greek story? *The Sleepwalkers*? Well, we already have that."

"I don't understand."

"We're buying some documents? There's like a package that tells the whole story. We're flying back out there next month to collect it."

My mind hurried to catch up.

"Who has the documents? Isabella?"

"Well, no, but—"

"The French man? From the curio shop?"

"Yeah, exactly. But that lady from the hotel? She has a pitch for the screenplay."

"Do the documents . . . ?" I wasn't sure how to ask it. "Is there a letter of mine in there?"

"Uh—"

"Because that belongs to me," I said. "I wrote that. And I lost a notebook as well."

"There are quite a few documents, doll. A letter from a wife, a letter from her husband, some—"

"Wait, a letter from a husband? Richard's letter to me?"

I wasn't sure I'd believed Richard when he'd said he'd been writing to me. I didn't think he'd actually done it, and that there was a letter for me that had been left behind.

"Please," I said. "I have to see that letter."

"I don't have it, sweetie. Not until next month."

"But—"

"You know," she said, "it does sound like maybe this *is* more your story."

"Yes!" I said. "I agree."

"I mean, I said that to Marcus originally."

"Well, then—"

"Yeah, Marcus believes movies nowadays are much more about synecdoche and metonymy, you know, like the adjacent stories? How you can open up one story using a totally different one? To be honest, I don't really get it myself."

"OK." I had no idea what she was talking about.

"So, I mean, if you wanna maybe go and locate the material we'd be just as happy to buy it from you. And you could probably pitch for the screenplay too. I'd need to check with Marcus, of course, and the lawyer."

An hour later I got an email from her saying that yes, they'd be glad to buy the documents from me, if they happened to be in my possession. And they'd be willing to hear my pitch for how I'd adapt it for their movie.

So I decided to go back.

I'd already begun waitressing at the classy hotel overlooking the waterfront. It was the one place I'd never frequented as a punter, in my early days here in Russell, when I still had money. I'd always preferred the lowly charm of the Swordfish Club, which I'd even joined, with its walls covered in pictures of Zane Grey and all the enormous fish he caught. On the few evenings I wasn't working I'd sit on the Swordfish Club balcony and watch huge sunsets bleed out over the harbor and the jetty, and check airfares and do calculations. It wasn't at all clear I'd be able to get to Greece before Marcus and Debbie did.

On the nicer evenings there'd be kids chucking each other in the water from a scruffy diving island. One time there was a girl, thin and lithe, in amongst several boys. The game seemed to be a version of King of the Castle. The tallest boy with the longest shorts was standing there, his chest aloft and proud, and whenever one of the other children got on the island he'd throw them in. After a while, one group of children were called out of the sea to eat chips with their parents on the beach, and only two boys and the girl remained. The boys picked the girl up by her arms and legs, her slight body like a skipping rope, and they swung her to and fro and then threw her in the bright blue water. They'd tossed her so high, she went in deep. It was a few moments before she came up, and I couldn't tell if she was laughing or crying.

The classy hotel was patronized mostly by European men with their long-suffering wives. They came from France, Switzerland, Germany, Austria. They reminded me of you, the wives, with their sensible haircuts and modest diamond jewelry. Their skin, like yours, was pale from years of sunblock and good cosmetics. They would drink one glass of wine out of the bottle their husband ordered, and never, ever eat dessert.

The men's tongues tasted like espresso and Gitanes. Their dicks were salty and wrinkled, but usually firmed up with a bit of encouragement.

The conversation would start when I brought the bill, carefully timed for when the wife had gone to freshen up in the toilets.

"And you keep all the tips?" he would say, or something like that, pressing a couple of fifties into my hand, or simply tossing them onto the saucer with the bill, if he was the kind of man who liked people to see him disgracing himself. I'd touch the money and then he'd ask where I lived, and was it nearby.

The wives would take a sleeping pill and not notice their husbands slipping out. Or maybe they just didn't care. By then it was late summer in the southern hemisphere and I'd left the motel and rented a cheaper room above the pizza place, all patchwork throws and complicated plants. I'd pour Cointreau into a shot glass and say it was a British delicacy, or sometimes I'd serve Japanese gin with just a squeeze of lime and one tiny ice cube. The drink usually remained untouched, though, not because the men thought it was poisoned, but because they wanted to fuck me as soon as possible. Or Hannah. I always let Hannah do the actual fucking.

Is it wrong that I earned my airfare back this way? You'd already managed to get Richard's assets frozen, including our joint account, and so I really had no option. I had to get back to Greece, and even economy tickets cost a lot then, in those early years after the worst of the pandemic, with everyone flying everywhere all of a sudden, and it always being summer somewhere, more or less.

It had actually begun with the private investigator you sent after me. He did a great job, by the way, picking up my trail at Athens and following it to Kerikeri, so long after I'd left. It only took him a few more weeks of all-expenses-paid travel in Northland to finally locate me. I can't believe I didn't suss him out immediately, but I'd become a little soft by then. He'd sat on the veranda of the hotel in a white polo shirt on Christmas Eve, nursing a single glass of Man O' War Syrah from Waiheke Island and staring out to sea. Sleigh-bell music and carols were playing on the sound system that night, reindeer and snow at the height of the summer. He's the only customer I regret fucking, and not only because he didn't leave a large tip. He was hard and brutal, although I still thought I deserved that then, after being so ruined by your son. Your detective—I never knew his real name—fucked me like it was a punishment, holding my shoulders and ramming me so hard it was like something you might see done to an animal at a country fair. He said if he could film himself deep-throating me with his hand around my neck he'd consider not telling you he'd found me, and that was when I realized you'd hired him. When I visibly considered his offer he laughed and said he was joking, that of course he was going to report back. But in his own way he was warning me, giving me notice to move on if I didn't want to be found.

I told him I had nothing to hide, and I didn't. I still don't.

I went so far away because I was traumatized, Annabelle; nothing more. Why can't you believe that? There would have been more convenient places for me to have hidden out, I promise you. Places it would have been so much easier to come back from.

Not that it isn't glorious here. Lemons grow on trees and although their outsides are knobbly and wretched, their soft flesh is the color of early sunrise. There are so many stars in the night sky. I've seen the Pleiades for the first time. They call them the "Matariki" here, and celebrate when they first appear in June or July, deep in their winter. Māori navigators once used them to travel in the Pacific and the Tasman, and the Greeks used them as a signal that it was time to begin sailing. Even though there are now only six visible stars, most cultures over history have mythologized them as seven sisters, or a mother and six daughters. Often, they are seven maidens being pursued by a man, and so there is always the fallen one, the one who disappeared, or was caught. Once she glowed bright in the heavens, but she's not there now. Maybe she's gone so far into the darkness we just don't see her; or perhaps she went into supernova and died a long time ago.

I don't imagine you ever thought twice about flying, not even long haul. I've always been a nervous flier—well, until I'm actually in the sky, at which point I love the freedom of it, and the sense of people moving around the planet, doing interesting things. I'm usually the only one with the window shade open, agog at the wondrousness of it all, mouth open for the vast pink sunsets and the insane twilight that covers the whole of Europe, with towns and cities twinkling below stars that have never seemed so close. This time the sky seemed bigger and the stars seemed brighter, and it was not just because it had been so hard to save up my fare, but because I was traveling so far to retrieve a part of myself that was so lost.

I spent my layover in Athens in the same airport hotel I'd gone to with Richard after the wedding, trying to remember the person I had been then. I even drank a glass of the same bad rosé. But it was as if I couldn't yet get that part of my mind to open back up. That place within me just felt numb.

The ferry crossing to Kathos was rougher than I'd thought it would be. I've never minded a choppy sea, but all around me people were vomiting. One elderly French lady was demurely throwing up into her handbag—she'd tucked a sick bag inside so it looked almost elegant. I waited in my cabin for the worst of the heaving and falling to subside, and then I went to the shop and bought an American fashion magazine, thinking it was something I could hide behind if I had to. The shop was in chaos: the mini shampoos and sun creams had fallen off the shelves, and other people seemed to care about this a lot more than I did. One man was taking photographs with a professional-looking camera while the woman who'd been vomiting into her handbag shouted at him in French and dabbed at her lips with a white handkerchief.

Memory is such a strange thing. When I'd looked at a map of Kathos when I was making my bookings, I'd initially been convinced Richard and I had honeymooned on the west coast of the island, although we can't have done, because I wouldn't have been able to see Turkey from there. In my mind we'd driven from the west coast to the east, on that strange humid night with Bob Dylan playing in the taxi, when we'd gone to the wrong restaurant, but it must have been the other way around. This time, I'd booked an anonymous-looking hotel in a bay on the southeast of the island. I was there for my letters, of course, but for something else too, something I'd never known I needed: the ability to stay perpetually in transit, to never go home, for the honeymoon to never end, even after the marriage itself has irrevocably broken down and the poor husband has been killed.

It was warm when I disembarked from the ferry, my legs unsteady from the crossing, and the anticipation of trauma. I felt more OK than I expected as I got in the cab to be taken to my hotel. But my chest tightened as the cab snaked through the dusty back streets, past the mopeds and whitewashed villas and—it came quicker than I remembered—the dapper little man's curio shop. My heart flipped. It was still there! But of course there was no reason why it wouldn't be. I wondered if my letters were tied in a bundle on his shelves or if Isabella now had them. I tried not to look too suspicious as I peered over my shoulder at the shop as we passed, the driver beeping for a couple of kids to get out of the road. The beep made a figure in the shop look around, startled. He moved out of the shadows and into the early evening sunlight. It was a skinny young man in a crop top. Hamza? Had he come back?

My hotel room had everything I needed. A bed, a sofa, and a small tiled balcony with a wooden table and two slightly rickety chairs. I sat on my balcony with a large glass of cold white wine and looked out across the bay toward the south of the island, oddly grateful I couldn't see Turkey, that the view was new to me and therefore neutral. For a few moments I pretended I was a single, innocent woman on holiday, and I didn't have anything to be afraid of. What would I do, if I were that woman? I supposed I'd read, and so I took the American magazine I'd bought on the ferry to dinner with me, and I flipped the glossy pages with their wrap dresses and cruise collections and diet advice disguised as "wellness" as I ate a grilled fish with a Greek salad. Afterwards, the tall young waiter brought me a complimentary bowl of Greek yogurt with lemon apparently preserved by his grandmother, and it really was as if I'd never been there before.

The next day was a Saturday. I got up early and went straight to the curio shop. I'd disguised myself as best I could, with bronzer-heavy makeup and my khaki cap. But the shop was closed, it seemed, for the whole weekend. A sign said it would reopen on Monday. I walked back to the hotel. As I did, I caught sight of myself in the window of a taverna and although I'd recently got used to finding myself unrecognizable—I saw that it was in fact me. Evelyn Masters. The woman who'd come here after marrying Richard. It didn't matter if I lost weight or wore a cap: here I was.

I spent the rest of the weekend daubing lemon in my hair and trying different styles of makeup to see if I could erase myself. I lay restlessly on a sun-lounger and planned and re-planned how I'd get my letters. I swam for miles, my head full of logistics and lies, with all the colorful fish underneath me. There were no tendrilous sea-plants on this part of the island, nothing to lick at my legs or pull me under. For each meal I ate a fish and a salad and shook my head when the preserved lemon arrived. I only wanted fresh lemons for my hair. The hours went past slowly, and sometimes it felt as if I wasn't even on Kathos and I imagined myself on a different island altogether, on a pleasant holiday or research trip. I tried to picture myself back in Russell but it really wasn't that similar at all, I realized. Everything on Kathos was so square and stony, and the light reflected off the whitewashed walls in a bluer way.

On Sunday I went for a longer swim than usual, around one bay and then into another. Back in New Zealand I'd been getting a buzz out of swimming as a form of transport, a way of actually getting from A to B. I'd take my sports watch, set it to swim mode, and when I arrived at the next bay or island I'd use its wallet app to pay for a plate of oysters, or an espresso, or if it was evening, a Japanese gin over ice. On that Sunday in Kathos I felt a great surge of energy, so much it almost frightened me, and instead of stopping at the first bay, I swam on to the next one. My tendency to mirror things and turn them upside down had persisted, because although I thought I was swimming southwest, I was actually going northeast. I thought I knew the shape of the coast, and I believed the next bay was closer than it really was. I ended up in a kind of no-man's-land, where I'd gone too far to turn back, but the nearest shore was still so far away. The last few hundred yards were difficult because choppy waves appeared in the water, and the current seemed to want to pull me back the way I'd come. I thought I was going to drown.

I ended up right by George's Taverna, where Paul and I had watched the fish devour the bread roll just six months before. There was hardly any beach, to tell you the truth—maybe it was because of the high tide, or perhaps George's spring storm had not yet brought it back after the winter. But otherwise the place was the same as before. I felt a little faint, but I couldn't draw attention to myself by passing out, so I slowly and carefully swam on, out of sight of George's Taverna.

When I'd swum the day before I hadn't cared about arriving at the next bay in my bikini—I almost relished the lack of shame I felt with my new body. But on this part of the island I needed more of a disguise, so I bought a cheap orange sarong and a pair of dark glasses in the general store by the motorcycle man's shop, and then found somewhere to sit before I lost consciousness. I'd also bought half a cantaloupe melon, a hunk of feta cheese and some water, and so I sat on the semi-beach and sucked the sweetness and moisture and fat into myself. What had I been thinking? I'd swum way too far and now here I was, in this terrible place where the sleepwalkers had drowned. I was like an animal that had unwittingly circled back to the hunt.

The wreath was still there, just about, storm-battered and withered. I sat next to it as I ate. Once I'd finished, I walked along the thin strip of beach toward George's Taverna. I couldn't help myself. And there was Christos, picking up a bowl from a table. In an instant, our eyes met. The effect was startling. I began shaking, and tried to cover it by walking faster. He looked away, but I was sure he knew it was me; he'd seen me as easily as I'd recognized my own reflection the day before. I walked on, feigning confidence, as if I had somewhere to go, but the path beyond George's Taverna only led up the mountain. I walked uphill and then sat in a grove until the sun went down, leaking orangey colors all over the jagged rocks. I half-wondered if Christos might follow me, perhaps even try to kill me again, but there were no footsteps, and nobody came. I pulled myself together and walked back as if I had just been on some innocent errand, as if that was something a lone tourist was likely to do on a mountain path. By then the evening service had begun and I could see George running back and forth, head down. Christos was gone.

As I walked past the taverna I noticed a table of beautiful young people; not the same ones I'd been so obsessed with the year before, of course. There were two girls and two boys. The girls wore heavy makeup, with false eyelashes and electric-blue eyeliner flicks. One wore a low-cut white camisole and the other wore a loose black halter-neck over a bandeau bikini top. The boys were slim and tanned, both with dyed blond hair. The two men they were with looked very much like the ones who'd been here last year. One of them was tearing the shell off a large prawn while the other one was glowering into his tablet with the bluebottle cover. I carried on walking. When I reached the harbor an hour or so later, I saw that the new beautiful people had got into a small boat with the men, and it was sailing back along the route I'd swum, perhaps heading for the marina. As the boat went past, the girl with the camisole peeled it off and dived into the water, topless. It looked at first as if she were attempting an escape, but she simply did a decorative backstroke alongside the boat until her friends laughed and hauled her back in.

I glanced at the fish restaurant across the harbor. Was Christos in there, I wondered, still doing his evening shifts as if nothing here had really changed? But how could he not have been affected by what had happened? He was the one who'd dragged me out of the storeroom in the Villa Rosa, while I was playing dead. He was the one who'd lain me on the grass next to the generator. I was pretty sure it was he who had killed Richard. I just had no idea why. If you've read the enclosed documents carefully enough, you'll know why Richard died. But I didn't, because I didn't yet have them.

The next day was Monday. I arrived at the curio shop at around eleven, before it shut for lunch. I had decided not to arrive like a hungry street cat when it opened at ten. As

I approached I could hear the faint sound of a goldfinch singing from within the next-door taverna. The silver bell tinkled when I opened the door of the curio shop. Inside, it was cool, not because of air-con but because the shutters were half closed, and pale curtains fluttered in front of the open windows. You can make rooms cool if you know how, even in hot countries.

He was there, the dapper little man, at the desk at the back of the shop, just as he had been the first time I'd ever seen him. Once again, he was working on a birdcage. He seemed to be securing a yellow wooden perch to the roof of the wire house.

Behind him were the shelves on which he kept the bundles of documents. They were there just as before, looking both real and fake, tied in string and browned and faded in all the right places. I glanced at them and then looked away, back down to the desk, on which there was a soft pack of Gitanes and a bronze Zippo lighter.

"*Kalimera*," I said, as if I were just a normal tourist.

The dapper little man glanced at me and then nodded and went back to his pliers and his wire, twisting it through a hole in the yellow piece of wood.

He was wearing a three-piece suit, despite the heat. His small paisley waistcoat was neatly done up, as if the buttons were glued to the fabric. His black hair appeared painted on or molded in plastic. I looked away and pretended to browse. Well, in fact, I really did browse. Acting has to be as close to life as possible to seem authentic. In *An Actor Prepares*, Stanislavski's Director asks students to search inside a curtain for an important brooch. When a woman is unable to do it convincingly enough, he tells her she'll be thrown out of class if she can't find it. Only then does she act with truth.

Last time I'd been in the curio shop I couldn't make myself swirl my hands through the drawer of starfish and seahorses as Beth had, but I did it now. I browsed the rails of peasant nightdresses and jodhpurs. I sincerely wondered how I'd look in loose, flowing white cotton, like a ghost that is secretly alive, or an invalid from a Victorian novel. In my mind I became the sort of woman who would wear clothes like that; the sort of woman who runs a hotel and is always looking for interesting interior design ideas and amusing things to pop on dressers. I could see it clearly in my head, my hotel. I could see its tiled entrance hall, and its large terracotta pots.

"Excuse me," I said, floating over to the front desk, but deliberately standing in shadow. "What are those?"

I pointed at the shelves of documents behind the dapper little man.

They were just out of reach, like prescription medicines.

"*Histoires*," he said, in French, and then shrugged.

I'd thought I was standing in shadow, but it must have been only a temporary cloud, as the sun suddenly shone in my eyes. I tried to move sideways out of the glare, but it was impossible. I stepped backwards, finally returning to the cool semi-darkness.

"For decoration?"

"Yes. Or you can read. They have genuine documents from the ages."

I let my eyes open wide with a sort of shallow excitement.

"They'd look amazing in my hotel. On the chests of drawers in the rooms."

His head jerked then, ever so slightly.

"Which subject you look for?"

"I'm sorry?"

"They have different subjects. Here." He stood and climbed onto a small wooden stepladder. "This one is about Italians who occupied the island during the war." He hooked his finger under the brown twine with which the documents were secured, turned and let the bundle of papers drop onto the counter in front of me. "There are love letters that were not sent; also a very sad journal of an Italian soldier just before the Germans came, and he was killed."

"Wow," I said.

"This one," he continued, dropping a smaller bundle on the desk, "is a collection of notes left for a cleaner from a man in a villa near the airport. They have many details about the tasks he asks her to do. Here in this one is also shopping lists and receipts for pharmaceuticals, and tailoring. I have others, from all around the world."

I had no idea the dapper little man could say so many words. Last year he'd been so sullen, and almost as mute as Hannah Kayak. I struggled to stay in character as he stared at me.

"How do you get the documents?" I asked innocently.

"People toss them away," he said, with a wave of his hand. "They send them to be recycled and I find them. Or my boy does. Or they leave them in boxes or the attic when they move, or die." He shrugged again.

Or you steal them, I wanted to say. *You fucking take them.*

Of course, I said nothing. Still, perhaps I am not that good an actress after all. Or perhaps he never believed in me. Perhaps at that moment the anger flashed in my eyes and he understood it all. Perhaps he'd understood from the moment I walked in the door. Perhaps he'd seen me as easily as Christos had.

He stared at me, and there was unkindness in his small eyes.

"Maybe they send them to the wrong person, who then loses them. Or perhaps they write in public, for anyone to take, in a hotel guest book."

I stared back at him. "Or leave them on a pillow, in a locked room."

He broke my gaze then. He picked up his Zippo lighter, turned it over in his hand, and put it down again.

"So you have come to search for your letters, after all this time?" he said, deadpan.

"They are mine," I said.

"You should have been more careful with them."

The way he said this chilled me. I rolled my eyes and shook my head, like I couldn't believe what he was saying.

He shrugged once again. "You know, if a photographer takes your picture, it belongs to him. Just because it is you in the photo does not means it belongs to you."

"Right. But these are not photographs, and what I wrote does belong to me. Are my letters here?"

I must have looked as if I was about to vault over his desk and start ransacking his shelves. He held up a hand as if to stop me.

"She have them. Isabella. She will burn them, perhaps, or maybe sell them to Hollywood. I don't know. But you must ask her. I see her no more."

"I suppose she's still at the Villa Rosa, murdering other women's husbands?"

"This is not true," he said, grimacing. "You misunderstand."

He shook his head and a long hissing sound emerged from between his teeth like a balloon deflating.

"Your husband." The dapper little man sneered. "He took a boat and left."

"No, that's not true!"

"Really? There was no dead body."

"I was there! I was locked in a cupboard and then—"

"Or maybe you put yourself in a cupboard while your husband packed and left you behind, and you had a breakdown and invented a ridiculous story. I know precisely what ridiculous story you invented, because I collected it and put it in order."

So you see, Annabelle, you're not the only one who has accused me of making things up. It's always been the same kind of dirt that sticks to me: slightly crazy actress who doesn't know what is real and what is fake, who imagines drama where there is no drama, who drives her husband away with her petty jealousy. The girl who kneels in puddles to give blow jobs to men she doesn't even like, because she simply must be in a story, even if she has to be the femme fatale, or, worse, the victim.

But even that girl rarely goes so fucking mad as to believe in an entirely different version of the world. But it was obvious this story about the cupboard and the breakdown was what they'd told the police. That must have been why you'd engaged your private investigator to find me.

"I don't understand you," I said to the dapper little man. "Why are you protecting Isabella?"

"I owe her," he said. "But not you."

He took a bundle of documents off the bottom shelf. It wasn't yet tied with string—it was as if this archive was still in progress.

"Here is a nice collection. A genuine blackmail letter, with some demands, and a few pictures. And then also a reply, negotiating. I am going to take the pictures out—they add nothing—and then ..." He pulled out the photographs and laid them on the desk in front of him. I thought I glimpsed Isabella, naked and possibly even handcuffed, before he turned the photos over. Then he took out two of the sheets of paper—they were blue, lightweight, made for letter-writing—and crumpled them into a ball before smoothing them out again. Then he took one of the pieces of paper and ripped it in half. He took one of these fragments—it had maybe two hand-written sentences on it—and held it in his thumb and forefinger, while with the other hand he picked up the bronze Zippo lighter from the counter. Then he set fire to the fragment. He let it burn to the last millimeter before dropping the burning ember to the desk, where it disappeared, like a hallucination.

He looked me deep in the eyes, and sneered.

"It is as Chekhov says: always delete the ending."

I bit my lip, said nothing, and left.

Actually, Chekhov says that you should delete the

beginning as well as the end, but only for short stories, not for plays. I always think plays need a proper ending, so everyone knows where they stand. Don't you agree?

After I left the curio shop, I walked back to my hotel and drank an iced coffee without tasting it and then had a long, cold shower.

I went over to the Villa Rosa late that afternoon, just as the sun was beginning to set. Perhaps you won't care, but when I originally began writing my letter to Richard I imagined it ending up as a one-act play with the title *The Honeymoon*. I was writing it partly to spite you and certainly to spite him. It was how I'd coped with the trauma of the wedding. I was planning to recast the whole thing as a tragic love story, or a melancholy tale of misunderstanding and loss where a couple splits up, but no one dies. Of course, that was before I knew the true story; before it had the chance to unfold. At one point I'd planned to end my play with the husband—Richard's character, whom I'd renamed Jay—coming back to the Villa Rosa many years later with his new wife. I visualized a moment of epiphany as he and the new wife go up the driveway and then into the cool tiled entrance hall, and Isabella, older but otherwise unchanged, treats the new wife exactly as she'd treated me. I'd even written in my notes something like, "And at that moment, he understood," although I was trying to work out how to translate that into an action, or a piece of believable dialogue. How do you convey a person's realization that they have been so wrong, and their whole life has pivoted as the result of a single mistake?

As I turned into the dusty road off the seafront now, a taxi overtook me. Then another one. Inside the first one had been a man and a woman of about my age. In the second one was an older couple. I had to blink a few times and steady myself because for a moment I imagined I was seeing myself and Richard, and the sleepwalkers, all arriving together, completely out of time. The road was not as dry as it had been the previous autumn, before the storm came. There was a damp freshness to everything, with flower buds on the trees and in the bushes. A few playful sparrows chased me down the path, twittering.

As I began walking up the driveway toward the Villa Rosa, the now empty taxis were leaving. I stepped aside and stood under the pomegranate tree to let them pass. Up ahead, a skinny young man was hacking at a large lemon bush with a machete. At first I assumed it was Kostas, and wondered how he'd lost so much weight. But as I approached, I saw the thin red silk scarf around his neck and realized it was Hamza. So he *was* back on the island. So much for claiming asylum in the UK or the US. But I guess I knew he was abandoning that plan when he'd made a run for it at Athens, that dreadful day we'd flown out of Kathos in the storm. And I had no idea why someone like Hamza would want to apply for asylum anyway. Not then.

I expect you don't care about stories of servants, and you may even agree with Aristotle that these can never be fully tragic stories, because they don't deal with great and powerful people. I've experienced the way you treat staff: never looking them quite in the eye and speaking to them in that crisp tone you reserve for giving instructions to people you

believe are beneath you. If you ever reflected on it, you'd realize that you think of servants as a lower class of human. So
I'm sure it won't be of any interest to you to hear that Hamza
had come back because he loved Christos. But I'm getting
ahead of myself.

Hamza turned and looked at me, startled.

"*Kalispera*," I said.

"You have come back," he said.

"So have you," I observed.

"Why are you here?"

"For my letters."

"Why?"

"Because they're mine. I think my husband wrote to
me. Before—"

Hamza looked frightened, as if I might actually say it.
So I didn't.

"Yes," Hamza said softly. "There is a long letter. It is a
sad letter."

"Wait, you've seen it?" I said. "Where is it?"

Hamza shrugged and turned back to the lemon tree.

"Come on," I said. "I helped you."

"I don't remember," said Hamza. It wasn't clear if he meant
that he didn't remember me helping him, or if he didn't
remember what was in the letter.

"Does Isabella have my letters?" I asked. "And my
notebook?"

"She won't give them to you."

"Why not?"

He bit his lip nervously. "She dreams of her movie deal.

She is writing her screenplay. She has planned a big dinner for the producers when they come back next week."

"Is her screenplay about how she murdered my husband?"

Hamza looked down, as if he was ashamed.

"Well?" I demanded.

"It is about how you murdered your husband," he said. "Because of your past."

This hit me like a sudden punch. I felt sharp pain, then numbness.

"You know I didn't kill Richard," I said. "How am I supposed to have done it?"

"With sleeping pills. And then drowning."

"But that's utterly ridiculous."

Hamza didn't reply. He turned and hacked another piece off the lemon tree.

"What if the producers actually want to do a deal with me?" I said.

"You are writing a screenplay too?"

"Maybe."

Hamza shrugged again, but I could tell this changed things somehow.

"They are my documents. It's my life," I said. "And you know what really happened."

"What really happened is no good."

"I know you want to get out of here," I said. "What if I helped you, again?"

He looked back at me then, and there was a thin sliver of hope in his eyes. Then he blinked and it was gone. He turned away and started hacking at the lemon bush once more.

I approached the main house.

Isabella was there in the tiled entrance hall, just as she'd been the previous September. She was wearing something that looked like a cast-off wedding dress with a wide brown belt buckled tight at her waist, and a pair of shining mahogany riding boots. She wore these items as if they'd been picked out for her by a drunk parent, or chosen by an older cousin from a dressing-up box. The cream gown hung limply off her slight shoulders, and the belt looked as if it had been pulled tight by another, more spiteful child. The boots had the air of being too stiff and too big. I strongly feel that you need to wear a dress like hers with a lot more enthusiasm.

As I approached, I saw that Isabella's face was partly obscured by a pair of thick, black-rimmed spectacles. She was holding some papers that looked like screenplay pages.

"Hello," I said. I'd like to think there was a lot of nuance in the way I said it. A twinge of regret, of course, plus the acknowledgment of time having passed, as well as our shared knowledge of her guilt. I also said it in a way that (I thought) implied I wasn't about to attack her in a crazed frenzy. After all, she had murdered my husband, or helped someone else to do it. And now it seemed that she was actually writing a version of events in which I'd killed Richard.

"Yes?" she said, putting the papers down and taking off the spectacles. She looked at me. "Can I help you? You have a booking?"

Can you believe she was the only person on the island who seemingly did not recognize me?

"I actually stayed here last year," I said.

"OK," she said, slightly mockingly, not quite meeting my eye. It was as if I were beginning a joke, or, perhaps more accurately, that I was the joke.

"I left something behind."

"Really?" she said. "I don't remember you. When did you stay?"

"September," I said. "There was a big storm."

"A storm?" she said, in the same half-amused mocking tone. "I don't remember. We have many storms in autumn months." Her voice then lost the amused tone and became serious. "It is a bad time to come."

In that moment, I realized that I hadn't ever accepted that Richard was dead. There was no way I could have come here if I'd thought I was going to confront his murderer. I suddenly realized I believed that he was still alive. Had he really taken a boat, like the dapper little man had suggested?

"Where is he?" I said.

"Where is who?" said Isabella.

"Oh, come on," I said, "stop messing around."

"You have lost someone?" she said, still deadpan. "I've seen no one except for my new guests. Such beautiful guests these are."

"My fucking husband," I said. "The one you're writing your fucking screenplay about. Where did he go?"

"You cannot keep track of your husband?" she said. "Oh dear."

"I want my letters," I said. "Don't pretend you don't know what I'm talking about."

She shrugged. "I'm sorry. You say you left a letter?"

Her eyes then revealed something, just for a moment. They darted just very slightly over my right shoulder and then back to somewhere on my face. For the whole exchange so far, Isabella hadn't completely caught my eye. She'd looked at my forehead or my nose but not into my eyes. Her gaze flicked once again to the right and then back. She looked anxious, suddenly. There was someone standing behind me. I turned. It was Hamza. He was holding the bundle of documents. The bundle was tied with string. Of course, I couldn't see what any of the documents were, but I knew instinctively that my letters were there.

"What is this?" said Isabella, with real emotion in her voice for the first time. "Hamza, what are you doing?"

Without thinking, I grabbed the bundle from Hamza's hands and went to make a run for it. Isabella saw what I was doing and lunged at me. She snatched at the documents but only managed to get hold of the string. The bundle loosened and some of the handwritten pages scattered on the floor. I didn't have time to try to retrieve them. I yanked the string out of Isabella's fingers, clutched the remaining documents to my chest and darted out of the hotel lobby. I started running, just as I had that night back in September. This time at the end of the driveway I turned right instead of left.

I kept running, holding the documents to my chest and not looking behind me, until I reached the main street that ran parallel to the sea. The motorcycle man was standing outside his shop. He gave me a big thumbs-up and then let his tongue fall out of his mouth and began miming "panting heavily" and I realized that's what I was doing. I could hardly breathe. I slowed and gasped for air and looked behind me. No one was there. No one had followed me. I tried to give the motorcycle man some kind of acknowledgment, which I think turned into a painful grimace, and then I jogged on to where there were taxis down by the big hotel.

I suppose anyone else on that street that day would have noticed the breathless and frightened woman running with a bundle of documents loosely tied with string. Maybe somebody saw me, maybe they didn't, but by the following afternoon the documents were gone. Obviously I took care to hide them in my hotel room, and locked the door. But none of this stopped whoever came and took the documents back.

Was it Isabella? She certainly created an interesting diversion when she turned up the following morning. But I'm getting ahead of myself again.

I arrived back at my room, still clutching the documents. I drank a whole bottle of mineral water, washed my hands and face, and then I sat on my bed and read everything, as I hope you've just done. But maybe you didn't even bother? Maybe you chose to leave the bundle unopened on the chiffonier, so to speak. Maybe you didn't think it contained anything important.

My own letter was familiar enough, and I read it wishing it had simply become the one-act play I'd had in mind when I'd begun it. My notebook was sobering. Richard's letter was less of a shock than you might think, especially as it stopped halfway through, just before his confession. You'll have read the confession by now, I suppose, but those pages—along with some from the guest book—were the ones that had fallen out of the bundle, and so at that point I didn't have them.

The next morning I woke to a furious pounding on the door of my room.

When I opened it I was surprised to find Isabella there, pink-faced and breathless.

"I hope you've brought the rest of my letter," I said.

"Where is he?" she demanded. "What have you done to him, you stupid bitch?"

It was the first time I'd seen her lose her cool.

"Who?" I said, but I guess I knew already that she meant Hamza.

"What have you done to him?" she said again. "Are you hiding him? You must give me back the pages that you stole. All of them. Including the fallen ones he took."

She held out her hands, as if I would simply put the bundle of documents in them.

"What *I* stole? You're even more brazen than I thought."

"Why are you here?" she hissed. "Why did you come back?"

"I came back for my husband," I said simply, letting the double meaning float in the air between us.

"You could never keep a husband. You are too ..." She looked me up and down. "You are too English," she said eventually.

"I guess once Richard knew you were involved in human trafficking he needed to be killed," I said. "And you thought I knew too, didn't you?"

You got that from the transcript as well, presumably, Annabelle?

"I do not know what you are talking about," Isabella said, biting her lip. She was back in her innocent child pose, as if she were about to blame everything on her cruel belt-tightening cousin. "You do not understand." She blushed and looked as if she was about to stamp her little foot.

"I know that Christos is a murderer," I said.

I should have been suspicious at the way Isabella reacted to that.

"I see," she said, dropping her head. "You have discovered everything. Well, then, I suppose there is nothing more to say."

She turned to leave, with the air of a performer about to exit the stage.

"I thought you were trying to find Hamza," I said scornfully.

"It's too late for him," she said, looking back at me. "I have tried to protect him, but Christos will be very angry with what you have discovered. He may think you mean to take Hamza away, which he will not like." She shook her head, and then she turned again and walked away, her buttocks bouncing in her pale jodhpurs like melons in a flimsy carrier bag. It was as if she wasn't wearing any underwear. Is that an odd thing to notice in that moment? It was certainly impossible to ignore.

Once I was dressed, I hid the documents at the bottom of my rucksack, and covered them with the fashion magazine. I can't believe I thought this was a good enough hiding place, but the hotel room had no safe, so I felt I had little choice. I went over to the harbor and got in a taxi and asked to be taken to George's Taverna.

When I arrived, the place seemed empty. It was not yet ten

o'clock. Christos was there, putting the umbrellas up at the outside tables.

"Where's Hamza?" I asked him.

"You tell me," said Christos wearily.

"He has something," I said. "Something I need. And I think he's in danger."

At this, Christos laughed coldly. "Really?" he said. "OK."

"I've read the transcript," I said. "I'd be happy to swap it for the pages he has."

On the word "transcript," Christos froze.

"What?" he said. "What the fuck are you talking about?"

"The transcript," I said, taking an instinctive step back. "The one I deleted?"

"I—"

"You kept a copy? You *lied*?"

Christos took a step toward me and then seemed to stop himself, just as I held my hands up.

"No. Hamza—"

"He downloaded it. At the airport. Fuck." Christos thumped the table. "That fucking treacherous snake."

"Christos, I've read everything," I said, as gently as I could.

"OK," he said, sinking into a chair by the table. "OK."

Are you at all worried for my safety here, Annabelle? Don't be. There was a steady trickle of traffic on the dusty road, and a few people off for their morning strolls. I felt sure someone would try to save me if Christos attempted to kill me, so I sat down opposite him. Out of lunging distance, I calculated. But you can never be sure, can you? No one knows the day they're going to die. Would you die for the truth? On that morning I thought I probably would if I had to, absurd as that may sound now.

And also, how do you feel about "manspreading"? I've never really minded it myself. It's just a way to sit, after all, especially if you have long legs and need to arrange them. Poor Christos looked less like a confident bro trying to take up the maximum space possible and more like a condemned prisoner trying to burrow into himself. After a few moments he took his head out of his hands and looked at me.

"What do you want?" he said.

"I want all my documents," I said. "And then I just want to leave. I'm not going to make trouble for anyone."

This wasn't a hundred percent true, but I felt like it was what Christos needed to hear.

"And I want to know Hamza's OK."

Christos scoffed. "What do you care about Hamza?"

"He tried to help me."

"Yeah? What did he think you'd give him in return?" Christos sighed, and visibly stopped himself continuing. He shook his head. "I take that back." He picked up the salt cellar from the table and weighed it in his hand as if it contained the truth. "I did love him, you know."

"Yeah."

"You have any idea what it means to be like Hamza, in Turkey?"

I shrugged. I'd read something once about people in the West thinking Muslim countries were much more homophobic than they actually are. But I'd never been to Turkey. I had no idea of what it would be like there for anyone. Was it even officially a Muslim country anyway? I didn't think so. I vaguely imagined that it would probably be fine if you knew what to do, just like most other places.

"Being used by men, being—"

"OK, we've all been used by men," I snapped. I dislike being lectured to about the patriarchy by its constituents, to be honest.

Christos looked at his feet, then back up at me. A pickup truck on the street behind him beeped at a moped that seemed to have stopped for no reason.

"Hamza wanted to be an artist," said Christos. "His father went crazy when he went to Istanbul and got a place at art school. Hamza worked in a nightclub to pay his fees. There were student nights, gay nights. Turned out the manager was trafficking and employing illegals. At first Hamza thought it was cool to be working with Syrians and Iraqis. They were queer, like him, or girls who'd got in trouble back home. When he realized they weren't being paid properly, he complained to the owner. The guy turned nasty and beat Hamza up. It's not difficult."

That hung in the air for half a minute.

"So then how did Hamza get involved in the trafficking himself?" I asked. "I mean, if he was so against it? That's what he was doing, right? Bringing kids over from Turkey, for, like, I don't know—"

"Photo shoots, marketing for a 'new band.' Yup."

"All organized by Isabella."

"There are worse people beyond her. Hamza's not scared of her so much, but he is scared of them."

"But how did he get involved with them?"

"He went back home for a big holiday, a few years back. Maybe Ramadan? It was pretty intense. Hamza came out to his dad, but it didn't go well. They had a big fight. Hamza stuck around, hoping they'd find some peace, only then his dad got Covid, no doubt from his son arriving from the big city. It was in the early days, and there were no antivirals or vaccines." Christos paused. "His dad died."

"Fucking hell."

"Right? So Hamza goes back to Istanbul, kinda broken, only now he has to make money to send his mom to pay for the house, and all the bills, and all his little sisters' shit, as they have zero income now his dad's dead. The dude who ran the nightclub gave Hamza a lot of extra shifts, but it wasn't enough, so he asked how he could make more money. All he had to do at first was befriend students or under-age kids who came to the club. They had to be vulnerable somehow, needy. He'd invite them for band auditions, or to do 'modeling.' There was a lot of bullshit, obviously, but eventually they'd end up on a private yacht to the island— all very impressive. They'd stay at Isabella's and get their pictures taken, and then on the last day their passports would disappear and they'd be sold on, to work in villas or on yachts or, if it was a pretty girl, to work as a personal maid in London or New York or Dubai."

"A 'personal maid'?"

"Yeah, I don't know if they were prostitutes exactly. They probably ended up in a better country than the one they'd come from anyway."

"I thought Turkey was quite a good place to live?"

"There are desperate kids everywhere. Kids get trafficked out of London and New York as well."

"And the refugee camps here of course."

"Yeah." Christos looked down at the floor. "That's on me. If he hadn't met me, he wouldn't have wanted to stay on the island. He—"

"Where's Hamza now?"

Christos shrugged. "I honestly don't know. Probably packing, now he's got your attention. He'll think you'll repay him by taking him back to the UK and sponsoring his visa. Or you'll help him claim asylum."

"Can Turkish people even get asylum in the UK? I mean, Turkey's in NATO. It's virtually the EU."

"He wants to report Isabella and the traffickers, but then he can never come back."

"Which would devastate you, right? Maybe even get you arrested."

"It's more complicated than that."

"Come on. You obviously still love him. Please say you haven't hurt him."

Christos said nothing. The street behind him was suddenly still and silent.

I stood up and took a couple of steps away from Christos.

"Because you killed the sleepwalkers in a jealous rage, right?"

Christos shook his head and rolled his eyes.

"Yeah, that's exactly how you kill people when you're in a jealous rage."

"So you admit you gave them the sleeping pills."

"Hardly."

"Come on, you as good as say it on the transcript. I think the software wrote 'slipping peels' but I knew what it meant."

"I don't think that's gonna stand up anywhere."

"What did Isabella do? Did she show you the letter Hamza wrote to James Border, the super-religious guy? All about giving Hamza love? I'm guessing James meant spiritual love, but you misunderstood, didn't you? You thought Hamza was going to meet him for sex."

Christos sighed. "It didn't matter if it was love or sex. The result would have been the same."

"You would have lost him."

"He thought if he could get to the US or the UK he'd finally be able to make enough money for his mother, but in a legitimate way, not by hurting people."

"And you wanted to stop him?"

"That makes it sound wrong. I wanted to support him, but—"

"Isabella told you Hamza and James were hooking up? And she showed you the note Hamza wrote, to prove it."

"Why does it matter?"

"You took away Hamza's one chance of freedom!"

"Did I? He didn't even want to go to the UK anyway. He was much more desperate to go to the US, the land of Lou Reed and Andy Warhol. We were going to get married, but—"

"Where is he, Christos?"

"He's exactly where he wants to be."

"Oh, for God's sake."

"Have you even stopped for one second to examine your own assumptions? You assume that all gay people are psychos who commit murder every time they feel jealous?"

I sighed. "Don't do that." I paused. "You tried to kill my fucking husband."

"No. I did not try to kill your fucking husband."

I grimaced. "Right."

"You wanna know why? Because I am nowhere near the biggest psycho on this island," he said. "You got the wrong guy."

"You tried to drive me into a fucking tree!"

"Yeah, but I didn't do it, did I? I've got issues, but I'm not a goddamn murderer."

"Who, then? Kostas?"

Christos laughed bitterly. "Poor stupid Kostas. She owns him too."

"So you're saying Isabella did everything?"

At that point, I felt we were going around in circles.

"Ask yourself who owns Isabella," he said, standing up. "And then you'll find Hamza. And the rest of your stupid documents."

"What happened to my husband?" I asked.

"I don't know."

"How can you not know?"

"I wasn't there. I told her not to do it. Just before we brought you out. She'd never gone that far before. You know, she's never actually killed anyone herself. Not even her husband. Far as the police are concerned, she's as innocent as a fucking baby."

"Then what happened to Richard? And how did the sleep-walkers die?"

"The sleepwalkers drowned, just like the autopsy said."

"Oh come on," I said. "We both know they were murdered."

"Isabella knows some pretty bad people," said Christos, as if that explained it. He paused. "I knew you were faking, by the way. And I ignored your passport—did you not wonder about that? I told her to wait, to find some other way. I was trying to save you, and your ridiculous husband. I guess you didn't realize that I was running after Kostas while he chased you."

"I—"

"You didn't think it was weird when he just stopped running after you?"

"I assumed I'd outrun him," I said.

"I brought him down," said Christos. "I fucking saved you."

"But why? I mean, before that, when I heard a buzz, I thought it was you electrocuting Richard."

"No. She was just testing it."

"So then where is he?" I asked. "Where's my husband?"

Christos shook his head. "I don't know."

As I walked down the street after leaving the taverna, I thought back to a particularly rainy day in Russell, just a couple of weeks before. It hadn't yet turned into a full-blown cyclone and they were still calling it a "tropical low." The sun had unexpectedly come out, late in the day, and I'd attempted to clean the wooden deck of my flat above the pizza restaurant. I'd seen a native pigeon that day, a *kererū*, its fat white legs like something you'd usually see covered in gravy, pecking away at a soaked cabbage palm for its unripe berries, its bright orange eyes flashing in the brief sunlight. I'd begun to clean the deck's major eyesore: a rotten old bird table that had been hanging from the branches of another tree for several winters and summers, and which now housed several different spiders. I was trying to clean it without killing the spiders when a tiny moth landed on its small roof. One of the spiders saw it and it darted out, ready to pounce. My instinct told me to give the moth a little push to make it fly away, thus saving its life. I did it—anyone would have done the same—but as the spider scuttled back to its web, disappointed, I realized that saving the moth meant killing the spider, or at least starving it to death. And maybe I hadn't even saved the moth, because you're not really supposed to touch their wings, however gently.

I arrived at the curio shop before I'd even thought about what I was going to do or say. I'd believed I was calm, but when I got there I realized I was so pumped with adrenaline I was ready to bust my way in and rip the shop apart. Looking back now, I guess I was a little unhinged—not the way you thought, though. I wanted to find out what had happened to Richard, and I wanted my documents, and I wanted to help Hamza. His story had touched me deeply. Maybe the reasons for that are obvious; maybe not. I wanted so many things at once it was all a tangle. I felt stronger than I really am, fiercer.

But the door to the curio shop was locked and bolted, which was odd, because it was a weekday, and some time before lunch. I peered in through the window. At first, all I could see were the silent shadows of bookshelves and riding crops, and the ghostly outlines of all the long white dresses that you could sleep in if you were rich or get married in if you were poor.

Then I saw the wooden chair in the center of the back room. Hamza was sitting on it, naked from the waist up. Where was his usual scarf? His shoulders were thrust forward at a slightly unnatural angle and I could see the sharp jut of his collarbones. I realized with a gasp that his hands were behind the chair: indeed, that's where his scarf was, tied in a brutal-looking knot around his tiny wrists while the ends trailed on the floor like a spilled drink. Across the room was the dapper little man, sketching the scene with a stick of charcoal.

It all made sense once I'd put it together. The dapper little man was the reason for everything. It was he, after all, who had been negotiating with Marcus and Debbie to sell the story of the sleepwalkers. It was he who had stolen all the documents and put them together in the first place. He had been Speaker 4 on the transcript. He was the one I'd originally thought was getting a fetishistic kind of pleasure from controlling everything around him, the one Christos had described on the transcript as a "little vampire."

I was just about to try and kick the door in when I saw Hamza smile, and then laugh. He said something to the dapper little man, who smiled back and nodded. I suddenly couldn't understand the scene at all. Its meaning fluttered away from me like an uncaged bird. Then Hamza spotted me looking in the window. The dapper little man had his head bent over his sketch, and Hamza frowned at me and shook his head. His shoulders lifted into a nonchalant shrug. He seemed to be saying, *I'm fine. Go away.* I wasn't sure, so I kept staring for a few moments, but all I saw was more easy laughter and banter between them. The scene seemed to be telling me to leave. So I did, feeling utterly confused.

When I got back to the hotel, as I said, the bundle of documents was gone.

But don't worry, Annabelle, I took pictures of everything. I'd photographed each sheet of paper as I'd read it earlier that day, just as any sensible person would have done. So, yes, I no longer had the originals, but I had the material itself. I had what I'd come for, more or less. I was still missing a few pages, but I'd already read the guest book entry, and I suppose I thought I knew by then what Richard's confession was. As I reflected on this, I felt the spark of something creative, the same as the feeling I'd had back in Athens after the wedding, when I was so traumatized I'd decided my life from then on would be fictional, like a play I was only acting in. The documents did make a good story, although not in the exact order the dapper little man had arranged them. I wondered about a different way of telling things. A new focus. Certainly an alternative to Isabella's murder mystery with me as the killer. Then I called Debbie's number.

She didn't pick up, which was disappointing. Ideas were racing through my mind like spirited reindeer and I wanted to make them real by telling them to someone. Perhaps that's also when I thought I should write to you, but of course I didn't begin this letter until much later, when I was back in New Zealand.

It was a couple of hours after dinner when the package was slipped under my hotel room door.

It was an A4 brown envelope, unsealed, like a thirsty mouth.

Did it contain my missing pages? I opened the flap and pulled out what appeared to be a short series of charcoal sketches, on thick creamy paper. On the first page, I was puzzled to see the girl with the "Istanbul is Contemporary" bag. She had been drawn inside a framed panel like in a comic book, with tables from a café scattered along the edge of the sea behind her.

The next sketch zoomed out to show a woman—did she look unnervingly like me?—reading the comic book with this panel in it. The woman's face *was* mine, I realized, and her hands somehow were too: the nails cut square, with the same chipped nail polish I was wearing right now. The woman had her fingers poised to turn the page, to see what happens next. There was another sheet under the first two, and so I had to turn the page just as cartoon-me did. Nice touch, I half-thought.

When I saw what was on the next sheet, I retched, and dropped everything. But then I forced myself to pick it up and look at it. Brace yourself, Annabelle. The focus of the scene had been expanded again so that the entire woman was now shown, reading her comic book. The face and hands remained realistic, but the body was both too skinny and too voluptuous. The woman's breasts pushed against a tight white shirt and almost touched the desk she'd bent over to read the comic book, which she held in both hands, her elbows resting schoolgirlishly beside her breasts, which were not as a schoolgirl's breasts should be. The woman's tiny skirt had been roughly pulled up over her shapely arse, all the way to her waist. You could tell the skirt had been roughly pulled up because the man's hands were still gripping it with some force as he penetrated her with his large penis. His expression was one of violence and pain, but on the woman's face was a simple, innocent smile.

The man looked exactly like Peter.

When I retrieved the envelope from the floor where I'd dropped it, my hand trembling, I saw there was a plane ticket back to Athens for the next morning. I'd been planning to take the ferry again in a few days' time, but suddenly I wanted to leave as soon as possible. I had to get away from that terrible place, with its cruelty and drama. Much as I hated doing it, I heeded the warning. I packed quickly and left the next day.

When I paid my bill at reception there was another envelope for me, of the same sort as the one that had been pushed under my door. This time it was sealed. I didn't want to open it, of course.

When I did, it contained the remains of the guest-book pages, and the second part of Richard's letter, both crudely photocopied.

I'd much rather have read the rest of Richard's letter in private than on the tiny plane with the whirring propellers and happy tourists. I must have looked a mess, sobbing without a tissue.

Paul, I kept thinking. *Paul.*

Even now, his name still turns me inside out.

I hung around Athens for the two remaining days until my flight back to London. It was hot and dusty, with long traffic jams down roads lined with parked mopeds and orange trees. Street cats sunbathed on ancient ruins. I walked up to the Acropolis—or at least, until the point where you have to pay. There were street-hawkers, scammers and beggars. How many of them were doing it through choice, I wondered. There were men who would get chatting to tourists, asking where they were from and if they liked music. They'd then give a friendship bracelet as a "gift." Presumably they would demand money once the offering was accepted. Gifts so often come with an edge or a threat, don't you think, Annabelle?

I began noticing the people you probably never see, the quiet cleaners, and the invisible staff washing up in the backs of kitchens, and I wondered how they'd got there. I tried Debbie and Marcus a couple more times. I drank a lot. I sat in the hotel bar, hating myself and the world I'd been born into. I stared at the curious framed prints in the airport lounge, the ones that depicted happy balloon rides and picnics, all in the same two-dimensional sunlit world.

There was nothing left for me in the UK. I stayed for only three days before flying back to Auckland. I didn't even have a window seat.

And now here I am, back on the balcony of the Swordfish Club, looking out at the pohutukawa tree and the jetty, as I was when I began this letter. The tables here are comfortable to write on, and I am inspired, somehow, by Zane Grey and all his novels and his many large fish. Right now I am trying to spend as much time as possible in public, and not simply because I am afraid of what might be slipped under my door when I am alone. I keep thinking I've seen him here, Annabelle. The dapper little man. I know that sounds crazy. But I was almost certain it was him—a white linen napkin tucked into his paisley waistcoat—in the classy hotel just yesterday when I was running past, and I balked, and ran faster. And then this morning I thought I saw him coming out of the public toilets near the museum. He was holding his brown briefcase with the bronze clasp.

So I must finish this quickly, and send it sooner than I'd like.

I don't even know what I expect you to do with all this material. But I hope you understand it, and give me back what is rightfully mine. If Richard is out there somewhere, don't you think he needs his bank account as well? But please, Annabelle, give me my money. The proceeds from the sale of my house would be a good start. Whether you like it or not, Richard married me, and I didn't kill him and I am not dead, so what he left behind should be mine, however cleverly you have hidden it. I'm unlikely to earn any money from this story. Marcus and Debbie decided not to go ahead with any version of *The Sleepwalkers* in the end. They said it wasn't clear enough whose story it was, and what actually happened. They felt it was too experimental and too dark. They said they still didn't know who the sleepwalkers really were and who, if anyone, had killed them.

"This story," said Marcus, when I finally got him to speak to me, "is missing something. You gotta make it clearer what actually happened. And I have to admit, sweetheart, I don't like trafficking. Tragic love—that I do like. But trafficking? Does anyone really care? And even if they do—which I doubt—is it even your story to tell?"

"But Hamza," I said. "He wanted to tell it, and you—"

"That kid didn't know how to pick his moment," said Marcus.

You know what I keep asking myself, Annabelle? Why did Richard drink the coffee? Maybe he didn't. Maybe he poured his away too. Now I've read the transcript I can see that he was telling me he knew about the trafficking. Did he escape? Is he out there somewhere? It's worth keeping an open mind on that, don't you think? But then again, maybe he was so ashamed he just wanted to die.

I don't even blame Isabella anymore. Where had she come from, with her disguised Texan accent and her layers of costume and armor and other people's kink? When I think of Isabella now she blurs in my mind with Chloe, the girl from Richard's story, who disappeared into the back streets of Europe. Chloe returned in the end, but I wonder if there are people waiting for Isabella back in Texas, or wherever it is she came from. Or maybe not. Maybe that's why.

Of course, I sent an anonymous email to Interpol as soon as I got back to New Zealand. Is that why the dapper little man is haunting me now? I imagine all kinds of ghastly weapons in his briefcase, plus his sketch pad and sticks of charcoal, to record the way he kills me. Whatever authorities ever arrived on Kathos, I imagine he will have got away with everything, and Isabella too. They are white, Western, silver-tongued. I hesitated before I reported their crimes at all, thinking it most likely that poor Hamza would take the blame like the whipping boy he always seemed to be. But then I remembered the sleek heron girl with her "Istanbul is Contemporary" bag, and how happy she'd appeared that day, and how much I'd longed to be her, because I didn't understand who she really was.

There are tsunami hazard warnings everywhere here. They freaked me out when I first arrived, with their image of a stick figure frantically clawing his way up a steep cliff, a jagged wave rearing up behind him like the open mouth of a shark. There is absolutely no way he's going to make it, but he scrambles for high ground anyway, wanting to stay alive, as we all do. I do hope you'll read all of this, or even if you don't read it, please keep it safe, for

Acknowledgments

Thank you to my family and all my friends for your love and support. In particular, I'd like to thank Rod, and also Mum, Gordian, Sam, Hari, Nia and Ivy, for your constant encouragement. Couze and Ruth, you are loved and remembered. Marion and Lyndy, thank you for the wonderful late-night chats about the Matariki. Kat, David and Amy, thank you for your unfailing friendship and camaraderie. Rosa, Sarah, Charlotte and Emma, thank you so much for reading an early draft of this with such love and care. I am so grateful for my brilliant agents, Dan and Veronique, and my editors, Olivia and Chris. Many thanks also to Ella and Brittany. Without you all, I would never have been able to get this book into the world. Blessings to every one of you.